KAMA'S LAST SUTRA

Trisha Das is the author of *Ms Draupadi Kuru: After the Pandavas, The Mahabharata Re-imagined, The Art of the Television Interview* and the internationally acclaimed *How to write a Documentary Script*. She has written and directed over 40 documentaries in her film-making career. She's also won an Indian National Film Award (2005) and was UGA's 'International Artist of the year' (2003). Her films have been broadcast and screened on the Discovery Channel, the STAR Network, NDTV, Doordarshan, at Indian and international film festivals, university campuses and conferences all over the world.

You can find Trisha on Facebook @trishadasauthor, Twitter @thetrishadas or contact her via email: trishadasauthor@gmail.com.

KAMA'S LAST SUTRA

TRISHA DAS

HarperCollins *Publishers* India

First published in India by
HarperCollins *Publishers* in 2018

HarperCollins Publishers India, Cyber City, Building 10-A, Gurugram,
Haryana-122002, India
www.harpercollins.co.in

2 4 6 8 10 9 7 5 3 1

P-ISBN: 978-93-5302-022-4
E-ISBN: 978-93-5302-023-1

Typeset in 11/14.1 Bembo at
Manipal Digital Systems, Manipal

Printed and bound at
MicroPrints India, New Delhi

MIX
Paper
FSC FSC® C218906

This product is made of FSC®-certified and other controlled material.

HarperCollins Publishers, Macken House, 39/40 Mayor Street
Upper, Dublin 1, D01 C9W8, Ireland

For Deeps, who is neither the breath in my lungs nor the wind beneath my wings and does not complete me. Here's to a pair of independently-breathing, fully-complete, wingless mortals who choose each other. Every day. Always.

1

Victory to the king. '*Maharaj ki jai ho*!' The battery-operated, short-wave radio blared across the excavated mound. Loud, yet muffled sounds of drums, conches, temple bells and other unidentifiable instruments, mixed with crackles and white noise, crashed through the air straight into my skull where they wreaked havoc on my long-suffering brain.

I screamed silently, balling my fists and willing myself to ignore the clamour instead of walking over and giving that radio the proper burial it deserved.

Then, suddenly, I spotted something lodged in the mud where I was paring it with my brush and trowel. A tiny, sharp, metallic tip.

'Oh!' I exclaimed, and then clamped a hand over my mouth as I looked around to check if anyone had heard. No one had. Luckily.

I started brushing, a little too frantically, around the tip. Professionalism and years of training often went to hell during moments like these. Moments when you felt more like a hunter who's caught a whiff of a potential prey in the distance than an archaeologist who might be about to dig up something important out of a pile of rocky mud.

'Slowly, Tara,' I chided myself as I took a deep breath and tried to focus. My mind fought the adrenaline pumping through my system, egging me on to use my fingers instead of the brush and make faster work of digging around the rusty metal sticking out of the earth. As a wide brim and sharp, refined cut lines started peeping out from under my brush, however, I lost my battle against the excitement. Throwing all thoughts of tetanus and septicaemia aside, I dove into the mud with my fingers. It looked like a sword tip. Not a knife, not an arrowhead, but a sword.

I held my breath. Swords were rare. Archaeological digs usually produced the most mundane things – pots, plates, fossilized crap – all of which were useful, of course, but let's face it, once you've seen a few thousand of the same, the novelty wears off quickly. Swords, on the other hand, you didn't usually find them in abandoned villages and temple sites. Swords were precious articles, handed down to family members over generations. They were polished and preserved, even worshipped. They were symbols of wealth and status.

'So what are you doing here, my precious?' I crooned to the sword tip, doing my best Gollum-from-the-Lord-of-the-Rings impression. I eased away the tightly packed mud from around it, pausing for a moment each time to feel the earth between my fingers. Ancient earth. Mud could tell so many stories if you looked close enough. So many people before me had been in this very spot … lived, prayed, worked and slept here. Each one in a different time, with a different story. And each one had left something, a piece of themselves, behind. For me to find.

'Found something, Tara?' yelled one of the men standing on the other side of the large mound we were excavating in Khajuraho, in the central Indian state of Madhya Pradesh. This was a UNESCO World Heritage site. Near us, shielded from view by the hefty barricades we had erected around our dig site, were the world-famous medieval temples of Khajuraho.

I wasn't ready to share. Especially not with those assholes. I shouted across the mound, 'Uh, no. Just talking to myself.'

He probably thought I was a bit loopy. Tara Singh, loopy archaeologist. The one who owns the same straight-cut jeans in every colour and little else. The one who shows up to work every day wearing the hat that Harrison Ford immortalized in the Indiana Jones films. The one who says she's 'from Delhi' but talks with a funny accent acquired from a childhood spent following the Indian Foreign Service drum – where life is neatly sliced into two-year chunks, each one spent in a new country, in a new school, trying to make new friends, and not having anything in common with your cousins when you visit India every summer.

The memory of holidays spent with my cousins in Delhi still made me chuckle ruefully. While my mother, ever the social butterfly, would push off to the Gymkhana Club with her friends after slathering me in sunscreen – to protect her 'pretty little mongrel' from the evil Delhi sun, you see – I would be left at home with my maternal aunt and her two daughters. Who were very nice to me. And patient. Especially when I bored them with stories about Indiana Jones and ghostly lions from Narnia. Or when I talked about eating bratwurst for dinner and how I hated anything with fish sauce even though it didn't make things taste fishy precisely. Or how I wore shorts under my skirt. That always made them giggle.

There were some good times though. Some of the best times, in fact. When my aunt taught us how to make rotis and we flew them like Frisbees across the kitchen when she turned her back. When we'd attack a pile of Dussehri and Langda mangoes and leave the table with sticky mango juice in every crevice of our upper bodies. When we drank cold coffee in Janpath and roamed decrepit bookstores in Connaught Place, where I would buy armfuls of *Archie* and *Amar Chitra Katha* comics to add to my *Tintin* and *Asterix* collections.

A glint, bouncing off the untarnished sword tip, brought me back to the present. Ah, yes, I was excited about the sword just a minute ago. Focus, Tara! I continued to remove the mud around it, using all my training from my four years as an undergrad student of archaeology at Columbia University in New York and the handful of years I had spent assisting in digs since then. I could tell the metal went some way down but there was no way to be sure it was a complete sword. Unlikely. Far more probable was that the sword's blade got broken and buried in this mound before anyone could see and repurpose it. There were over fifty mounds scattered around in this area and I had spent the better part of two years bent over them, trying to uncover their secrets. Maybe even find a new temple in the bargain. Not a completely unrealistic goal, considering only twenty-five out of the original eighty-five Khajuraho temples had been discovered so far. Another group of archaeologists had recently discovered one in a village nearby – apparently the biggest yet.

I dismissed the little twinge I felt as indigestion even though I knew fully well it was jealousy. Two years of dedicating myself to this dig, studying the area and its traditions, its language and people, its history. Two years of putting up with blaring, local radio soap operas about god-like kings and their 'dutiful' wives while I worked, the searing summer heat and the biting winter cold of Bundelkhand, substandard hotels with sleazy caretakers and considerable dietary abstention because my diplomat-family upbringing meant that my passport was Indian but my digestive system was not. After all that, I really deserved to find a temple.

One last push and a chunk of rocky mud fell away. As I had suspected, it was only the top third of the blade. I swallowed my disappointment. Maybe, just maybe, the rest of it was further down in the mud. I'd need time to get there though. Meanwhile, I had to show the blade to Hari, back at the site office.

I sighed wistfully.

Hari Varma. My former college professor. He was the one who had invited me to join his Khajuraho dig team two years ago as part of a partnership between the Archaeological Survey of India (ASI) and the Archaeology Department of Columbia University. It was just one of the teams he supervised around the world. At thirty-four, he was one of the youngest professors at the university and one of the most highly regarded archaeologists in the business.

At this point, I might mention that he was also the sexiest, but that would be entirely beside the point and very unprofessional. I am not that kind of person. Now, had I ever thought about him in that way, completely inadvertently? Maybe. But it would've been unnatural if I hadn't. Young, good-looking, tall and rugged archaeologists, who are also professors at Ivy League universities and leaders in their field, are few and far between in a profession dominated by balding old men in baseball caps. Guys like Hari get fan-girled by their students along with preferred spots in Nat Geo documentaries. They are the archaeological equivalent of rock stars.

Although, to be fair to him, Hari didn't behave like a rock star. If anything, he was probably even more reticent about this kind of thing than I was. I had never once heard a rumour about him sleeping with a student or acting full of himself. And he had never been anything less than a gentleman in front of me or my friends. I caught myself before a rueful sigh escaped.

Glancing over at the men on the other side of the mound, I quickly covered the mud-caked blade in plastic, draped a cloth around it and put it in my oversized bag. They were local guys hired by Hari to assist the archaeologists on the dig. Although the word 'assist' would be a bit of a stretch. More than once, they had blatantly gone ahead and claimed credit for something dug up by one of the women on the team. Not to mention that they tended to look at us as if we were some kind of anomalies. Like: 'Look, women. Why are they here, trying to do a man's job? They wear tight jeans and funny hats and take themselves seriously. Let's laugh at them in a superior way while also getting a good look at their butts as they bend over. And then, if they find something worthwhile, let's pretend to take it for cleaning and grab credit for it so that the boss realizes that we men can do a better job on our own turf than these imported, indecently dressed bitches.'

I nodded perfunctorily as I passed them. I was done trying to be friendly, the way I had when we first got here two years ago. I had soon realized that this was a deeply patriarchal part of India and any friendly overtures on my part could be dangerously misinterpreted.

Passing through the barrier gate at the far end of the dig site, I took a deep breath and stretched, soaking in the silence, the surrounding trees, stones and manicured parklands of the temple complex. Nothing lavish or lush, but not wild and overgrown either. If there was a certain lack of imagination or whimsy in the landscaping though, it was more than made up for by the Western Group of Khajuraho temples that stood in it.

In front of me, some distance away, was the largest and most impressive of them all: the Kandariya Mahadeva temple, dedicated to Lord Shiva.

One never, no matter how many times they saw it, got over how magnificent it was. In the Nagara style, which resembled a mountain, it radiated power and personality, its peak rising higher than any of the twenty-five temples still standing in Khajuraho. Of course, there would have been many more temples a thousand years ago – perhaps even more than eighty-five, according to the legends of the Rajput Chandela dynasty that built them. I remembered a local man, who happened to be a descendant of the Chandelas, telling us the story behind the temples.

Hemavati, he explained, was a beautiful princess, who was said to have bathed in a moonlit pool on a sultry night when the Moon God saw her and got randy (not his words, obviously). He came down from the sky and seduced her. Hemavati got pregnant, naturally – god-sperm was pretty potent. Ashamed and alone, like most young, beautiful princesses who do the deed outside matrimony, Hemavati came to Khajuravahaka –

the ancient name for Khajuraho – and gave birth to a son whom she named Chandra Varman, after his father. Apparently, Chandra was a stand-up guy, according to our storyteller, who very magnanimously built the temples to atone for his mother's 'sin'. As a result of this effort on his part, his mum went to heaven instead of hell.

I remembered listening to all of this in incredulous silence until the man finished. Then I blurted out, 'So what was her sin exactly?'

The man looked embarrassed. 'She ... she consorted with the Moon God.'

'But I thought you said she was having a bath and he was the one who came down and seduced her?'

'Yes, but we cannot blame the god. He is a god. Besides, she should not have been bathing at night.'

I was peeved. 'Why? Is the Sun God less horny?'

Hari intervened at that point with a, 'Right. Thanks for that. Can we get back to business...' and changed the subject while our storyteller glared at me.

I was unrepentant. Most Indian myths and legends were far too chauvinistic for me. With history, on the other hand, I was far more forgiving. And the history of Khajuraho, I pondered as I strolled towards the massive Kandariya temple, was nothing short of fascinating. Built over hundreds of years by the Chandelas as their religious capital, Khajuraho's name came from the word 'khajur' or dates, a sweet fruit. A thousand years ago, the area surrounding the temple complex was a dense, seemingly impenetrable jungle, while inside were lush orchards full of date trees, including two solid gold ones at the gate, apparently. The dense jungle was what had protected the complex from being destroyed by invading armies from the northwest, particularly Sultan Mahmud of Ghazni, who conquered many of the kingdoms surrounding the Chandelas, took their wealth and razed their places of worship to the ground. The Destroyer of Temples and Idol Breaker were Mahmud of Ghazni's nicknames, given after he crushed a united army of Rajput kings in the Battle of Waihind and raided their temples and forts.

However, Sultan Mahmud of Ghazni had never beaten the Chandelas on their own turf. The Chandela king, Vidyadhara, the builder of the Kandariya Mahadeva temple standing tall before my eyes, had single-handedly faced off the Sultan in battle twice. And sent him packing both times. By the time the Khajuraho complex, abandoned and inconspicuous after the Chandela dynasty died out, had been rediscovered, a more tolerant age had begun and the temples survived to tell the tales carved into their walls. Unlike many of their counterparts.

This one, the Kandariya temple, had been commissioned by Vidyadhara to commemorate his second victory over the Sultan in the year 1022 CE. On its walls were carved numerous scenes of mortal and immortal life from a thousand years ago. Gods, goddesses, divine avatars, heavenly nymphs – or apsaras, as they were more commonly known – kings, queens, courtesans, soldiers, priests, regular people doing everything from bathing to eating to fighting battles to praying to having sex. A lot of sex. Not just regular sex, but wall upon wall of graphic nakedness – orgies, men-on-men and women-on-women action, oral and acrobatic sex and even bestiality – it was pretty full-on. In exquisite detail as well, right down to nail marks on the bodies of those involved in more vigorous copulating.

I smiled as I remembered one of the local experts telling me that the sex carvings were a mixed boon for the temple complex. On the one hand, they were just a small part of a much larger bank of equally spectacular carvings, each of which intricately explained different aspects of the lives and belief systems of medieval Indians and which were largely ignored by the people visiting the temples. On the other hand, the sex carvings on the Kandariya temple alone brought in millions of tourist rupees a year, which paid the maintenance bills for the entire complex. Even now, as I glanced along its large, elevated base, I could see a small scaffolding on the side. Minus a maintenance crew, of course.

I walked up to its foundation and looked around. A few tourist groups, mostly foreigners, milled about, two of them being led by umbrella-carrying local tour guides. On the side, in a quiet corner, sat a Caucasian man with long, ragged dreadlocks and a large cloth bag chanting 'Hare Krishna, Radhe Krishna, Hare Hare Hare Krishna' at the top of his voice.

I said loudly in his direction, 'You've got the wrong temple. This one's Shiva. Vishnu is down the road.'

He looked past me with glazed eyes and continued his chant without missing a beat. I figured there was probably more than just mineral water in the bag and walked on.

I climbed up the steps to the temple's raised dais and craned my neck upwards to see the carvings that had become so familiar in these last two years. I could hear a tourist guide's voice on my right. 'And now, please follow me … here, *here*, please look for my umbrella,' only it sounded like 'umreila', and it was a big, red one that he was waving in the air over his head so that an elderly group of American tourists could gather around him.

I stood still, waiting for the inevitable reference to one of the carvings directly ahead of us, where a man was being held upside down by two female attendants as he copulated with an upright woman who was hanging off the attendants' shoulders, her fingers bunched in their hair. It was a very explicit depiction – shaded by the woman's curvaceous bottom was the man's erect penis penetrating her vagina. His hands were as busy as his penis – they were in the attendants' vaginas, potentially giving them some finger action. Basically this one, extremely acrobatic dude was doing three women at the same time. And all four of them looked like they were enjoying it.

The tourist guide continued in a sing-song, heavy voice, 'And here we are having the males and the females in a position from the Kamasutra. Kama, meaning love, and Sutra, meaning thread, for stitching and also like a teaching in school. Teaching of love – that is the meaning. This one is called the "international position", that is because only the international people are doing this. No Indians are doing any more.'

I choked on my laughter just as an elderly tourist asked him, with an American twang, 'So how come they put this stuff on a temple wall? Isn't that sacrilegious or something?'

It was a common question and one I had heard asked many times before. I think the most entertaining answer I had heard so far was that these positions were supposed to be good for blood circulation. I waited with bated breath for the guide to reply.

He didn't disappoint. 'No, it is for teaching. The bottom of the temple, there are bad things, wrong things. These positions, they are for bad people. When you are going higher, you must conquer all the bad things. Then, higher, there are only good things and mind is clean and body is clean. The top of the temple, that is like Mount Kailasa, the home of Lord Shiva. Over there, there is no peoples carving and they are only showing flowers and symbols, which is like purity. The meaning is that when mind and body is clean, then the person can go higher and be closer to God.'

The elderly man's face lit up as he replied, 'Like a pyramid of enlightenment.'

The guide shook his head furiously. 'No, not a pyramid. It is a mountain. The pyramids, they are in Dubai.'

Smiling, I turned to the group. I couldn't resist. 'Actually, experts think that the sexual depictions on the walls of the temples have to do with tantric practices that were popular in India a thousand years ago. Some people also believe that the carvings are geometric representations of yogic philosophy or even coded messages for disciples of Tantra, illustrated using a symbolic, double-meaning language called Sandhya Bhasha.'

The guide was not happy with the interruption but an elderly woman spoke up before he could. 'What's all them double meanings for? Why can't they just tell it like they mean?'

Why indeed? I smiled again and shrugged. 'Your guess is as good as mine.'

The guide quickly moved his group along to the next part of the tour, glancing nervously towards me to make sure I wasn't following. I stared back up at the carving. Most old Hindu temples had erotic sculptures on them but this temple far exceeded the bounds of acceptability. Experts had spent decades trying to come up with valid reasons for why its sculptures were so much more explicit than other temples, their themes so much more twisted, a few even strictly taboo. Why would a medieval king put seriously kinky stuff like that on the walls of a sacred place of worship? That too in such a feudal, patriarchal part of India. The dichotomy, the blasphemy, the secrecy, the sheer pornographic pleasure of the carvings … it was confounding!

As for me, I wondered less about the carvings themselves than the man who had commissioned them. What kind of a man was King Vidyadhara? Obviously, a brave warrior. History says he was a follower of Shiva and fairly liberal. For a Rajput. That still didn't explain what he was thinking when he commissioned these sculptures. Was he really trying to warn his subjects about the evils of kinky sex or was he trying to turn them on? Was it the medieval equivalent of free porn? Or was it a business venture – to attract people to visit and then spend their money making offerings to the gods (i.e., the king's coffers) inside. Was he trying to speak in some double-meaning language, like the experts believed or was he just playing an elaborate, private joke? Was he into any of this stuff himself?

A slight quiver ran up my back as I heard a familiar voice behind me. 'Stop staring at it, girl. You're beginning to drool.'

2

I smiled. Sumithra Subramaniam. One of the Columbia graduate students whom Hari had assigned to the dig team as interns during their summer break. A second-generation Indian-American, just like Hari, Sumithra had grown up in Manhattan and gave the word 'diva' a whole new dimension. She hadn't broken a single, talon-like, gel-painted nail since she got to Khajuraho. We only met a month back but I felt an instant connection with her and we'd become friends very quickly. She was the one who gave me all the gossip about the rest of our team – Sarah, the second-in-command senior archaeologist who worked with Hari to supervise his teams around the world, Joanne and Erico, the two other grad students/interns on our team for the summer, and Gopa and Vik, short for Vikram Aditya, the only Indians and resident archaeologists, apart from me. Gopa was a senior archaeologist and supervised Vik, me and our local crew when Sarah, Hari and the interns were in New York.

Sumithra sauntered up to me, her generous proportions clad in a long, flowy black dress and her feet encased in black gladiator sandals. I had never seen her wear any other colour. I shook my head. 'I'm not staring or drooling. I'm thinking.'

'Well, I hope not about Erico, darling.' She winked. 'We got cosy last night.'

In Sumithra speak, that could have meant anything from a chaste hug to full-blown sex to hanging blindfolded from the ceiling and being whipped with a belt. She vacillated between crushes on Erico and Vik, and even though Portuguese-born Erico flirted with her outrageously, I doubted he was really interested. I decided to spare myself the details. 'Good for you. Look what I found.'

I opened the bag and unwrapped the edge of the sword tip so she could have a look. Her eyes widened. 'Oooh, that's so cool. Have you shown it to Hari?'

'Not yet. I'm going to his office now.'

She looked relieved. 'I'll walk with you. I wasn't looking forward to running into those creeps at the site. I still can't believe they took that land grant plaque we found!'

I nodded as I started walking. 'I know. Hari should have told them off properly instead of giving that tired speech about teamwork.'

She rolled her eyes. 'He's too busy trying to play the diplomat to stand up for us. Trust me, I know. All Indian-Americans feel the same guilt. We're not Indian enough over here and we're not American enough over there. We're perpetually stuck in the middle, trying to please everyone.'

She fluttered her eyelashes and titled her head coyly. 'Not that I would mind pleasing Vik one of these days before we leave … Maybe I'll go sit on his lap today and whisper "hukam" into his ear. Isn't that Rajput for "your wish is my command"?'

I laughed. 'Yes, although I doubt it was meant to be used in that way. You'd better not try. He's the traditional type.' That was the understatement of the year. Vik was part of some Rajput royal family or the other and he recently showed me a stack of bio-datas that his mother had sent him to consider for marriage. They included photos of Vik's future-bride candidates dressed in chiffon saris with simpering, professionally made-up faces in front of soft-focus backgrounds with liberal amounts of photo filters to make them look as attractive as possible. Vik had gone through them with a toothcomb and had also looked legitimately concerned when I remarked that the prettiest of the lot didn't look like she had child-bearing hips. Enough said.

Sumithra fake-pouted before her face turned mischievous. 'Well, I'll tell you who Hari is definitely pleasing. Sarah. She's like a bitch in heat around him – I can feel the pheromones emanating out of her fake blonde roots!'

I blinked and replied carefully, 'In that case, I wish them well.'

She gave me a penetrating look and huffed, 'Oh don't be such a wuss, Tara. You're hot, you're smart *and* you're into all the same stuff Hari is. You could totally have him. If you'd just comb your hair, slap on some eyeliner and make the slightest bit of effort to hook up with him.'

Now it was my turn to roll my eyes. 'Why is everything about "hooking up" with you? He's my professor. There are … rules about that sort of thing.'

'He's not your professor anymore!'

'I'm not interested!'

There was that arched eyebrow again. 'Really?'

I felt a flush creep into my face but stretched my lips into a fake smile, just to irritate her even more. 'Really. Besides, he had a fake blonde girlfriend back when I was his student too. So maybe Sarah's his type.'

She gave me another look and then shrugged. 'I think you're crazy. I'd be all over him if he didn't clutch his forehead every time I opened my mouth.'

I chuckled and shook my head again just as we reached the small complex of portable cabins and tents that was our site office. Luckily, the cabins were air-conditioned. A blessing, when one spent most of one's time baking in the summer sun outside. Sumithra waved me off and went into the lounge cabin where the team usually hung out. I tried to forget about our conversation before I entered the adjacent cabin that was Hari's office.

I was about to push the door open when I heard Sarah's voice inside. It sounded low, intimate. I stopped, unsure about whether to go inside or quietly close the door and walk away.

I heard her say huskily, 'Hari' – she pronounced it like 'Harry', which didn't suit him at all – 'have I ever told you I *love* your tattoo?'

Hari had a Stone Age arrowhead tattooed into his forearm. The kind that cavemen used to attach to spears and hunt with millions of years ago. I heard his deep voice answer her in an unsure, slightly hesitant way, 'Er, you might have mentioned it. Did you need to ask me something?' That last bit was more business-like.

Sarah, if she heard the dismissal in his voice, ignored it. 'I have a tattoo as well.'

There was a pause before he said, 'Really.'

I heard footsteps shuffling along the PVC floor as she said, 'It's in a … private place.'

Another pause. 'Okay.'

'Want to see it?'

My eyes widened. That was an invitation if I'd ever heard one. I waited, with bated breath, for his reply.

He cleared his throat and said firmly, 'Maybe another time, Sarah. Did you happen to see last week's report lying around anywhere?'

I heard a huff and decided that it was as good a time as any to make my entrance. I pushed open the door and walked into the office.

Sarah, tall, willowy, slightly horsey and blonde-with-dark-roots, turned and stared at me with narrowed eyes, unsure about whether I'd overheard what had just transpired. She was dressed in a pink tank top under a safari waistcoat and tight cargo pants, the delicate Caucasian skin on her arms looking uncomfortably lobster-red after four weeks in the summer sun.

Next to her, seated behind his desk, was Hari. His skin had been tanned, rather than burnt, by his native Indian sun and he had two frown lines on his forehead that never seemed to smoothen out, even when he smiled. Which was when that tiny, elusive dimple on his right cheek made an appearance. He was dressed casually, in a grey T-shirt over cargo pants, and my eyes unintentionally dropped to the large arrowhead tattooed across his muscled forearm. I couldn't help myself.

That made him look even more awkward than he already did at my sudden arrival and made Sarah's eyes widen as they swept over me. I could sense her sizing me up – my longish, slightly wavy hair tucked into a dishevelled bun under my

Indiana Jones hat, my black T-shirt that had the words 'I needs a nap' emblazoned on it and my muddy jeans. Finally, probably deciding I wasn't worth feeling embarrassed over, she flicked her hair off her face and turned to walk out, saying over her shoulder at Hari, 'I'll take a look in my office in case the report's there. See you at dinner. Bye, Tara.'

She shut the door with a little more force than necessary and Hari and I were left alone, staring after her. I cleared my throat. 'Is this a bad time?'

He gave me a long, assessing look before saying, 'Not at all. What's up?'

'I found something,' I said, as I came over to his desk, took out the sword piece from my bag and handed it to him. His eyes lit up as he held it carefully and examined it. He got up, walked to his examination table and flicked on the overhead light before meticulously peeling away the mud to reveal a rusty but remarkably well-preserved blade. I walked over to stand beside him. He smelled of mild deodorant and warmth. I didn't stand too close. I never did.

He said softly, almost to himself, 'It's definitely Rajput … double-edged… I'm guessing an earlier version of the Khanda sword. Feels slightly narrower and heavier than the Prithviraj version and doesn't seem to have any indications of the traditional spine along the back edge, although it could have started lower down on the blade … No way to be sure until we see the full thing.' He stroked the edges gently, confidently, and I felt a little uncomfortable looking at his fingers, almost lover-like, on the metal. Despite years of knowing him, being around him, I could never switch off that part of my belly that started buzzing whenever he was in the same room as me.

I turned away, took a quick breath and said, 'I haven't dug any deeper yet. Thought I'd show this to you before I tried to find the rest. Besides, I didn't want the local assistance guys to catch a whiff of it.' I strolled over to some shelves near the window and looked at the English daily newspaper lying on top. Its headline screamed, 'Entire Clan Murdered in revenge Killings: Thakur Claims His Family's Honour Insulted.' I sighed.

Hari looked up at me and then at the newspaper under my gaze. 'What? I hope those guys are behaving themselves?'

I shrugged. 'I guess. If you count ignoring us and staring occasionally as behaving.' I held up the newspaper for him to see the headline. 'How does something like this even happen in this day and age?'

He put the sword down, turned off the light and came over, taking the newspaper from my hands. 'Yeah, pretty rough. I was speaking to the ASI guy about this in the morning. Turns out he knows the accused – the thakur is the same caste as him. Apparently, there was something about someone refusing a marriage offer and then insulting the family and so they went back, got guns and blew everyone's heads off. Women and children too.'

He shook his head sadly. 'Honour, pride, clans – the whole feudal culture – it's deeply ingrained around here. This place is still, in many ways, stuck in the middle ages.'

I bit my lip in frustration. Thakurs were the local overlords – men from higher castes – who owned much of the land and its resources, were related to the local politicians and government officials and, therefore, controlled much of the local economy. Mostly under-educated and given to alcohol abuse, with an overblown sense of honour and self-importance, they also regularly feuded with rival clans and terrorized people from lower castes. Incidents of murder, rape, slavery, fraud and violence were commonplace. Didn't greet a thakur with the proper respect? At best, he might beat you; at worst, he might rape your wife. Or he might cut off one of your limbs or your nose. He might send his goons over to your house at night to set it on fire. They might even drive their jeep over your son as he walked to school or gang-rape your daughter and hang her, naked, from a tree.

The local law enforcement was, of course, completely ineffectual. Just the other day, a policeman had come over to our dig site because we'd reported that it had been vandalized during the night. Instead of asking questions about the crime, the paunchy officer had said to me in Hindi, so that Hari wouldn't understand, 'You seem like a girl from a good family. You should be married by now, not hanging around with these kind of people and working in the sun. You're pretty, have a nice, fair complexion – you can find a good husband.' I obviously looked extremely irritated because the guy from the ASI had hurriedly intervened and taken the officer away.

Hari continued from behind me, 'Even keeping the team safe around here is a challenge. Sarah said someone tried to climb into her balcony at the hotel last night. Luckily she managed to lock the balcony door before ringing me.'

A little devil in my head wondered if that was actually the truth or just Sarah's way of getting Hari into her hotel room at night, before I swatted the thought away. All the women in the team had had close calls. I had gotten into the habit of walking down crowded streets with my elbows sticking out to discourage boob grabbers and feeler-uppers. Once I had caught a man watching me with his hand inside his pants. I didn't even notice the stares any more – they came with the territory.

I looked over at Hari. 'What happened?'

He shrugged. 'I rushed over, but whoever it was had disappeared by then.'

I heard the door open and turned to see the rest of the team – Joanne, Erico, Vik, Sumithra and Gopa – walk into the cabin. Sumithra winked at me and I rolled my eyes.

Hari smiled. 'Good, I'm glad you're all here. The ASI people have invited us to visit Kalinjar Fort tomorrow and stay for lunch. They're organizing a tour and a dance performance in our honour. I've agreed. I hope that's Okay with everyone?'

Gopa smiled back. 'That should be nice. Now that you're all here for only a little more time, you should see everything, no?'

I liked Gopa. She was sort of like the team mum, even though she was only in her thirties. She was also a huge prude. The sculptures on the temples made her stiffen and look away uncomfortably and she got immediately offended if any of us laughed at her. She was the opposite of Sumithra and they couldn't stand each other.

I looked over at Joanne, a mild, bespectacled, second-generation Filipino American who said, 'I wanted to see it actually. But it's a few hours' drive away, right? I always get motion sickness on these roads – they're so bad.' Joanne was delicate and was having the hardest time adjusting to the heat, the spicy food and the lack of American-style amenities. Not a good start for a future archaeologist.

Erico piped up in his heavily accented voice, 'Come now, Joanne! We cannot leave you behind alone, yes? Sumithra, she will give you one of her magic pills and you will be, how you Americans say, awesome!' He winked broadly at Sumithra, who beamed back at him saucily.

Joanne shrugged and said in a slightly passive-aggressive voice, 'I guess.'

Vik, meanwhile, spread out in one of the armchairs on the side as if he was about to take a nap and mumbled, 'I'm fine with anything,' in a voice that suggested he was already half-asleep.

Hari had a slightly pained expression on his face – like a babysitter who had to constantly cajole toddlers into doing every little thing. 'Er, great. So, Mr Chauhan ...' Groans and exclamations interrupted him, which brought a smile to his lips but he pressed on, '... is going to pick us up at 6 a.m. from the hotel. I know he's a handful, but he means well so let's be nice, children.'

Sumithra looked over at me, fluttered her eyelashes and mouthed, 'Yes, daddy.' I glared back.

3

'Yes, the honour killings … big tragedy. The whole family is gone – not even one son is left to carry the name. But, you know Hariji, it happens sometimes… Pat is very important to the Bundela people,' Mr Chauhan said as he twisted his distended stomach from the front passenger seat of the Toyota Innova to face us.

'Who's Pat?' Joanne, huddled in the third row of seats between Hari and Gopa, looked like she was trying hard not to lose her breakfast. Sarah sat opposite me in the middle row and Sumithra had chosen to ride with Erico and Vik in the other car. Of course.

'Pat is not a person, Joanneji. *Pat* is the word for honour,' replied Mr Chauhan, whose first name none of us knew because he always referred to himself as Mr-Chauhan-from-the-ASI. He had taken it upon himself to play host to all the foreign teams who participated in excavations at Khajuraho. 'Honour is more important than anything else. One time, a very poor Bundela man was taken to the magistrate for hitting a government official with his sword. The magistrate asked the man why he did it and the Bundela replied that the government official should be grateful that he hit him with a sword and not his shoe. You see, the government official was from a lower caste than him.'

I turned and looked out the window. This kind of talk always set my blood boiling even though I knew that everything the well-meaning Mr Chauhan said was true.

We drove past a water tank, or kund, as the locals called them. Stone steps led down to a large pond around which were gathered small groups of people performing their early morning ablutions. Some prayed, some washed clothes and utensils, and some bathed. An elderly woman perched on a mossy step splashed water over herself while fully clothed in a sari, petticoat and blouse while a man waded in for a bath wearing nothing but a small loincloth. He was probably going to get a lot cleaner than the woman, I thought. In a land where much of the rural population had to bathe and defecate out in the open, women definitely got the short end of the stick. Village women even had to go into fields in groups so that they could take turns defecating and standing guard.

I shook my head to lighten my thoughts. Spending so much time in this area during the last couple of years had completely changed my perspective on life. I no longer complained when the electricity went out or the tap in the bathroom ran dry. I was well aware of how incredibly lucky I was to have a roof over my head and a bathroom at all.

'Rupee for your thoughts, Tara?' Hari teased from the back seat. He knew I'd have something to say, vehemently, about Mr Chauhan's story.

I smiled back and said sarcastically, 'I could tell you what I'm thinking but we're in the middle of nowhere and I don't want to walk back to the hotel.'

Sarah smirked. 'I think we're all thinking the same thing.' She looked at Mr Chauhan's back and rolled her eyes in a way that immediately set my back up.

Funny how I criticized the unfair, the depraved and the deplorable in my own culture so freely all the time but I hated it when any foreigner voiced exactly the same thoughts. However messed up it all was, it was mine and I belonged to it. I looked away before Sarah saw the disgust in my eyes.

Mr Chauhan, happily oblivious to the undercurrents in the back seats, continued, 'Anyway, let us talk about more pleasant things. Kalinjar Fort is really the most underrated attraction in this area. Its name means "destroyer of time", from the words "kal", meaning time, and "jar", which means to destroy. Implying the Lord Shiva, of course, who is the god of destruction and also known to be the master of time. The fort itself is carved out of solid stone on a very high, sheer cliff at the top of a hill – the walls are 10 feet thick and used to be three floors high. You know, it once held an army of 65,000 soldiers, 36,000 horses and 640 elephants. A complete township existed inside, with its own water supply fed from a system of underwater springs. In fact, it was because of the water that the fort was almost impossible to conquer. As long as they could keep the enemy out, the people inside could survive indefinitely. There is also a network of natural catacombs and reservoirs underneath the fort which was extremely difficult to navigate. We have closed most of it now due to safety reasons, but some small caves are still accessible. You must see it.'

He shifted in his seat uncomfortably as the car sped over a ditch. 'And then, of course, there is the Neelkanth temple. Very nice. It is the oldest part of the fort. The cave in which it sits is said to be from mythological times. The Shivalinga inside is always wet at the neck, from a natural stream, so that is why they call it Neelkanth.'

Gopa added helpfully, '"Neel" means blue and "kanth" means neck. It is one of the names for Lord Shiva because he drank poison to save the gods and kept it in his throat, which went blue. It's a story from the ancient Vedic texts.'

Mr Chauhan looked very pleased with Gopa and nodded enthusiastically, 'Yes, yes, thank you, Gopaji. Sorry, I forgot you must not know these stories, Hariji – you look Indian so I sometimes forget that you're a foreigner!'

A tiny flash of something flickered across Hari's face before he said, 'Actually, I do know the story. My grandmother lived with us in New Jersey while growing up so I know many of the stories. But thank you for telling it, Gopa – for Sarah and Joanne's benefit. And probably Tara's as well.' He looked at me and smiled again.

I got a warm feeling inside and quickly squashed it. 'Yeah, definitely for mine. Many Indian-Americans I met during university knew this kind of stuff but many of us Indian-Indians often don't pay attention. I mean, I know that Krishna is blue, but I can't tell you why.'

Hari nodded. 'It's because he was dark-complexioned and possibly had a blue aura which came from absorbing the evil around him. You're right – my parents and grandma left India in the eighties and tried as hard as possible to inculcate as many Indian values into me as possible. Which is probably why I get a mini culture shock every time I travel here –

India doesn't live in the eighties any more but my idea of it still does!'

Mr Chauhan laughed and said, 'Very interesting, Hariji. I am happy that your Dadiji taught you about our gods. In fact, Neelkanth is just one aspect of Lord Shiva depicted in the fort. The other prominent one is Kal Bhairava! That one is really something, but I will keep it as a surprise for our young students.' He did the clichéd bobble-head-doll-thing with his head and smiled cheekily, his own excitement far exceeding any enthusiasm the 'young students' would have for his surprise.

The rest of the drive was completed in companionable silence, apart from the occasional groan by Joanne followed by soothing, clucking noises from Gopa as she rubbed Joanne's back and upper arms. The great Indian countryside flew by outside our air-conditioned cocoon. Laughing children chased each other or a runaway bicycle wheel, colourfully dressed village women walked across the landscape with water pots stacked on heads and perched on hips as their skirts and draped veils, or odhnas, fluttered in the wind. Turbaned men strolled in the middle of nowhere as if their destination was mere minutes away. Bullock carts plodded patiently next to more zealous motorcycles. Tractors teetered with more produce and people than one could ever have thought possible. And, more infrequently, there was the sight of a car much like ours – with white-kurta clad men in front and a gaggle of women and children at the back. These were the rural elite, and our driver waved respectfully at each of them.

As the mild morning sun intensified and waves of heat began to radiate in the distance, we got our first glimpse of the hill on which Kalinjar Fort stood. The cliff underneath the structure was breathtakingly sheer, a 700-foot-high incline that used to be thick jungle in the old days. The fort itself was like a massive beast stretched out on top, its taut, undulating sinew of stone radiating strength and at-oneness with the landscape.

I had visited Kalinjar once before when I first started working on this dig. At that time, however, I hadn't really settled in and the heat, dust and lack of conveniences had made me crabby and unable to appreciate it. I was hoping this time would be different.

We drove closer, past the old village that stood in the fort's shadow at the foot of the hill. Ruins of old ramparts lined the structures and, beyond them, stretched fields of paddy and vegetables. These fields would have fed the people who had lived inside the fort for over a thousand years until the British finally retired it and it fell into ruin. Now, the village was not much more than a sleepy relic to a forgotten, glorious past.

Mr Chauhan beamed. 'Ah, here we are! Now we will be driving up the south-eastern side road to the first of the seven dwars, or doors, that allow access inside. Of course, the road is a new one. In the old days, it was jungle, jungle and more jungle – very easy to get lost.' He shrugged but then continued excitedly, 'Except here, you see this plateau' – he pointed to a wide expanse of flat land – 'this is where the armies would meet. It is about a kilometre wide. The first attacking army to ever capture the fort was of Qutubuddin Aibek in 1203 CE. But, before that, many battles were fought here. Most notably, the Chandela King Vidyadhara against Sultan Mahmud of Ghazni, who tried to take the fort in the year 1022 CE.'

'And failed,' I added.

Mr Chauhan nodded smilingly at me. 'Yes, Taraji. This landscape, and intimate knowledge of it, was the best defence against foreign invaders. It is said that on his second attempt at defeating the Chandelas, the sultan encircled the fort for a full year before he got tired and negotiated peace with Vidyadhara.'

'They exchanged gifts, right?' I asked.

'Yes, yes. It is said that Vidyadhara only gave him 300 elephants and a poem he had personally composed whereas Sultan Mahmud gave fifteen forts in return. It shows that he was scared of our king!' Mr Chauhan grinned.

Sarah raised her eyebrows. 'Did he give Vidyadhara forts he had already ransacked? Wouldn't be much left in them in that case.' She chuckled.

Mr Chauhan's grin faded and he gave Sarah a half-lidded look, the closest I had ever seen him to looking put off. Sarah seemed to have that effect on everybody – cultural sensitivity was obviously not her strong point.

I turned to Sarah. 'Well, even if they were ransacked, the forts came complete with land and whatever was left of the surrounding villages. Sultan Mahmud of Ghazni was a pure looter – he didn't care for land, but Vidyadhara would have valued it much higher than gold. He was considered one of the most powerful kings of his day. Jejabhukti, the Chandela kingdom, was quite possibly one of the two largest dominions in the subcontinent, land-wise. The Chola empire being the other big one.'

Sarah shot me a sidelong glance which probably implied that she wasn't impressed with my general knowledge. Or maybe she was still embarrassed about yesterday's tattoo debacle. That would explain why she hadn't looked me in the eye all morning.

The car pulled up and parked next to another one from which piled out a radiant Sumithra, a stiff-looking Vik and a smiling Erico, who casually sauntered up to the back window of our car and grinned at Joanne's pathetic expression. She stuck her tongue out at him.

Mr Chauhan, back in his element, shepherded us up steep stone steps and through the large arched gateways that guarded the entrances to the fort, keeping up a steady stream of commentary in a tour-guide tone. 'Ah, now this is the Alamgir Darwaza, but the locals call it Pratham Dwar which just means "first door". Most of the structures you see, the seven palaces and gates, are in the Mughal style, but the kunds and temples are in older, Hindu styles – please watch your step, Ericoji, the rubble is loose – the Mughals rebuilt all this and also built two mosques inside the fort. There is a cave there where Goddess Sita is said to have bathed and another one where they say the Pandava brothers camped during their exile. Also the underground Ganga cave – yes, yes Joanneji, lots of caves – a whole network of them under this cliff, which most people do not know about ... There are many Shivalingas all over the fort, but we don't like to talk about them that way, Sumithraji, because they are for worship, please understand...'

He led us to the Neelkanth temple – or what was left of it. The temple, formerly in the Nagara style with a towering, carved roof that rose several stories high, was now just a bunch of huge, interconnected stone pillars in a courtyard in front of a cave entrance. The mountain-like roof had either caved in or been destroyed ages ago. We stood in line to enter the cave behind a group of local men and women who had come to pay their respects, our eyes squinting as we moved from bright daylight into a dim, clammy interior with a slightly sticky floor that smelled of damp rock and sweaty humans. A priest dressed in a saffron robe and turban and sporting a flowing beard pointed out the Shivalinga that was supposed to be the highlight of our visit – the Neelkanth idol, an ancient, dark, phallic-shaped rock that had a rudimentary mouth and nose in front and a perpetually wet throat.

Not being particularly religious myself, I looked around rather than bow down and take the rock's blessings as Mr Chauhan was encouraging the foreigners to do. The temple bells clanged and echoed loudly in the dark chamber and I could make out a few other idols off to the side. On the far right, recessed into the cave walls, was a small, closed wooden door that looked like it might lead into a cupboard of sorts. *Or a secret passage*, said a voice inside my mind that began to spin with possibility. I felt a strong urge to walk over and open it before I shook my head to reel my thoughts in. It was probably rude or, worse, sacrilegious. I might inadvertently bring about the apocalypse or something – you never knew when it came to the devout and their beliefs. Having had an agnostic father and a pretty laidback mother, my knowledge of religious customs and nuances was rather dismal. I regularly offended pious people without knowing why.

Mr Chauhan, however, didn't look at all offended when I skipped the praying and began to walk out – he even smiled at me. I smiled back and resolved to ask him his first name at lunch. He walked us next to a massive carving of Shiva chiselled out of the sheer cliff face that brought forth much ooh-ing and ahh-ing from the interns.

'This,' Mr Chauhan waved grandly at the giant carving, 'is the Kal Bhairava – 24 feet in height and 17 feet wide. It is Lord Shiva's most terrifying aspect – the one which he uses to kill demons and destroy the world. You will see that the carving has eighteen arms and a garland of skulls with snake earrings and armlets.'

'And I thought only Cartier and Bvlgari did good snake jewellery,' whispered Sumithra.

I chuckled softly. Hari, who was standing close by, looked over at me with questioning eyes. I shook my head in friendly dismissal just as Mr Chauhan continued, 'The Kal Bhairava is not only meant to be a protector of the fort and its people but is also supposed to strike fear into the hearts of an approaching enemy. They would have been able to see it from quite a distance away.'

Hari continued to look at me a little absently, as if a troubling thought had just occurred to him. After a few seconds of shifting uncomfortably under his scrutiny, I gave him an awkward 'what's up?' tilt of my eyebrows. He blinked, frowned and turned away with an equally uneasy shake of his head. I didn't know what to make of it.

'Tandav. The posture of the carving is called tandav, Ericoji. It is Lord Shiva's dance of destruction.' Mr Chauhan was still at it.

'Ten-dave,' intoned Erico.

'Taaan-duv,' Mr Chauhan enunciated cheerfully.

'Ten-dove.'

'Taaan, like paan, and duv, like glove.'

'Tan…'

'No, no, not tan, like frying pan – taan, like paan. Have you ever tried paan, by the way?'

4

I ran my hands over the carved stone, letting my fingers trail along the smooth ridges of a row of time-worn lotus flowers. It was a geometric pattern, typical of Indo-Mughal architecture all over India. The stone was cool, even though the day had been blazingly hot, and a light breeze caressed my face as I stood in a covered hallway of what used to be Rani Mahal – the palace inhabited by queens and royal women when Kalinjar Fort was in use. The breeze was flowing in through a wind tunnel. I felt a momentary rush of wonder at how adept the ancients had been at keeping their homes cool in the summer and warm in the winter simply by designing structures that harnessed seasonal solar and wind patterns.

I pressed my hand against the stone, trying in some weird way to connect to the thousands of women who must have stood in this very spot before me. Women, some of whom may have spent every day and night of their lives, from birth till death, within the confines of these walls. There would have been only two entrances into this palace during the Mughal age – one for the servants and one for the king. It would have been heavily guarded, so that no man, other than their immediate male family members and eunuch attendants, could ever lay eyes on them. The women who lived here would have remained unseen and unheard by the outside world. Like inmates in a lavish jailhouse, I thought, and shivered involuntarily as I looked around at the ornately carved doorways, arches and columns.

It was a small palace, by modern standards, containing one large courtyard that was flanked by a double-storied network of verandas, hallways, interconnecting rooms, much smaller courtyards and balconies. And, probably, like any self-respecting royal abode, a handful of secret passageways. It was also relatively new, having been constructed during the Mughal era, like the other seven palaces in the complex. Before the Mughal age, there would have been one or two older Rani Mahals, maybe even several of them, considering that medieval women were known to have more freedom of movement compared to their later, more conservative counterparts. What would have remained constant through the ages was the purpose of a Rani Mahal – to house the king's various women in a controlled environment, so that they could provide him with sexual and heir-producing services as per his convenience. There would have been hundreds, maybe even thousands of women who lived here, dormitory style, with only the queens and preferred concubines enjoying the luxury of their own apartments. As long as their king was alive, of course. The minute he died, the whole lot of them would jump into his funeral pyre in a ritual act of suicide called sati, making space in the apartments for the new king's queens and concubines. It was an incredibly efficient system … if you didn't mind treating women like old clothing.

A deep breath and a shake of the head did little to relieve me of my depressing thoughts. Today was supposed to be about enjoyment! I was supposed to stare at the beauty of the artefacts and architecture around me and rejoice in my rich heritage, not find fault with it. The others had gathered in the courtyard some distance away. I could hear Sumithra's loud and utterly contagious laughter and the thumping and clanking of folk instruments as the dancers and musicians set up their stuff. The ASI guys were treating us to a post-lunch performance by a local dance troupe. In the courtyard of Rani Mahal, no less.

I heard a scurrying behind me and let out a shriek as a large langur monkey belted past, brushing my jeans with its tail in the process. It leaped on a column, swung up on the roof and disappeared. I cursed it silently – the damned things were everywhere! A few months ago, a huge male langur had snatched a sandwich right out of my hands, sat on a tree and sneered at me as he ate it. Then he bared his very sharp teeth as I flipped him my middle finger and I had to make a hasty retreat.

I heard quick footsteps and Hari appeared in the hallway.

'Are you Okay?' he asked worriedly. 'I heard you scream.'

My heart, fresh from its adrenaline shot, had not yet comprehended that the danger had passed and was still racing wildly. That made my voice a bit breathless when I replied, 'I'm fine. A langur was trying to amuse himself at my expense, as usual. Are they starting the performance?'

Hari shook his head. 'Not yet.' Then he looked at me in the way he had earlier – as if pondering over a troubling thought.

This time I wasn't going to let it go. 'What's the matter? Have I done something to upset you?'

He cocked his head, feigning innocence. 'Not at all. Why do you ask?'

'You're looking at me funny.'

He raised his brows a tiny fraction. 'I didn't realize I was doing that. I'm sorry.'

Awkward silence followed. For how long, I can't be sure – maybe just a few seconds but it felt a lot longer. We both sort of hovered in the hallway, not saying anything but not moving away either. Then we both spoke at once:

'We got lucky with the weather.'

'Was it your Nani or Dadi?'

He drew his eyelids together as he smiled. It wasn't unattractive. 'You go first.'

I shrugged as nonchalantly as I could manage, 'Was it your mum's mother or your dad's mother? The grandmother who lived with you as a child?'

His smile turned slightly shy. 'Why do you ask?'

'Well, you said in the car that your grandmother, who lived with you, taught you all about Indian culture and Mr Chauhan assumed it was your Dadiji, your paternal grandmother. Was it?' I shuffled defensively as his eyebrows went up again. Maybe this was too-personal territory. 'Never mind, forget it. I don't know why I asked. It's just that Mr Chauhan sounded a bit presumptuous. Maybe he didn't mean it like that and I'm reading too much into it. I sometimes see issues where they don't exist.' I let out a breath in a huff, annoyed at myself for shooting my mouth off.

Hari looked as if he was trying to hold back a chuckle. He failed. Miserably. His teeth flashed in a mischievous grin and

I held my breath as I realized that brooding-serious Hari was not nearly as handsome as cheekily-grinning Hari. Damn.

'I should get going to the courtyard.' I began to move past him down the hallway, rushing to hide my discomfiture before he saw it written all over my face.

His hand shot out and touched my upper arm to stop me and immediately withdrew as if he'd gotten a jolt from my skin. He pushed his hair back and said, 'I … er, agree. It didn't necessarily have to be my Dadiji – although, as it turns out, it was. But you're right, there is an issue there. My mum's parents visited us only twice in my entire childhood because it was just too expensive to fly from India to New Jersey in those days. We couldn't afford to visit India more than once every few years. I do wish I had seen more of them. That my mum had seen more of them.'

He looked into my eyes. 'And, as far as being a feminist is concerned, I think that's good thing. A great thing. You should … continue.'

That made me laugh, which was a relief from feeling awkward. 'Thanks. For your permission. You know, men can also be feminists.'

He looked relieved too. 'Well, sign me up then. Do I have to take an oath or attend a ceremony or something?'

I grinned. 'You do, actually. I'd have to officially initiate you. It involves a full moon and dancing around a bonfire' – and then, before I could stop myself – 'naked.' Shit.

Hari's eyebrows did that thing again as he grinned back. 'Sounds interesting … do the initiators dance naked too? I might be up for it in that case.'

I blinked. Was he *flirting* with me? That definitely sounded like flirting. Was it? Or was I reading too much into it?

Sumithra would know, but Sumithra wasn't here. Oh God. My insides started churning as I looked everywhere except at him and made an engine-like 'errrr' sound that wouldn't become words no matter how hard I grappled with myself.

One second passed, then two and the moment was lost. Hari's grin faded and we went back to awkwardness, his face becoming brooding and troubled again. He was standing at least 4 feet away, but I was uncomfortably aware of his presence, feeling flushed and disjointed. And upset at myself for behaving like some blushing maiden out of a historical romance novel.

'We should get back – they'll be starting the dancing soon.' He didn't look at me as he turned to walk away.

'You go ahead. I'll be there in a minute.'

I waited until he had disappeared into another hallway before I turned and deliberately knocked my forehead against the pillar next to me. Bad idea. I tried to rub away the pain as I admonished myself. Why? Why did I have to be so … so … I didn't even know what. Afraid? That was silly. I had nothing to be afraid of. Tongue-tied? Not good at flirting? Confused, unsure, self-conscious? Yes, all of those things! And apprehensive. Of saying the wrong thing or doing something I might regret. Of putting myself out there. Of getting hurt.

I sighed and rubbed my temples. I was usually very good with men … when they were just friends. When it came to romantic involvements, however, my brain just seemed to freeze up and become a dithering mess. My one and only relationship with a man, a DJ who wore sunglasses at night, carried cocaine in his back pocket and seemed very exciting and charming at the time, had ended with me walking in on him getting a blow job from a stoned girl in a bathroom stall.

In the ladies room of a nightclub. While the girl's equally-stoned friend was throwing up in the neighbouring stall. I remembered thinking how anyone could possibly have an orgasm with the heavy, acrid smell of fresh vomit around them.

Not that I knew much about orgasms. I had no idea how to give myself one and my few, furtive encounters with BJ Vomit, as I now called the ex-boyfriend, in the back seat of his car had resulted in multiple neck sprains, a lot of time wasted in trying to avoid people who might peek into shaking cars and one rather painfully broken hymen – but zero orgasms. For me, not him. I was officially an orgasm virgin. And apparently too uptight to let anyone else actually have a shot at giving me one, I thought with a snort of disgust.

I glanced at the spot where Hari had just stood. There was no point denying that I was attracted to him. Sumithra had been right, as usual. Had I responded to his semi-flirting with a witty comeback or even just smiled back without saying a word, it might have actually led to something. Now he would go into boss/ex-professor mode with me again and Sarah, the flirting samurai, would end up becoming his girlfriend.

The sounds of folk instruments coupled with the tinkling of the dancers' anklets snapped me out of my mental self-flagellation and sent me scurrying towards the main courtyard of Rani Mahal. My eyes squinted as I emerged from the darkened hallway into the huge, bright openness of the enclosure, with its numerous pillared arches and flowery carvings. The sun was dropping slowly towards the horizon and most of the courtyard was shaded, the small, pointy domes of the rooftops casting almost Daliesque shadows on the floor and pillars. The ASI team had set up two rows of plastic chairs on one side, and in the centre was a brightly dressed dance troupe and musicians getting ready to perform. I saw Mr Chauhan insisting that Hari sit in the centre-front, chief guest-style, while the others fell back in two groups, looking exhausted after a full day of moving around the fort looking at palaces, temples, mosques, reservoirs, caves and ruins – not to mention devouring a coma-inducing lunch at the on-site office.

I slunk to the back and sat at the far end, crossing my arms in front of me and avoiding the where-have-you-been glances from the rest of the team. As the music started, everyone took a seat and I was glad that it was Vik who ended up next to me. No pressure to make conversation there. I was free to continue the pity party in my head, where I believed myself – a well-travelled, empowered, intelligent woman with an Ivy League education, a successful career, better-than-average looks and every opportunity in the world at my feet – somehow deprived.

5

'Tara beti?'

My heart sank when I heard the softly spoken word from behind a tree as I exited the dig site through the gate. The voice was hoarse and masculine-sounding, as if its owner's pharynx had spent a lifetime marinated in tobacco, but it belonged to quite possibly the tiniest and oldest woman I had ever met.

Kala Devi, a hunched woman dressed scantily in a maroon dhoti-style sari without a blouse or a petticoat, looked like she might be a century old. Her wrinkled, dark face was framed by very few strands of matted grey hair and the veins on her claw-like hands looked like the roots of the ancient tree we stood under. She had no teeth to speak of and her body was barely more than sagging skin and bone. But then you looked at her blacker-than-black eyes that burned rather than sparkled and the energetic and strangely supple way she walked, you figured she must look older than she is.

I met Kala Devi two months ago. She came up behind me while I was studying some carvings in the Kandariya temple. We started talking and she told me some really interesting things about the temple and its history. I figured she must be a lonely widow from the village nearby and, on the infrequent occasions we met, I made sure to exchange some pleasantries with her. Until the last time I ran into her, two weeks ago, when she told me she was a time-travelling yogini from a thousand years ago. That's when I realized she was batshit crazy.

'Namaste, Kala Devi.' I eyed her warily.

Her eyes seared into me as she came closer. 'You're fighting with yourself again, beti.'

I mentally rolled my eyes at the soothsayer-ish comment.

She smiled. 'It's better to let go and leave yourself open to all that comes your way. Hurt might come, but so will possibility.'

After my flirting debacle with Hari the day before, I wasn't in the mood for a lecture from a lunatic. 'Thanks. I'll keep that in mind.' I half-turned to walk away.

'I am telling you the truth, Tara. I am who I say I am. I can prove it.'

I wanted to walk away but an inherent respect for elderly people made me reluctantly reply, 'You don't need to. It's fine. I believe you, Okay?'

'No, you don't. Open your mind. What have you got to lose? Let me prove it to you.'

That was the thing about Kala Devi – she didn't sound insane. Had she twitched and rambled, had her eyes seemed shifty or glazed over in confusion, I might have offered sympathy and dismissed what she said as some form of dementia. But her gaze was steady, her body radiated energy and confidence, and her voice sounded perfectly rational and even astute. Especially when it said crazy things like 'I've travelled through time from a thousand years ago'.

'I have, you know.' She grinned as she read my thoughts. 'I'm one of the very few who can. Others have tried, but the secrets of the Scorpion Bearer are not so easily understood.'

'The Scorpion Bearer?'

She waved her hand at the Kandariya temple behind us. 'The one you all think lives there. People of my age call him the Mahesvara. You call him Shiva.'

Right. So God is into time travel. I sighed. 'Look, you don't need to prove anything to me. It doesn't matter whether I believe you or not. I've got to get back to work now…'

'It *does* matter. It matters more than you can imagine. You don't understand right now, beti, but you will. Soon.'

I shook my head impassively and began to walk away. There was no point in arguing with her.

She reached out and rested her hand lightly on my arm, whispering, 'I'm sorry. I've waited long enough. You've left me no choice.'

Her fingers were unnaturally warm, like she had a fever. My arm tingled in response and I felt her black eyes, now much closer than before, bore right into my soul. In the quiet moment that passed, I could hear the distant sound of a chirping insect coupled with my own breathing, heavy and intrusive, against the silence engulfing me. In a remote part of my brain, I knew something wasn't right, but I didn't … couldn't, understand what that was. I felt separated from myself and a little sleepy. All I could see were her eyes, all I could feel was her touch, all I could comprehend without effort was her voice. I couldn't pull away.

She almost whispered, 'This must be done today. I will prove to you that I'm telling you the truth. That I am who I say I am.'

'Who are you?'

'I am Kala. Kala is time and I am its servant. I've come all this way to see you, Tara Singh.'

'Why?'

'Come with me.'

I think we walked. We must have. I'm sure I would have noticed if we'd gotten into a vehicle. Either way, we ended up in a village – inside a decrepit little mud hut next to a thatched, enclosed cowshed that was ripe with the smell of fresh dung and unwashed cattle. I gagged involuntarily as Kala Devi turned around to close the rickety, hole-ridden wooden door behind us. The hold she had over my mind was broken the minute her eyes and touch were no longer on me.

'Where am I?' My voice sounded high-pitched and fearful as I suddenly realized I had blindly followed this woman into an isolated hut and my team had no idea where I was. The worst was, I couldn't even remember following her! Had she drugged me? I didn't feel drugged, just a little … disoriented. Had I been hypnotized?

I looked at Kala Devi's back as she pottered around in the hut. She was tiny – I could easily overpower her if needed. That's when I noticed that she no longer had a hunched back. Her movements were fluid and strong, completely belying the look of her crumbling body. I was in trouble.

'Don't be scared, beti. I'm sorry I had to bring you here like that, but you people these days are so distrustful. In my day, we were more open-minded.'

I kept the door of the hut in my peripheral vision as I rounded on her angrily. 'You're wondering why I'm distrustful?? You've bloody kidnapped me! Where am I?' I almost screeched.

She sighed and shook her head, saying firmly, 'Calm down. You're in no danger from me. You just need to listen to what I have to say.'

I crossed my arms in front of me. 'What? That you came here from a thousand years ago? That God somehow brought you here? Spare me the drivel. Which village is this?' I felt my bag in my arms and knew my phone was in there. I needed to call the team but I was worried she might do the eye thing on me again.

'The name of the village is not important and I *am* from a thousand years ago. God' – she smiled – 'means different things to different people. To you and your kind, maybe God is a mysterious figure who resides in a temple or an invisible force that controls your lives. To others, God is someone who understands how our world works and knows how to use that knowledge.'

I rolled my eyes. 'Like you?'

She chuckled and shook her head. 'No, I don't claim to know everything. That claim only the Scorpion Bearer himself can make.'

I took off my hat and pushed a floppy lock of hair behind my ear. 'Look, Kala Devi, I don't know what's going on here, but my team is going to start missing me soon…'

'Time is like a wheel, Tara. It spins continuously, without a beginning or an end. What has happened before will happen again and is already happening, right now. You and I can't change that. Sometimes, however, it is possible to fold the wheel – for those who know how to do it. The person you call Krishna was a master at folding time for his teachings and even his own enjoyment – he couldn't possibly have kept so many women happy without it. For novices like me, however, it's more difficult. I only do it when there is a purpose.'

'What purpose? What are you talking about?'

She stared at me again but stayed at the other end of the room. 'I'm here to send you back about a thousand summers, to the time your people call the eleventh century.'

Seriously? She was a freaking psychopath! Visions of me strung up naked on some cross-like contraption while she stuck needles into me, voodoo style, ran through my head. I needed to get out of there before she did her hypnosis thing on me again!

She laughed as if she knew exactly what I was thinking. 'I'm not crazy and, for the last time, I'm not going to hurt you, I promise. Do you want to see something from my time? Maybe proof will help your doubting heart to believe.'

She bent down and picked up a long, narrow, heavy-looking cloth package. She then proceeded to unwrap the dirty, tattered fabric layer by layer until I saw something glint off a ray of sunlight coming in through a hole in the door.

I gasped.

In Kala Devi's hand was an intact version of the medieval khanda sword I had dug up a few days ago. Except that this one was inlaid with solid gold and precious stones. And it looked new.

I reached out, my fear forgotten, and touched it carefully. I barely noticed my handbag slide down my arm to the floor as I took the sword in my hands, breathing like I had just run up a flight of stairs. It was heavy and unwieldly, its vicious double-edged blade capable of slicing my fingers off if I wasn't careful. I knelt and rested the broad sword tip on the cloth now lying on the floor, and ran my fingers along the base of the blade and the hilt. The metal on the blade was etched with the most intricate patterns. And the carved hilt was gold-plated, set with dozens of shimmering rubies, emeralds and, in the centre, a glittering blue sapphire the size of a quail egg.

My mind was whirling with awe and utter confusion. If it didn't look brand new, I would have assumed it was stolen from a museum or a private collection. And yet, this was no flea market fake – it had to have been made by a specialist of the highest order, obviously without any budget restrictions. I squeezed my fingers around the sword hilt and again took in its weight, the carved patterns, the setting, the clarity and size of the precious stones. This wasn't a soldier's or even a rich man's sword. This was the sword of a king.

'Where did you get this?' I whispered.

Kala cackled with mirth. 'I didn't steal it. Yes, I know that's what you're thinking, beti. It was a gift. From a very desperate man.'

I looked at her. 'This is not the sword of an ordinary man.'

'Yes, it is. Except that the ordinary man happened to be a king. But even kings, with all their trinkets, cannot buy their destiny. As he quickly discovered.' She shook her head. 'He asked me to help him, to use the secrets of the Scorpion Bearer in a deceitful way. I refused him many times. He thought this gift would change my mind.' Kala cackled again.

She sounded like a cross between a hyena and the wicked witch from *The Wizard of Oz*. I didn't know what to think. How would an old woman who lived in a hut next to a cowshed in a small Indian village gain possession of a sword that would probably sell for millions of dollars at an international auction? If she or someone else had stolen it, wouldn't it be in the news?

This was definitely a medieval khanda design, but it was new. Could a modern sword maker have fashioned it that way? Sure, but why? Why wouldn't you make a modern, more efficiently designed khanda instead? This old design, specifically intended only for stabbing and not slashing, had proved so inefficient in battle that Prithviraj Chauhan had changed it. Anybody who commissioned a khanda sword would want the better design. Especially if they wanted to stick walnut-sized gemstones into it. Nothing added up.

Not to mention I still had no idea where I was or how I got there! I needed to get back to Hari and the team. I could figure this out later – maybe confront Kala in a group situation where I wouldn't feel so powerless. I responded in my best archaeologist voice, 'Look, this needs further examination by someone more experienced than me, Kala Devi. It's obviously very valuable. I can ask my boss to look at it if I could just contact him…'

Kala shook her head. 'Nobody else needs to examine it, beti. It has no value to me. The sword is yours to keep for the moment – you'll need it where you're going.'

'I'm not going anywhere,' I said as firmly as the panic swirling inside would let me. I was not going to allow her to … to … I had no idea what she had in mind but I'd seen enough movies about women being held hostage in basements for decades to know I was not going to be one of them.

I swung the sword up into the air, holding the hilt with both hands and pointing the tip at her. It was large and cumbersome and highly impractical since I didn't have the foggiest idea how to use it, but I was desperate and whacking her with my handbag was probably not going to work. Then I realized my handbag was on the floor. I gulped.

This time her cackle was so loud it bounced off the walls and I heard a cow next door moo loudly in response. 'Brave girl. You'll need that feisty spirit for what is to come. Remember, Tara, show courage and hold your head up high. In my time, valour is the only thing that will earn you respect. Farewell, and good luck.'

She touched the tip of her finger to the tip of the sword blade and I felt the hilt tug at my hands with such force that I was pulled off my feet. I felt my beloved hat blown off my head as my feet dangled uselessly in thin air, the ground having vanished from beneath. It felt like I was waterskiing without the water, my death grip on the sword's hilt being the only connection to something tangible. The walls of the hut fell away and the world spun around me in a dizzying circle, round and round, until I thought I might throw up if I didn't close my eyes. The air pressure increased, pressing down on me from all sides. I moaned as my ears began to roar. Then I blacked out.

6

A mosquito whined relentlessly in my ear. I tried to brush it away, but it persisted and I had no choice but to wake up. That was when I realized I was lying on a very hard, very cold floor instead of my usual hotel room bed. I opened my eyes and let them adjust to the dim light around me. I was in a room … no, it was a hallway. There were pillars everywhere and a dank, incense-like smell … Oh God, I was lying on the floor inside one of the temples!

It all came back to me in a rush – Kala Devi, the hut, the surreal roller-coaster ride with the sword … had it all really happened? I looked around and saw carvings, typical of the temples, on pillars, walls and ceilings around me. Except that they seemed to be a lighter, clearer shade of sandstone and … smoother, a lot smoother, than I remembered. Confused, I cast a glance along the floor where I was sitting and gasped. Kala Devi's sword was lying at my side.

I stood up quickly, a sliver of fear chilling its way around my stomach. What had she done to me? My senses sprang into action. I could hear noises coming from outside – like crowds of people cheering, along with drums, a lot of drums, rhythmically beating away in the distance. I made my way towards a beam of light entering from down the hallway, passing idols carved into the pillars that had been dressed in gold cloths and smeared with vermilion paste and looked completely unfamiliar. Which temple was this, I wondered, as I stepped out into the light onto an open-air ledge and looked outside, expecting to see the usual lacklustre temple gardens, town buildings with their hoardings and criss-crossed electricity and phone wires, and busy roads with impatient vehicles beeping at sleepy livestock.

All I saw were trees. Not a few trees. A jungle. A dense, overgrown, virgin jungle full of trees. Everywhere. No town, no roads, no electricity wires slung over makeshift poles, no fences, no tourist guides, nothing. Just big, bushy, gnarly trees.

'Oh God.' I blinked. Then I closed my eyes, took a couple of slow, deep breaths and opened them again. They were still there.

Don't panic, I told myself as I turned around and started down the hallway in the opposite direction. There had to be a perfectly reasonable explanation for why I seemed to be in an unfamiliar temple in the middle of an unfamiliar jungle…

'This is a dream. One of those dreams when you think you're awake but you're actually not,' I murmured to myself. I just needed to go lie down on the floor again, close my eyes and will myself to wake up in my hotel room. And realize that everything that had happened to me in the last hour or two had been the combination of an overactive imagination and after-dinner indigestion. I lay down next to a darkened wall and mentally chanted *Wake up, wake up, wake up* to myself for a few minutes. Then I opened my eyes. I was still there.

Disoriented, I got up and began to walk around absently. I stumbled on something on the floor – it was the sword, its glistening lines and sparkling gemstones in stark contrast to the unadorned stone floor. I stared at it for a long moment as the reality of Kala's words echoed in my ears. *'You'll need it where you're going…'*

So much for the dream theory.

I cursed her silently. When I got back to the hotel, I was going to file a bloody police report and have her locked up for kidnapping. Still, if this place was unsafe, it would help to have a very sharp blade at hand, no matter how heavy it was or how unskilled I was at using it. I looked around for my bag and wasn't surprised when I didn't find it. Kala had probably kept its contents for herself – she'd likely emptied my wallet and sold my smartphone and watch by now. I was going to kill her.

Locking my fingers around the hilt so I had a firm enough grip to lift the sword upwards and rest the flat of the blade lightly against my shoulder, I began to make my way down the dim hallway. The faraway drums beat in a steady rhythm that was muffled by the thick stone of the temple. I tried to examine the carvings on the walls and pillars as I walked. They seemed fairly typical of the Khajuraho style and period – scenes of daily life, gods killing demons, battle scenes … the usual. Except that they didn't look like they were a thousand years old and, despite having studied all the Khajuraho temples, I had never seen these ones before. Once again, Kala's words rang in my ears. *'I'm here to send you back about a thousand summers, to the time your people call the eleventh century.'*

I shook my head. Better to not get on to the crazy, time-travel train of thought. *Reasonable explanation, reasonable explanation*, I started chanting in my mind like a mantra.

There isn't one, said an irritating little voice in my head.

There must be. I frowned at the voice. This was probably some remote village in a remote jungle with a temple that no one had any idea existed.

There are no more remote temples or jungles in this area, replied the voice. *It's well-chartered territory. The forests around here all have eco-friendly resorts that offer early morning safaris so sleepy tourists can drive around aimlessly for hours, looking for tigers that don't exist any more.*

It could happen, I argued. Not every place is GPS-ready.

Ever heard of Google Earth?

Shut up.

A couple of turns, and the hallway turned into a chamber which featured a huge marble Shivalinga on one end and a door leading outside on the other. There was no one around, not even a priest, despite the fresh incense burning on the platters of fruit, flowers and leaves that adorned the floor in front of the Shivalinga.

I took a deep breath and stepped out through the door. There was a courtyard in front of the temple and, beyond it, dense jungle. A narrow mud path had been cut through it, although the foliage was so thick, I couldn't make out where it led. The temple itself was surprisingly large, I noticed as I turned around to take it in. I had definitely never seen it before even though it was in the same Nagara style of all the Khajuraho temples. The sounds of drums were no longer muffled and, now that I was outside, they seemed to be much closer than I had previously thought. I looked around but there was no one in sight.

I began to walk around to the back of the temple to see if I could find anybody. That's when I noticed something that stopped me in my tracks.

It wasn't hot. I was outdoors, it was midday, but I wasn't sweating. The air around me felt crisp and dewy. The imposing foliage around smelled strongly of … foliage. Fresh, damp and heavy – like when you blended a bunch of spinach leaves and opened the blender lid to realize that spinach had a smell after all.

I immediately looked up at the sky and gasped. It was blue! Not the wishy-washy, cloudy blue I had grown so used to looking at in the last two years, but a sharp, clear blue. Like someone had photoshopped the sky.

'Oh God, this isn't happening,' I whispered.

Yes it is. That scrawny little witch sent you back in time.

'No, no … that isn't possible!' I ran to the rear of the temple. There was another clearing but that was deserted too. Where were the people? I reluctantly peered at the mud path leading into the jungle. I wasn't ready to be that adventurous.

'Hello?' I shouted, over the drums. '*Hello!* Anybody here?'

A scream answered my question. And then another scream, and another. It sounded like a child.

'Oh God.' I looked around frantically, biting back the urge to scream myself. The screams were coming from inside the jungle. I stared hard into its dark recesses. There was no other choice – I had to go in.

Taking deep breaths and fighting against the relentless slamming of my heart against my ribcage, I clutched at the sword and barged into the opening between the trees. Blindly,

I pushed against leaf-laden branches and stumbled over roots until the cries became louder. Then I heard a shuffling in the bushes nearby and turned towards it. A girl was crying hysterically and a man was cursing loudly. There were sounds of a desperate struggle. It sounded like … My eyes widened. 'No!' I shouted as I charged in their direction.

I took them by surprise. A man, obviously a priest by the looks of his bald head, sacred thread and elaborate white dhoti, held a young girl down on the ground with one arm. His other arm was busy trying to release his penis from the numerous folds of his dhoti. The girl's skirt was hitched up over her naked legs, her tiny body thrashing against the weight of a fully grown man, her face contorted with tears and terror. She couldn't have been more than ten years old.

Fury, cold and hard, washed over me. I bared my teeth and lashed out clumsily at the man with the sword. The blade struck him on his back, ripping through his skin and sending blood spurting all over the three of us. He screamed in pain and collapsed in a heap on the ground, his eyes widened in fear as he turned his head and saw me standing over him with the blood-stained blade pointed directly at him.

'You bastard!' I bellowed and lifted the sword over my head to bring it down on him again and stab his brains out. His eyes became as round as saucers and he whimpered loudly, putting his hands over his head in a useless attempt to protect it from being skewered by the blade. This is it, I thought wildly, I'm going to kill him.

'Na!'

The girl's voice took a moment to penetrate through the frenzy of feral rage coursing through my body. I stopped the sword mid-air and looked over at her, almost in confusion.

She scrambled up off the ground, pulled her skirt over her nakedness and stood up. Her face, streaked with tears and the priest's blood, held a pleading look as she gestured towards the sword.

'Tum kah karat ho! He's a Brahman!' she burst out in Bundeli, a local dialect close enough to Hindi for me to understand, especially after two years of living in Bundelkhand.

She gave the priest, now writhing on the ground in pain, a quick, scared glance and then caught hold of my hand. 'Run!'

Run? I shook my head. 'Don't worry, I won't let him hurt you.' I spoke to her in Hindi, trying to catch her panic-stricken eyes with my own, but she shook her head wildly.

'No, no … we have to run. They'll catch us!'

I was confounded. 'Who?'

Her eyes were desperate as she pulled my hands harder. 'The soldiers!'

Soldiers?

She tugged at my arm with more strength than I would have thought possible and pulled me into a frantic run. More branches and leaves hit my face as I chased after her through the jungle. I had no idea where she was taking me but it sure as hell wasn't back to the temple I had just left. The path was nowhere in sight now and I felt panic rising once again in my throat.

'Stop! Listen to me!' I shouted at her breathlessly. 'I need to go back to the temple.' It was my only link to home. If I had really travelled back in time, maybe I could figure out a way to travel back. Maybe the temple had a … what did they call those things in sci-fi movies … a portal!

'Please stop!' I yelled at her.

She quickly glanced my way before increasing her pace as she leaped over gnarly branches sticking out of the ground with the practised ease of a doe. I could barely keep up with her.

Suddenly, she rounded a corner and disappeared. I stopped and looked around, my fear going into overdrive. What was worse than being stuck in a temple a thousand years in the past? Being stuck in the middle of a jungle a thousand years in the past!

That was when I noticed a small entrance to a semi-camouflaged, underground cave a few feet away with the girl inside it, beckoning me. I scrambled into it and squeezed myself into a small trench, barely big enough to fit our huddled bodies and the sword by my side.

I had to catch my breath for a few seconds before I could look into her scared little face and ask, 'Are you alright?'

She nodded and then looked at me with guilt-ridden, petrified eyes and said in a voice that sounded older than it should have been, 'You shouldn't have struck him with the sword. They execute people who harm Brahmans.'

I blinked and sputtered, 'He was about to … to … hurt you.'

She looked away and blinked back tears, saying in that same voice, 'I know. But I must let him. It is my fate.'

No one should ever have to hear a child say that it was her fate to be raped by a grown man. I felt the force of my revulsion crush down on my chest and it was a moment before I could bring myself to whisper, 'How can you say that?'

She looked up at me, her eyes brimming. 'I'm a devadasi.'

Devadasi … a temple dancing girl. Pubescent girls who were formally married off by their families to a temple God so they could serve him for the rest of their lives. These girls were taught religious scriptures, classical music and dancing, and were supposed to dedicate themselves to worshipping their 'husband' through dance and song. In theory, they were second in status only to the temple priest. The wretched truth, however, was that they were more often than not used as a source of entertainment and free prostitution for the men around them. I took in for the first time her ragged state – her torn, moss-coloured cholaka, a longer, looser version of a choli blouse that reached the waist in front, and limp ghagra skirt of the same colour, her bare feet and the lack of any ornamentation. She didn't look like the wife of a god. She looked like a scared child desperately in need of help.

I shook my head vigorously. 'That's no excuse. He had no right to do what he did. Don't worry, I'm not going to let him hurt you. What's your name?'

'Puppa,' she said softly, shaking her head as tears began to drop silently onto her lap. 'You can't help me. I'm already married to the deity. They had my ceremony two days ago. Bari Didi told me I must do whatever the priest wants or he will be angry with all of us. She knew he would…' A small sob escaped her.

'Who's Bari Didi?'

She looked up at me. 'The eldest wife. She's been a devadasi at the temple for more than forty summers. She told me my family cannot keep me any longer. I have crossed eleven summers and no offers of marriage have come for me. My younger sisters cannot wait much longer. My grandparents are getting old.' More tears rolled down her cheeks as her chest heaved with low sobs. 'I must do my duty.'

'Where are your parents?'

Another onslaught of fresh tears. 'They died crossing the river. My father's brother has four girls of his own and said he can't afford to feed three more. They took in my younger brother and sent us to live with my mother's parents.'

I pursed my lips in helplessness. Puppa's situation was hardly unusual, even in modern times – thousands of girls regularly entered the sex slave market every year because their families couldn't afford to keep them. Before I could say anything though, she wiped her tears and shook her head resolutely. 'This is the way it must be.' Then she seemed to notice, for the first time, my muddy jeans, T-shirt and heavy-duty hiking boots. She tilted her head and asked, 'Why are you dressed like that?'

That brought me firmly back to my own problem at hand – the one which potentially involved me being stuck a thousand years in the past with nowhere to go and no idea how to get back to where, or when, I came from. I was reluctantly coming to terms with the idea, as ludicrous as it seemed. There were no soldiers or devadasis in modern-day Khajuraho and I knew for a fact that there were no unexplored jungles with large temples in them.

I looked carefully at Puppa's face. I couldn't tell her I was from the twenty-first century, obviously. Not only because she wouldn't believe I had travelled back in time (I hardly believed it myself) but because she'd probably run from the cave screaming 'Witch!' at the top of her lungs. Did they believe in witches in eleventh-century India? I had no idea but I wasn't taking any chances.

'I, er … am a traveller. From a distant land. They wear clothes like this over there.' Not the most original idea but I was hoping she'd buy it.

She tilted her head. 'Is it in the north?' She pointed at my arms. 'You have beautiful skin – fair and soft. Are you a concubine? I've heard the king has concubines with light skin like yours. They come from the Turuska lands.'

Oh God. This was getting worse by the second. Turuska was the medieval term for the raiding Muslim armies from the northwest. I looked down at the pale, almost-white undersides of my arms with growing dread – a fair-complexioned woman in these parts, in this day and age, would probably be considered at best a foreigner, at worst a spy. International borders were between kingdoms, not countries, and they were constantly changing. I didn't even know which year this was. 'No, no, I'm just a normal woman. Not a concubine or anything. From the north, yes, but I'm not Turuska, no, I'm just … I'm...' – think, Tara, think – 'I'm a noblewoman. From a *Hindu* northern kingdom.'

Puppa blinked. She obviously had no idea what the word 'Hindu' meant, which made sense, I quickly realized, because Hindu was still a Persian word at this point in time. I made a mental note to be more careful about what I said – there was no better way to get myself into trouble than by using Persian words. She looked at my clothes again and a tiny bit of suspicion crept into her voice. 'So women dress like men in your land?'

My jeans were obviously going to be as much of a challenge as my complexion. 'Sometimes. Now look, we can't stay in this hole forever. I need to get back to the temple urgently.'

'Which one?'

'The one close by.'

'There are many close to here. Khajuravahaka is a complex of temples. Which one do you want to go to?'

I hung my head in my hands, fighting panic once again. I had no idea what to do.

'What is your name?' Puppa suddenly whispered.

'Tara.'

'Tara,' she repeated. 'I can hear soldiers coming.'

7

It all happened so quickly I barely had time to react. One moment we were squeezed into the hole trying to be as quiet as possible while footsteps shuffled all around us, the next we were being propelled out of it by a wrinkled, claw-like hand that was a hell of a lot stronger than it looked. Bari Didi apparently knew where Puppa would be hiding and had led the still-bleeding priest and a handful of soldiers to the runaway devadasi.

I knew it was hopeless to try and fight off the soldiers – three of them, dressed in dull orange turbans and angarkhi-like tunics that tied up at their shoulders and waists with menacing swords hanging from leather cummerbands. They wore white dhotis just like the priest, but theirs were shorter, more serviceable and less ample, with minimal folds and flares. They would have been able to overpower me even if there weren't three of them. Still, after one glance at that priest's blood-ridden, child-molester face, I lifted up the sword and prepared to go down with a fight.

They froze when they saw my sword. All of them. Bari Didi, after exchanging a look with the equally shocked soldiers, spoke to me, 'Who are you and where did you get that?'

Puppa, struggling against the firm hold of one of the soldiers, shouted before I could say anything, 'She's a noblewoman!'

Bari Didi turned and slapped Puppa hard. But not before I saw her slight hesitation at the girl's words. Puppa burst into tears.

My heart broke for her and anger surged through me. Okay Tara, I thought, either you take a chance and play the part or you give it up and die. I decided to play the part.

'Unhand that girl,' I commanded. I straightened my back and looked around me in haughty disgust as if I were Cate Blanchett in *Elizabeth*. If I projected enough authority, they might … I didn't know what they might do, but I was hoping they might think twice before hanging me and sending Puppa back into the jungle with the priest. He would probably torture and kill her as punishment.

'I have taken this girl under my protection. Anybody who harms either me or her will be answerable to my father, who is an ally of your king in the north.' This was a long shot, since I had no idea who the king was or whether he even had any allies in the north at this point. Still, since Puppa had mentioned this was Khajuravahaka, I supposed that the king would be far away in Kalinjar and the people in this area would have little idea about their king's allies.

'You lie!' shouted the priest at me, his eyes bulging from hysterical outrage and pain. His back was still bleeding where I had cut him and, despite it being a superficial wound, he was going to have his revenge. He turned to the rest of them. 'She ran out of the jungle and attacked me!'

Then he spun back towards me. His voice turned slithery. 'What is a noblewoman in Turuska men's clothing doing in a jungle attacking Brahmans? With a king's sword?'

The soldiers had begun to look a little uneasy after I had spoken but now they nodded in agreement with the priest. Bari Didi just kept staring at me with half-lidded eyes.

I had no idea how to respond so I hedged. 'I am not answerable to the likes of you. A common priest. How dare you question me?' I raised my chin and pointed my sword at him with as much hauteur as I could muster.

The soldiers began to look unsure again. I drove home my point. 'Now unhand that girl or I will make sure you pay for it with your lives!'

One of the soldiers replied hesitantly, 'But she is a devadasi.'

I rounded on him in dramatic fury. 'And I am related to a king!'

He took a small step back and gulped, but still said, 'That may be so but it doesn't explain what you were doing in the jungle alone or why you are' – he pointed in awkward embarrassment to my clothes – 'dressed like that.' He blinked a few times in indecision before speaking again. 'If you won't answer to us, you'll have to answer to the mukhya mantri. Or the king himself. Come with us.'

He turned and began to lead the way through the jungle. I must have looked confused because Puppa, still being held by one of the soldiers, looked at me and murmured, with a small, heartbreakingly hopeful smile, 'The king is here.'

Bile rose in my throat and I fought the sudden urge to cry out. This was officially the worst day of my life. Probably the last day of my life too. Maybe, I thought, I should just give up and beg for a quick death instead of entangling myself inside a giant cobweb of deceit that would probably strangle me in the end anyway. Then I thought about my parents – they would be devastated if I just disappeared off the face of the earth. I couldn't give up. I had to try.

The pointy end of a sword nudged the back of my shoulders ever so gently. I swallowed hard, tightened my grip on Kala's sword and began to follow the soldier listlessly through the jungle. The priest, Bari Didi and the two other soldiers followed behind me. No one touched me, which I took as a good sign. Even if they didn't believe my 'noblewoman from the north' story, they were obviously treating me like a person of high birth. Puppa had said I had skin like a concubine – soft skin would be a precious commodity in an age before commercially manufactured sunscreens and body lotions. Only occupation-less, high-born women would have the time and money to invest in it. On the other hand, my clothes and the lack of any escort, not to mention the fact that I had attacked a priest, wouldn't exactly work in my favour. Maybe I could pull it off if I had a convincing enough story to tell. I took a deep breath, willing myself to think clearly. If I could just stay alive long enough to get back to that temple, I might have a chance of returning to my own time.

The rhythmic drums that had got fainter when Puppa and I had run through the jungle now began to grow louder amidst the hum of what sounded like a very large and rowdy crowd.

As we approached the sounds, I looked around. The trees blocked out any view I might have had of anything other than the rudimentary jungle path ahead. But the voices of the crowd were beginning to make sense. They were calling out in regular intervals:

'Jai ho!'

'Jai ho!'

I could hear a man's voice shouting between the pauses. At first he sounded muffled but as we walked closer, I could make sense of his words.

'Maharaja dhiraj ki...' and the crowd would yell, 'Jai ho!' Victory to the king of kings.

'Kalinjara maharaja ki ... jai ho!' Victory to the king of Kalinjara.

'Nanda Deva ki ... jai ho!' Victory to Nanda, the divine.

Nanda. I knew that name. It was a pet name. It belonged to...

'Maharaja Rao Vidyadhara ki ... jai ho!'

Vidyadhara. That made the year sometime between 1003 and 1035 CE, roughly the period when he could have reigned. I looked at the impassive faces of the soldiers around me. Were they taking me to the Kandariya Mahadeva temple? If so, then perhaps I could get a sense of my bearings and retrace my steps.

We walked into a clearing and I stopped, my heart torn between disappointment and awe. The temple in front of me was not the Kandariya temple. It was bigger, grander and it shone, like burnished gold, against the trees and sky behind it. The top of its elaborately carved, mountain-like peak was plated in actual gold, which glinted and gleamed as sunlight bounced off it. Flags, hundreds of them, protruded from everywhere, and thousands of buntings and garlands made from leaves and flowers hung overhead, suspended between the imposing temple pillars and the tops of the trees. Underneath this festive canopy must have been a thousand-strong crowd of men, women and children cheering and waving their arms as they stared with wide, toothy grins at the temple's imposing, raised dais.

On the dais burned a sacred fire complete with a gaggle of priests around it, and a large group of richly dressed soldiers standing guard. Nearby, stood a giant silver weighing scale that was as tall as an elephant and had been polished to the point where it almost hurt the eyes to look directly at its elaborately carved fulcrum, balancing beam and two massive, sturdy looking weighing pans. Sitting on top of one of the pans, being weighed against an enormous pile of gold, was the king.

I squinted but couldn't get a good look at him. The soldier in front of me gestured to Bari Didi, who nodded and grasped my arm firmly with both hands. Her hold wasn't overly tight or rough, but I knew that would change if I tried to make a run for it when we entered the crowd. The four of them made a tight circle around Puppa and me as we weaved through the gathering. Despite my fear, I looked keenly at the weathered faces around me. Most were bright-eyed and smiling, as if this event was the highlight of their year. Many of the men wore dhotis of muted colours under loosely tied tunics and turbans on their heads. Some of them wore just dhotis and a few holy men walked around wearing nothing at all. The women were dressed in short, tie-up choli blouses that covered their breasts and either saris that were draped in dhoti style around their legs or in flowing ghagra skirts and draped odhnas. Surprisingly, many of their heads were uncovered and they moved freely among the men. I also noticed many of the middle-aged and older women, like Kala Devi, hadn't bothered with a choli at all and had simply slung their saris over the shoulders and tied them at the back. I could see their breasts swinging out when they moved.

I looked across the sea of turbans and smiled, for a tiny moment forgetting the predicament I was in. It was refreshing to know there was a time in Khajuraho when women could walk around with their boobs and tummies hanging out and men were fine with it. I was soon reminded of where I was by Bari Didi who, irritated by my pace, pushed me to move faster towards the dais.

I looked up again at the figure sitting in the weighing pan when we got closer. The weighing ceremony was a popular one among Rajput kings throughout the ages. The king would be weighed and the equivalent of his weight in gold would be distributed among his subjects. With the bulk of it going to the Brahmans. Rajput kings were dependent upon Brahmans for good reason – they legitimized the divine right of the Rajputs to rule over their domains by writing and interpreting Hindu scriptures accordingly.

Most dominant Rajput clans were descended either from indigenous tribes or from ancient, immigrant groups of men that entered the Indian subcontinent from the northwest and married into existing communities – supposedly part of the 'Aryan invasion' that was so hotly debated among historians. This rather humble origin didn't sound very kingly, obviously, so Rajput clans constructed divine lineages for themselves as their power and influence grew. Some were descended from the Sun or Fire God, others from the Moon God, etc. This heavenly connection positioned them as rightful rulers in the eyes of their subjects. There was just one caveat – the Brahmans had always been the undisputed custodians of everything holy and divine since Vedic times, and they were the link between the king and the common man. Therefore their help and support in shaping belief systems and local culture was crucial. Which was why there were numerous ceremonies like the one that was taking place before my eyes. They were elaborate opportunities for the king to make payments for services rendered without looking like he was actually paying for them. Other, similar ceremonies took place every time there were solar or lunar events, Hindu festivals and auspicious days. The many plates and plaques archaeologists had unearthed at Khajuraho showed that the Chandelas, who considered themselves descendants of the Moon God, gave Brahmans gifts every time there was a lunar eclipse, or a full moon, or a new moon, or a half-moon, or no moon – basically, almost every day.

Which was probably why Puppa thought it was a bad idea to attack a Brahman with a sword. I took an unsteady breath and tried to temper a wave of panic.

The crowd cheered loudly and I saw that, since the king was still slightly heavier than the gold, he had waved for more gold coins to be added to the counterweight pan. We reached a line of guards that surrounded the dais and stopped behind them – waiting, I supposed, for the ceremony to conclude. I tried to find the king's face in the cluster of people around him. He was dressed to attract attention in a bright red, gilded angarkhi tunic, a gold-laden odhna draped over his shoulder and secured in folds at his waist with a chunky gold cummerbund. More gold profusions hung around his neck, shoulders and the turban he wore. A huge stone was set in a gold brooch at the front of his turban and more precious stones glinted on the golden hoops in his ears. I could see he had a well-groomed handlebar moustache but not much more of his face. The king sat with his back ramrod straight and looked straight ahead as the priests chanted loudly and the crowd egged on the man who was adding gold coins to the opposite weighing pan. He cut a resplendent figure that was somehow very masculine despite all the finery.

Finally, the gold and the king were the same weight and the scale was level. The crowd erupted into even louder cheers as a well-built priest put a huge conch to his mouth and released a deep, excruciatingly loud, reverberating sound that would have put modern conches to shame. It was a lot for the senses to take in – the noise, the crowds, the giant temple and the heavy smell of the forest and moist earth combined with pungent incense, spicy smoke from the rather large sacred fire, human sweat and oil. I felt a little dizzy as I watched the king get off the scale, inspect the gold that was being unloaded and sorted into cloth bags and come to the edge of the dais to wave to his subjects. The crowds shouted and cheered some more. Then, he disappeared into the temple with the priests.

I took another deep breath as Bari Didi's hands tightened on my arm and she pulled me towards the rear of the temple. The crowds had started dispersing and the priests continued with their chanting and invocations next to the sacred fire. I got a lot of curious glances on the way. The line of tall, well-built, lavishly decorated guards that had formed a formidable perimeter around the base of the temple stopped us and questioned the soldiers in hushed voices. After a brief discussion, they let us past and we trudged on, eventually turning the corner towards the backyard.

Here, I was surprised to see a large enclosure with a luxurious, gold-embroidered canopy above it and lush carpets on the ground. More guards were stationed around it and, inside, seated on divans filled with gold-embellished cushions and bolsters were a group of richly attired men. At the head, the king's seat was higher and more elaborately decorated than the rest and surrounded with fruit and finely carved gold and silver utensils. It was empty. Obviously, the king was still inside the temple and these were his … courtiers? Noblemen? Warlords? I had no idea. They were all dressed in a similar style as the king, with slightly less lavish jewellery and turbans.

One of them, a slim, distinguished-looking man in his fifties, with a giant grey moustache and grey hair brushing the nape of his neck, spotted me and Puppa with the soldiers, standing to the side. He looked me up and down with barely open eyes, seemingly disinterested, but I could feel his stare taking in every detail of my muddy clothes, my dishevelled hair and the sword in my hands. Then he looked away and proceeded to talk to another man beside him, ignoring us completely.

My chin went up and I straightened my back. These were extremely hierarchical people and I needed to look worthy of respect if I was going to pull off the noblewoman act. I couldn't let them see fear on my face.

Another man – shorter, plumper, younger and more richly dressed – glanced over at me, curiosity evident in his eyes. He got up and walked towards us.

'What is it?' he asked the soldier who stood in the front of our little group.

The soldier folded his hands and bowed low. 'Khajuravahaka pradhan ki jai ho.' Victory to the head official of Khajuravahaka. 'We found this woman in the jungle. She attacked this priest and then tried to smuggle a devadasi out of the complex.'

I turned on the soldier in anger. 'That's not true! I was trying to save her from the priest. He was the one doing the attacking –'

The pradhan reached me in a couple of quick strides and, before I could react, slapped me across the face. Hard. My head whipped to the side and my cheek burnt with pain. Through a haze of involuntary tears, I saw a glint of pleasure in his eye and my temper boiled over.

'How *dare* you!' I lunged at him, only to be held back by Bari Didi and then one of the soldiers, who looped his arms around mine from the back and clutched the sword grip so I couldn't use it.

The pradhan looked me over with disgust. 'You will speak when you are asked a question, woman.'

'I will not,' I shouted back at him in rage. 'I *will* speak. He was raping her! Do you hear me? That priest was raping this child. I was trying to save her!'

The injured priest, cowering on the side, now sprang into action. 'She lies! She attacked me with that sword.'

'Quiet!' The pradhan glared at me before clutching my throat in a vice-like grip. 'You dare speak to me like that, woman. Do you know who I am? I could choke the life out of you right here if I wanted.'

His fingers pressed down on my windpipe relentlessly. I couldn't breathe. I struggled against the soldier in a pathetic attempt to break free. Puppa screamed behind me as my lungs desperately grasped in vain for air.

'Let her go, Vidana.'

It was said in a calm, almost conversational voice, but the pradhan jumped back and let go of me as if my touch had burnt him. The soldier also quickly released his grip on me and the entire gathering dropped into bows, their heads lowered as their king casually strode down from the temple platform onto the ground. Everyone except me, that is. I clutched my throbbing throat and gasped for air as I straightened my back once more and looked King Vidyadhara straight in the eye.

He was magnificent. Long-legged, broad-shouldered, strong-jawed, bronzed, manly magnificence. I didn't normally like men with moustaches but this one wore his like a lion wore its mane. You couldn't imagine his face being more handsome without it. His eyes were like a lion's as well – deep, piercing and watchful, combined with the casual indolence that comes from knowing you're the one in charge. There was nothing indolent about the rest of him though – he moved with taut grace and radiated strength, energy and magnetism with every step. This guy was seriously hot.

And he was smiling at me. While everyone else had their heads bowed down.

I felt my back being pushed downwards roughly by the soldier behind me. I strained against his hand and stood ramrod straight. This was my only chance to make an impression. If Vidyadhara walked past me now, I was a dead woman. '*Show courage,*' Kala had said.

Vidyadhara walked over to me, his amused smile never faltering as he murmured, 'Now what do we have here?' as though I were an unusual-looking deer his men had caught in the jungle. He walked around me and checked out the sword clutched tightly behind my back as I followed him nervously with my eyes. Just for a second, I thought his eyes flicked over my butt, but I couldn't be sure.

He came around to face me and said softly, 'That's a very nice sword you have there. Where did you get it?'

'It's mine.' My voice came out hoarse and a little trembly.

His smile widened. 'No, it's not. You're not holding it correctly. In fact, I'd say you've probably never held a sword in your life.'

I gulped. 'It was a gift.'

He tilted his head to the side and gave me an amused look. 'I'm sure it was. And now you have the chance to gift it to a king.' He left the words hanging.

He wanted the sword? No! It was my only link to Kala and I might need it to get back to the twenty-first century. I couldn't give it to him.

'Please' – I hated that my voice trembled even more – 'I need it.'

Again, that smile. 'Ah, but so do I. Give it to me.' He stretched out his hand.

'No!' I stepped back and brought the sword up for the fourth time since I'd had the misfortune of running into Kala. I held it with both hands and pointed its blade at Vidyadhara.

Which was probably the worst idea in the world because each and every man and guard that stood around us – a hundred of them at least – drew his sword and aimed it at me. Two guards who stood directly behind the king now started to advance upon me. This was the end, I thought. This was how I would die.

'Stand back!' Vidyadhara ordered his guards. He looked at me, the sword clutched tightly in my hands, and his smile turned into a grin. Then, very slowly, he unsheathed the equally elaborate sword at his waist and stroked the blade of my sword with his own blade very gently, almost caressingly. It made a hissing, metallic sound that vibrated all the way down into my fingers.

He said, 'If you want to fight me, woman, you have to hold it properly. With one hand, like this.' He gestured to his own grip. 'Aim higher, put your feet apart and loosen your stance. You won't last very long if you insist on standing as stiff as a stick. Now, attack me.'

I shook my head. 'Look, I don't want to fight. I just want...'

'If you want something, fight for it.'

Maybe it was the indignity of being pushed around, slapped, then throttled, maybe it was just sheer frustration at my helplessness or maybe it was the goading tone of his voice, but I just lost it. I charged at him with the sword, flailing wildly at his blade and, judging from the momentary widening of his eyes, obviously taking him by surprise.

Not for long though, because he took a step back and held his sword flat against mine to easily block each blow I attempted. The air around us twanged and heaved but all I saw were his laughing eyes through a haze of anger.

Very quickly though, my arms began to ache and the sword became even heavier and more unwieldy. Vidyadhara clearly knew this would happen because he said, 'You need to hurry up and kill me before you get tired. Do it quickly – distract me and thrust at my heart or my neck.' He pointed to the vein in his neck with his free hand and grinned again. 'One jab here and I'll choke on my own blood.'

I cried out as I summoned the last bits of my strength to lash out at him, knowing fully well it was useless. My breaths came in short sobs and my arms burnt. To think that just hours ago, working at the excavation site, I had no idea I would be run through with a sword by the end of the day.

I knew the moment he decided to stop playing because his eyes flashed with excitement and he leaned forward. Then, as easily as if he was taking candy from a child, he thrust his blade on top of mine and pushed it around in circles, grinding down against my hands until I was forced to let go of my grip. Then he tossed the falling blade up sharply into the air with his own blade and, before I knew it, had caught the hilt of my sword in his other hand. It was over.

8

I willed myself not to cry as I massaged my throbbing arms, desperately trying to catch my breath. Crying was exactly what all these sadistic bastards would want a woman to do. I wouldn't give them that pleasure.

Vidyadhara was ignoring me for the moment as he examined my sword very closely, his own firmly sheathed under his cummerbund once again. He squinted slightly as he looked at the carvings on the hilt, the etchings on the blade, the massive sapphire in the centre. After a minute or two, he looked up, his amused smile firmly in place.

'You fight with courage, I'll give you that. Now let's find out if you have the courage to tell the truth. There's no name, seal or crest on this sword. To whom does it belong?'

I half-laughed as I let out a gasping breath. They were far more interested in the sword than they were in me. Maybe that was the reason Kala had given it to me. She would have known I couldn't possibly tell them the truth.

I answered slowly, making sure I committed the details to memory so I could repeat them if necessary, 'It belongs to my father. He gave it to me as a gift.'

'Who is your father?'

I had told Puppa I was from a Hindu northern kingdom. Which was technically true since my father's family was Punjabi. But Punjab was probably under the sultan of Ghazni's rule at this point and that would make me the enemy. However, Singh didn't become a common surname until at least a few hundred years from now so it probably wouldn't be identifiable with any particular family or area. I hoped. I had to stick to the truth as far as possible. 'My father's name is Gautam Singh' – which was true – 'and he is a minister' – which was a slight exaggeration considering he was a diplomat – 'in the kingdom of … Chandigarh.'

A light danced in Vidyadhara's eyes. I couldn't tell if he believed me or not as he replied, 'Chandigarh? I haven't heard of it.' He turned and loudly addressed the grey-haired man in the tent, 'Thakur Jajuka, have you heard of Chandigarh?'

Thakur Jajuka, the man who had glanced at me earlier, looked serious and a little bored as he replied, 'No, Maharaj.'

Vidyadhara turned to an elderly, overweight Brahman, expensively draped with various white odhnas and dhoti folds. 'Mukhya Mantri Sivanagaji, have you heard of the kingdom of Chandigarh?'

Mukhya Mantri Sivanaga looked at me as if I were a fly in his food. 'No, Maharaj.'

I persisted. 'It's a small kingdom, in the foothills of the mountains. Our ruler … er, Guru Gobind Singh, is a…' – what was the old, native word for Hindu? – 'a Bharatiya king.'

Vidyadhara smiled. 'I see. And you? What are you doing so far away from home? Without any attendants. Dressed like that.' He waved a casual hand towards my jeans.

This was the difficult part. 'I was kidnapped. By gypsies. I've only just escaped with my sword.'

He raised his brows slightly. 'Which gypsy would dare kidnap a minister's daughter? Your husband didn't do a very good job of protecting you, did he?'

The most straightforward options for my marital status – spinsterhood or widowhood – were both inauspicious. Then I remembered what happened to women of this time when their husbands died. I stammered, 'I … I have no husband. I decided to stay unmarried.'

The unwavering amusement on Vidyadhara's face told me he didn't believe a single word I was saying but he kept going anyway. 'That's a shame. Why? A beautiful noblewoman like you would be a worthy prize for any man.'

I kept silent. There was no point talking any more – he knew I was lying. Still, he continued, 'Such soft skin, untarnished by the sun and hard labour.' He gently nudged my chin up with the flat of the sword's blade. 'Such a beautiful face with a smooth, graceful neck. Such – ' he raked his eyes over my body – 'well-placed curves.' His gaze returned to meet mine and I saw that amusement had been replaced with something far darker – desire. 'What man wouldn't want you?'

Oh God. He was going to rape me. My eyes widened and I sucked in a breath. But before I could give voice to the terror that gripped me, he said, 'Don't worry' – leaning in and murmuring so softly that only I could hear – 'I find willing women far more enjoyable.'

He stepped back and looked at the priest whom I had attacked in the jungle. 'Panditji, concentrate on your prayers in the future. Devadasis are for the deity's pleasure, not yours.'

The priest made a few whimpering noises of denial but Vidyadhara cut him off with a quiet command. 'Go.'

The priest gave me a quick glare before stumbling off. I saw that the Brahman Sivanaga wasn't looking too happy about what had just happened. Obviously, Vidyadhara had gone against protocol by giving an unknown woman precedence over a Brahman.

The king turned back to me and scratched his chin before speaking loudly, 'What should I do with her, Thakurji?' This made Sivanaga look even more irritated.

Thakur Jajuka had the smallest of smiles on his face as he replied, 'As Maharaja Dhiraj wishes.'

Sivanaga said softly, almost involuntarily, 'Forgive my insolence, Maharaj, but she should be punished.'

Vidyadhara continued to look at me and scratch his chin. 'Perhaps. What is your name?'

I lifted my chin. 'Tara.'

'Tara,' he repeated softy in his deep voice and I felt a tiny shiver go up my spine. Then he leaned in again and murmured, 'Your story is a lie. Perhaps I can persuade you to tell me the truth.' He leaned even closer so I could feel his warm breath brush against my ear as he whispered again, 'I can be very persuasive.'

He turned around and announced, 'Tara Bai, from the kingdom of Chandigarh, will be a guest of the kingdom of Jejabhukti. She returns with us to Kalinjara until we can restore her to her family.'

My heart sank. Kalinjar was over a hundred kilometres away. I was never going to get back to my own time at this rate. Still, I was alive at least. For the moment. That would have to do until I figured out a way home.

A shuffling to my side reminded me that Puppa was still being held by the soldier. I quickly looked up at Vidyadhara, who was about to walk away. 'Maharaj, the devadasi … if I leave her here, she will be harmed, maybe even killed. She has not started her training yet. Please have mercy on her.'

The king briefly glanced over at Puppa and said, 'You may keep her as your servant.' He looked at the guards. 'Take them to the thakur's house. They ride with us at dawn.'

He swivelled around and strode into the tented enclosure. The guards bowed after him and turned to me, gesturing that I follow them. I gathered Puppa close and began to walk slowly, looking around quickly at the temple, the jungle, the position of the sun, trying desperately to find something familiar – anything that could help me identify the coordinates of this location. If I ever found my way back to the twenty-first century, I would need to return here and dig this temple out of the ground.

9

'You must wear it or the thakurain will be angry.' The middle-aged maid's face looked worried.

Despite her diminutive size, the thakurain, Thakur Jajuka's wife, had certainly looked formidable when she welcomed me at the threshold of her home a few hours ago. Pretty reluctantly, I might add. The hairs on my neck had stood on end as her heavily kohled, deeply wrinkled eyes took in every inch of my face, hair and clothing before condescendingly suggesting that, as their *guest*, I might like a bath and some clean clothes before the evening's festivities began.

Fiddling with the gold-embroidered yet surprisingly flimsy sari and tie-up blouse in my hands, I sighed. The only times in my life I had worn a sari were school performances, college cultural events and weddings. Someone else had always been at hand to drape them around me while I fidgeted uncomfortably and spent the rest of the evening moving around like a stiff zombie because I was worried I'd trip over the pleats in front.

'Isn't there anything else I can wear?' I eyed the maid's relatively simple, gilt-bordered skirt and blouse with a sturdy-looking odhna that covered most of her upper body and head.

The maid shook her head patiently, making the thick gold hoops in her ears swing from side to side. 'This is a royal Kayastha household. The thakurain and the kuwarani only wear saris. As do all the other women of the household. And you cannot wear servants' clothing.'

Kayasthas were an important part of the king's court. Traditionally, Brahmans had always been the only educated caste, taking care of all administrative and record-keeping activities for royal families. The problem was that Brahmans, who tied everything together with religious scripture, only propagated their own belief systems and had become power hungry and corrupt over the ages. The Kayasthas were a relatively new community, born outside of the regular caste hierarchy, who provided a viable alternative to the Brahmans as administrators and record-keepers. They were educated but weren't affiliated to any particular religious lifestyle and were culturally adaptable. This allowed kings to keep religion and state separate in a multicultural and secular society and also gave them a certain amount of personal freedom from Brahmanical doctrine. That was probably a big reason why Thakur Jajuka was obviously such a powerful man in this kingdom. Vidyadhara didn't look like a king who appreciated being told what to do by someone like Mukhya Mantri Sivanaga.

I held the sari up at the maid and huffed in exasperation. 'I don't know how to drape this.'

The maid smiled. 'I can help you.' She began to remove the large cloth I had wrapped myself in after a hurried bath in the small enclosed garden adjoining the room I was in. The thought of undressing in the open air, where anyone could just peep over the wall for an eyeful, would have dissuaded me from a wash had I not been covered in mud and sweat. I had ended up crouching in one corner in my underclothes while hurriedly scrubbing my skin with a paste that smelled of raw lentils and pouring warmed water over myself from a copper pot.

Which unfortunately meant that my bra and panty were soaking wet and I had to go commando and wear the sari and choli directly over my skin. Along with no petticoat, barely any back or belly coverage and not even the slimmest of linings to the thin tie-up choli that was to cover and support my far-from-negligible breasts. Worst of all, there were no safety pins to hold everything together. Not only would I feel half-naked walking around in this thing, I'd probably end up a fully naked, unravelled heap on the floor before the evening was over.

The maid, not privy to my thoughts, briskly went about getting me dressed while I stood still and looked around the palatial room. Carved pillars were covered in gold and silver leaf, and silken curtains wafted around embellished archways. A massive bed, with a plethora of gilded cushions and bolsters, stood in the centre of the room and a huge, elaborately decorated chest stood off to the side. The walls were painted with intricate frescos and dotted with arches, alcoves and nooks. The thakur was obviously a very wealthy man.

I asked, 'So who lives here?'

The maid went on draping the sari as she replied, 'Thakurji's family.'

'Who are they?'

'His wife, the thakurain, stays here with two of her unmarried daughters while Thakurji is in Kalinjara. Thakurji's nephew and adopted son, Kuwarji, also stays here with his family. He manages the affairs of Khajuravahaka for our king. Thakurji's three sons are managing other parts of the kingdom. You have come here on a very auspicious day, Tara Bai. Not only is our beloved Nanda Deva our guest for the night but also one of Thakurji's granddaughters is home to deliver her firstborn. Her pains started yesterday morning so we will pray for a healthy baby boy today.'

She bent down to pleat the material at my legs and I caught a whiff of oil from her hair. 'What if she has a girl?'

The maid's eyes widened momentarily but she continued in an unruffled way, 'It's inauspicious to say that. But if it is a girl, we will pray that the little bride-to-be is blessed with a healthy husband.'

I rolled my eyes but held my tongue. Instead, I remarked, 'The king is very young.'

The maid smiled. 'Our Nanda Deva is the greatest of kings. Jejabhukti is the most powerful kingdom in this world. We are very fortunate. He is not very young – already about thirty-four summers now – but he still has the strength, courage and vitality of a tiger. We will be cooking tiger meat for him tonight so he may become even stronger. It is from a very special tiger – the strongest, most feared, most virile one in the forest. The kuwarani, Kuwarji's wife, has commissioned a necklace made from its teeth for Nanda Deva. With this particular tiger's teeth around his neck, he will be invincible.'

Too bad the teeth didn't make this particular tiger invincible, I thought, cringing in shock and disgust. A thousand years from now, tigers would be an endangered species because of this kind of habitual disregard.

Before I could say anything though, the maid stood up, gave me a quick once over and said, 'Now you look like a proper Kayastha noblewoman, Tara Bai. Come, we must go. The thakurain will want to see you before she gets busy.'

I looked down and saw that the front of the sari had been pulled in between my legs and tucked in at the small of my back, creating a low-slung dhoti that didn't feel too different from wearing harem pants. Part of the sari had also been draped tightly across my chest, preventing my renegade breasts from bouncing around too freely under the loose blouse that obviously belonged to someone plumper than me. Outside of the fact that my stomach, arms and almost my entire back were uncovered and it was a bit too breezy around my lady-parts for comfort, it actually felt pretty comfortable. I did a little shimmy to check if the whole thing would fall off. It didn't. I sighed with relief.

The maid slid embellished leather slippers on to my feet and cast a dubious glance at my damp hair, which I had combed and twisted into a loose knot at the top of my head. 'Don't you want to oil and tie it?' She fingered the shorter wavy tendrils that had escaped from the knot to frame my face. 'It looks untidy.'

She sounded like my mother. 'No,' I replied as I brushed her hand away automatically. Every Saturday morning of my childhood had been spent pacing around indoors with various pastes and oils on my hair and body, thanks to my beauty-conscious mother. Once, she added dubious, ready-made turmeric powder to a face pack and we were both bright yellow for a week. I dispensed with all of it when I left home for college, thankfully embracing the expediency of store-bought products. Still, every time I walked into my parents' house, my mother would finger my face and hair, let out a little shriek and run off to mix something gross into honey and milk.

The maid shrugged and led me out of the room into a darkened hallway, with small windows near the ceiling that let in enough daylight for us to see our way. As we walked, I noticed the grooves in the walls where oil lamps would be placed later, when it got dark outside. I shivered just a little thinking about the approaching night, the thought of it somehow making me feel even further away from home than I already did.

We stepped out through a rather small door, onto a covered veranda which was part of a much larger outer courtyard. I looked out and saw lush gardens and orchards for hundreds of metres surrounding the house, which sat on top of a rolling hill. Beyond the gardens, in the distance, was the jungle – as dense and forbidding as before.

I asked the maid as we walked, 'How many temples are there in Khajuravahaka?'

The maid looked unsure. 'Many.'

'What about the big ones? The ones built by Chandra Varman.'

'Who?'

I blinked. 'Chandra Varman? He built eighty-five temples?'

The maid looked at me blankly.

I tried again. 'Hemavati? The princess who consorted with the Moon God? The one from whom your king has descended?'

The maid shook her head. 'Our king's forefathers certainly descended from the Moon God, Tara Bai, but I don't know about any princesses. Nanda Deva is from the blood of the great Sage Chandratreya and he is the direct descendant of the heroic brothers, Jay and Vijay. Khajuravahaka is the home of gods from many faiths and it is named after the Scorpion

Bearer, the Mahesvara. Most of those who come here for pilgrimage come for the Mahesvara. Like our Nanda Deva.'

'Has the Kandariya Mahadeva temple been built yet?' I asked absently and instantly regretted my carelessness. I was supposed to behave like a foreigner, not betray intimate knowledge of the area.

The maid frowned. 'I don't know of which temple you speak. As I said, there are many temples here. The king is building one more.'

'He is?'

'Yes, it will be as big as the temples his grandfather, Maharaj Dhanga Deva, built. May Nanda Deva be blessed with the same long life as him. His grandfather survived most of his own children and grandchildren. He lived more than one hundred summers before he immersed himself in the confluence of holy rivers at the edge of the kingdom! It is believed that he had a dream where the Mahesvara came to him and said it was time to join him on the heavenly peak of Mount Kailasa.' She smiled.

So the Kandariya temple was still being built. I wondered if I could figure out what year it was without arousing too much suspicion. 'Has the kingdom been … er … peaceful lately?'

'What do you mean?'

I swallowed. 'Any … invasions?'

The maid frowned again as she led me through another door and into another hallway. 'No one would dare enter Nanda Deva's kingdom! He has defeated the evil Hamira in foreign lands twice! He is invincible.' She looked away with pursed lips and I knew our conversation was over.

10

I chewed slowly, taking in the subtle flavours of the food. The silver thali in front of where I was sitting on a mat was crowded with silver bowls full of vegetables and lentils cooked in different ways. There were rotis made out of an unfamiliar, coarsely ground but soft grain. Surprisingly, there were also batis – balls of grain which crumbled and softened when mixed with ghee and lentils and were typical of the desert cuisine of Rajasthan. I absently wondered what they were doing all the way over here in Bundelkhand … and how Indian food could taste so flavourful even in the complete absence of chillies, which wouldn't reach India for a few hundred years yet.

Across from me, on a carved and gilded wooden divan in a breezy indoor courtyard, sat the thakur's wife, getting her jewelled feet pressed very solicitously by a younger woman, whom I now knew was the wife of the thakur's nephew and adopted son, Vidana, the pradhan of Khajuravahaka. The man who had slapped and then tried to throttle me. Despite my obvious misgivings about her husband, I couldn't feel any animosity for this woman the others called Kuwarani – she was a wispy, scared-looking thing who seemed like she was completely under the thumb of the short and plump force of nature that was her mother-in-law, the thakurain.

A little to the side sat one of the thakur's unmarried daughters, playing a game with a young child. They giggled as they rolled what looked like stones on the floor and paid little heed to me. Servants scurried around and I looked among them for Puppa, whom I hadn't seen since she had been whisked away by one of the maids for a bath.

No one spoke to me as I ate, but the minute the thali was removed and I was done washing my hands, the thakurain asked in an authoritative voice, 'You are comfortable here, Tara Bai?'

I took a deep breath, knowing an interrogation was about to begin. 'Yes, I am. Thank you for your hospitality.'

'You are the king's guest. We are honoured to serve you.' She didn't look in the least bit honoured.

'The king has been very kind.'

There was a moment of silence as she nodded. The kuwarani gave me a quick, nervous glance from under her lashes.

'You are from a kingdom called Chandigarh. Tell us about this place.'

I smiled as confidently as I could. 'Well, it's not very much different from here. We have a good king and we worship the same gods.'

She didn't look satisfied, so I continued, 'The summer is cooler than here but the winter is very harsh. The food is not as delicious.' I hoped that a bit of flattery might thaw her attitude a bit.

It didn't. 'Today is a fasting day for the women of this house.' She cast a disapproving glance at the spot where my thali had lain.

My insides cringed. No wonder she was so cranky. I tried to change the subject. 'I believe your granddaughter is about to give birth? You must be very happy.'

She finally smiled fondly. 'Yes.'

'I will pray for a healthy child,' I said politely. It seemed like the appropriate thing to say.

She peered at me carefully. 'Are you familiar with birthing?'

When I didn't reply immediately, she continued, 'The girl has had her pains for almost two days now. It is her first child and she is tired. We will appreciate any help.'

I looked at her nervously. I knew the mechanics of childbirth as much as any other modern woman who had only ever witnessed it in movies. Most of which involved screaming women with the messy bits strategically covered with hospital sheets. The only actual childbirth experience I ever had was visiting the hospital when my cousin was about to have her baby. I spent an hour sitting on a couch next to the bed, chatting with her while she updated her social media accounts and periodically told the nurse to adjust the epidural tube in her back. Still, I could potentially bring some up-to-date medical knowledge to the table which might help the thakurain's granddaughter. 'I know a little. I would be happy to help.'

She smiled again and motioned to the kuwarani, who stood up and timidly gestured that I should follow her. I semi-bowed and thanked the thakurain for the meal before following the kuwarani from the courtyard.

The kuwarani tinkled as she walked in front of me, the countless gold drops in her necklaces, waistband, armbands, bangles, anklets, earrings, toe-rings all colliding with each other as she moved. I was amazed at how much jewellery everyone in this house wore. There must have been at least two kilos of gold on this woman alone. The thakurain had sported a gold collar that looked an inch thick and half an arm full of bangles with giant rubies on them. Even the servants wore heavy gold hoops in their ears, gold armbands and anklets. No wonder Sultan Mahmud kept invading these kingdoms. They were loaded.

The thought of the sultan brought my mind back to my earlier conversation with the maid. She said Vidyadhara had fought Hamira, which was the local, medieval name for Sultan Mahmud, twice in foreign lands. The first time would probably have been in the battle of Waihind in 1008 CE and the second time would have been on the banks of a river in the Pratihara kingdom in 1019 CE. But Sultan Mahmud had obviously not tried to attack the Chandela kingdom. Yet. History knew that he showed up at Kalinjar Fort with an invading army in the year 1022 CE, to purportedly punish Vidyadhara for having his vassal king, Rajyapala of Kannauj, assassinated and installing his own vassal, Trilochanpala, on the throne.

A chill went down my spine and spread to the very tips of my fingers and toes as I digested that information. That meant it was sometime between 1019 and 1022 CE right now. There was an impending war at Kalinjar Fort sometime in the immediate to short-term future. *Not* a good time for me to be going there. I needed to escape. Maybe I could sneak out of the house tonight while everyone was busy with the festivities and find my way back to the temple. There *had* to be a portal of some sort or…

A woman's weak cries brought me abruptly back to the task at hand. We entered an antechamber where two female servants were dipping cloths into a large copper vessel filled with a pungent-smelling, dark green liquid. Beyond a pair of curtains, in a darkened room, was the granddaughter – a heavily pregnant, young girl of maybe sixteen, laying naked on a mat on the floor. She was being propped up at the back by an older woman, who was massaging her lower back and breasts in rhythmic motions with oil. In front of her squatted an elderly woman who was obviously a dai, a midwife, laying the soaked green cloths on her stomach and giving instructions to everyone else. The unadorned room stank of the green liquid, oil, vagina and sweat.

We walked closer to the mother-to-be and the kuwarani bent to stroke her sweat-soaked forehead gently. She said softly, 'Don't worry, beti. The Brahmans are chanting and laying offerings for you outside. It won't be long now. You will have your son at your breast soon.'

The poor girl was completely exhausted and her glazed eyes barely registered the words. The two dais attending to her bowed their heads at us, their gazes solemn and slightly worried. I noticed a line of metal implements lying on a cloth near the elderly dai. Razors, knives, long metal rods with all kinds of shapes at the end, long spoons and a pile of cloths, along with a selection of pastes and oils.

I saw my first opportunity to help and said in a firm voice, 'Have those instruments boiled in water before using them. The cloths also. That will clean them thoroughly.'

The elderly dai looked at me in an assessing way for a moment but bowed her head again before calling to one of the servants in attendance. Dais were lower caste women and I was dressed like a noblewoman. She may not have agreed with what I said but she wouldn't argue or call me inexperienced to my face. I felt slightly guilty for ordering her about but I had to play the part or the kuwarani would get suspicious.

I leaned over and felt the girl's forehead. It felt cold and clammy. 'Is she drinking water?'

The dai nodded. 'Yes. We are giving her sips of water from the fastest stream in the jungle. It will quicken her pains.'

I rolled my eyes. 'Please mix some salt, lemon and sugarcane juice in the water and then make her drink a glass of it immediately. It will give her energy. Has her water broken?'

'Yes. The womb's water came yesterday.'

I wracked my brains and tried to remember what I'd seen on a maternity reality show I had stumbled upon while channel surfing one day. While I'd gawked, both horrified and transfixed, a naked woman had popped a baby out into a bathtub and caught it with her own hands under the water. What did people like her do to quicken labour in these situations?

'Walk!' I exclaimed.

Everyone looked at me, startled.

I hurriedly explained, 'Walking around will help the baby come faster. Also, she should alternate walking and sitting with her stomach submerged in a large vessel of water. The water should be boiled and cooled enough to be warm. She must keep moving though – the more movement there is, the faster the baby will come.'

The dai looked intently at the kuwarani who looked at me nervously and asked, 'Are you sure this will help?'

I nodded firmly. 'Yes it will.'

'This is what they do in your land?'

No, in my land women go to a hospital where a doctor injects them with painkillers so they don't feel a bloody thing and slices their belly open if the baby delays its arrival for a minute longer than expected. Once it does make an appearance, they place the newborn in the mother's arms and take a photo to upload on to social media so that everyone she ever met at a party can share that magical moment with her. 'Yes.'

The kuwarani nodded shakily at the dai. 'Very well then. Let her walk and prepare a vessel that will fit her.'

We sat on stools as the servants rushed to do her bidding. Five women carried a gigantic silver serving bowl into the chamber and began to fill it with warm boiled water. The girl was given sweetened lemon water with salt in between moans and encouraged to walk around with the assistance of two servants. When the contractions came, I called out to her to keep breathing through her mouth and did my best imitation of expectant mums huffing and puffing in B-grade Hollywood romcoms.

After about an hour, as my butt started going numb from the hard stool I was perched on, the dai slipped her hand into the girl's vagina and turned her face to me with gleaming eyes. 'Her womb has begun to open!'

There were sighs of relief all around the room and the kuwarani smiled, putting her hand on mine. 'Thank you.'

I shrugged, genuinely happy I had been able to help the poor girl. In my time, she'd probably still be a schoolgirl, thinking about exams, make-up and boys rather than giving birth to a child. I took a moment to appreciate how far women had already come in my day. Modern women like me had walked on the shoulders of countless girls like this one – each small step forward for women like her had eventually laid the foundation for the freedoms I took for granted every day in my life. It was something to be deeply grateful for.

'I'm glad I could help. Please keep doing more of the same and I pray it won't be much longer,' I replied. Then I stood up. 'Perhaps I will take a walk in that garden we passed on the way here. I could use some fresh air.' And figure out a way to get out of the house without being caught.

The kuwarani nodded and smiled, her gratitude erasing any suspicions about me or my movements.

I walked out as casually as I could, trying to find my way not to the interior garden, but to an outer veranda or courtyard. I could hear sounds of revelry and music. The light coming into the house through the windows and columns was muted and shaded with the rosiness of dusk. The men of the house were probably entertaining the king and the courtiers in his entourage somewhere close by. I peeked around every corner before turning and made sure to steer clear of any rooms. Traditional Indian houses typically had separate areas for men and women, and I hoped not to inadvertently stray into the men's quarters.

No such luck. As I passed down an unknown hallway, a hand shot out of the shadows and grabbed me. It was the pradhan, Kuwar Vidana. And he had a drunken glint in his eyes. I screamed.

He clamped his hand over my mouth and pulled me into the shadows. I could smell the alcohol on his breath as he hissed at my ear, 'You'd better be quiet if you know what's good for you.' He pushed me against the wall with the force of his body.

Anger fused with panic as I struggled frantically and shouted in a muffled voice against his hand, 'The king! The king!'

His eyes widened for a brief moment. Then he sneered. 'You think the king will save you again? You think he gave you another thought once you were out of his sight? No, my beauty. He's forgotten about you already. But I haven't. You will regret the humiliation you caused me today, make no mistake about it.'

His free hand grabbed my bare waist and then slid up to squeeze my breast roughly. His expression turned lewd as his grip on my breast turned painful. 'But maybe I can sample the fine wares of Chandigarh before I have my revenge. A maiden, are you? Perhaps it's time you knew a man!' He giggled absurdly, his protruding tummy pushing against me harder.

His hand uncovered my mouth to move over me and I bared my teeth. 'Over my dead body, you asshole.' As I was about to poke his eyes with my nails and knee him in the crotch, I saw something move behind him.

'Kuwarji, what am I going to do with you?' Thakur Jajuka's voice, filled with annoyance, came from beyond the shadows.

Vidana jumped away from me for the second time that day, his unsteady eyes looking behind him guiltily as he swayed a little. Thakur Jajuka stood a few feet away, his demeanour and expression calm but his eyes full of anger.

The thakur glanced at me briefly and barked, 'Get back to the women.'

I scrambled, ran down the hallway and around the corner just as I heard him say to Vidana, 'If you used your intelligence half as much as you use your shaft, you might have been a mantri, a minister, in the council by now. You must know the king wants her for himself.'

I stopped in my tracks. Slowly, I slunk against the wall and inched quietly closer to the corner so I could hear them.

Vidana sounded wheedling. 'But, Kakaji…'

'Quiet. I promised your dying father that I would give you precedence over my own sons and have done everything in my power to ensure your rise at court. It's bad enough that Maharaj sent you here, away from Kalinjara, to a mere pilgrimage town. Had you taken that woman he would have cast you off to some tribal outpost or, worse, to the borders in the south or the west, where your tender neck wouldn't survive either the living conditions or the raids.'

Vidana was silent. The thakur continued in a scathing voice, 'Even now, Sivanaga continues to quietly implant his own men inside court and line his coffers. Every position lost to one of his people is a challenge to our influence with the king. I will not have you damage this family's honour, Kuwarji. Do you understand?'

'I understand. It was a momentary temptation. Forgive me.' Vidana's voice sounded a little sulky.

'Make sure the work on his precious temple goes smoothly and according to his plans, no matter how much the Brahmans or the treasurers protest. Make sure it's bigger and grander than the others. The chief architect is our man – keep him happy with gold. The collections from within the temple complex are off limits but collect what you can from the pilgrims in the surrounding areas and contribute more than just taxes to his coffers. Keep your head down and behave yourself. I will see to it that you come back to court in time.'

'Yes, Kakaji.'

'And send word to the thakurain that the foreign woman is wandering about. She must be watched at all times. Alert the soldiers around the house to be on guard in case she tries to escape tonight. And keep the devadasi locked in the servants' quarters.'

I pressed my back against the wall as my heart sank with the sudden realization that, in my hurry to escape, I had completely forgotten about Puppa. If I disappeared now, they would send her back to the temple priest and Bari Didi. I imagined her at the mercy of those monsters. My shoulders slumped and I squeezed my lips together to stop from crying out in frustration. I was going to Kalinjar.

11

My butt was on fire.

Not literally, but it definitely felt that way after an hour of holding on to a horse as it sprinted across the landscape. A soldier rode next to me, holding my horse's reins in his hands while Puppa clung to him from behind. Around us were a few hundred men on horses, riding in a thundering mass at the same furious pace. Vidyadhara had commanded that I travel with him and his soldiers on horseback, instead of following sedately in canopied and cushioned horse-drawn tangas, or wagons, along with the other, older members of his convoy. The tangas hadn't even been loaded when we set off this morning at dawn – the king didn't wait for them. Apparently, he liked to travel light. And fast.

I thought of our encounter just before we departed the thakur's house – I had sleepily tugged at my oversized, travelling odhna and bowed as the thakurain directed spicy incense smoke from a prayer thali in my direction with her hand. The king had walked by just then and the thakurain had quickly turned the thali in his direction, anointing his forehead with vermilion and praying for his safe journey back to Kalinjara.

I had rolled my eyes discreetly but then turned to find the king smiling in amusement again as he watched me.

He said in a laughing voice, 'I hear Tara Bai has captured the hearts of the thakur's household in just one day.'

Thakur Jajuka, who was standing directly behind him, stiffened for a split second before Vidyadhara continued, 'My men tell me that she helped in the birthing yesterday.'

The thakurain replied with a smile, 'Yes, Maharaj. My granddaughter's son is healthy and was born at an auspicious hour. Her husband's family will be very pleased. We are greatly indebted to Tara Bai.'

The baby had been born a couple of hours after I had left the birthing room. It was a boy, a fact that had led to frenzied celebration in the house. The women had sung songs and danced in the interior courtyard and the men had gotten even drunker than they were before. The sounds of conches had filled the air and a feast had been laid out for the king in the gardens. I had eaten indoors with the other women, who had broken their fast after a prayer ceremony. I had also eyed the meat on my thali dubiously, thinking about the unfortunate tiger whose teeth would soon be hanging around Vidyadhara's neck.

I folded my hands and bowed to the thakur and his wife. 'I'm happy I was able to repay your kind hospitality in a small way.'

The thakurain smiled again as we turned to mount the horses. Vidyadhara walked with me to my horse, waving the accompanying soldier away and whispering, 'You look even more beautiful in women's clothing,' in my ear before picking me up and firmly seating me on the horse.

Despite the odhna that had separated his hands from my waist, it was a while before I stopped feeling my skin tingle from the contact. Then, as the horse started trotting, I was too busy trying to hang on for dear life.

The king rode hard at the head of the riding party, with his personal bodyguards and a few courtiers at his side. There were no umbrellas over his head or rose petals in his path, no fanfare as he swiftly moved past jungle settlements. Behind them were the bulk of the guards and soldiers, while I rode towards the rear of the convoy. The cleared jungle paths soon turned into wider mud roads and, as we crossed the main square of a town, I was able to see a large open area in the distance. In the centre of the clearing stood a marketplace that was currently shuttered and would probably open later in the morning. On one side stood a massive stone gateway, an intricately carved lintel seated on top of a pair of pillars, flanked by two huge palm trees. Made from gold.

I sucked in my breath and gazed up at them. They were breathtaking, their intricate, radiating artistry and magnificence in stark contrast with the lush natural jungle that was their backdrop. I could see why this was a place of pilgrimage – not only did you get to pay homage to the gods, you could gawk at gold trees. These were the tourist attractions of the medieval world.

The king didn't stop to admire them though – he just rode straight through, entering the Khajuravahaka temple complex that stood on the other side. I realized that even though it was a jungle, the paths were laid out in an organized manner and there were generous clearings for communal spaces and the smaller temples, most of which I didn't recognize. Even if any of them were from the twenty-five that stood in my time, they were completely unrecognizable. Most of the temples we passed were surrounded by wooden structures, covered in bunting and flags, and were a much lighter shade of sandstone than I was familiar with. The mild, irrelevant and decaying park-like aura that emanated from the Khajuraho complex during modern times was absent here. This place felt visceral, evocative and throbbing with life, even though there were no crowds to be seen this early in the morning.

I had the strongest urge to slip off my horse and make a run for it. I was so close. If the paths were laid out in a grid, I could navigate them, comb the complex and find the temple I had woken up in. Yesterday, I had been disoriented and upset. Today, it could be easier.

Then I looked at Puppa, bouncing on the horse's rear end awkwardly and clinging on to the soldier's waist with all her strength. She turned her face towards me and smiled, despite her obvious discomfort. She was so innocent, so grateful to have been saved from her horrible fate. How would I ever live with myself if I abandoned her now? I sighed and gripped the saddle harder. I had no idea how I was going to get home, but I knew I needed make sure Puppa was safe before I tried.

The king led the way into another large clearing, which had a construction site at the centre of it. Finally, I knew where I was. In front of us was the half-built foundation of the Kandariya Mahadeva temple. Huge stones lay around in piles of many sizes. There were wooden structures in which half-carved stones were lined up against one another. On one end of the site was a line of wagons minus the horses, and on the other end, a sacred fire with priests in attendance. Hundreds of construction workers and craftsmen stood around, sleepily waiting for the king.

The guards jumped off their horses and made a line in front of Vidyadhara's horse. The gathered men all fell to the ground with bowed heads and folded hands as one of them yelled at the top of his voice, 'Maharaja Dhiraj ki…' – and everyone joined in – 'Jai ho!'

Vidyadhara got off his horse and waved away the guards. His gaze fell on me, shifting uneasily on my now-stationary horse at the back.

His lips twitched as he strolled towards me. 'Tara Bai, perhaps you need a break. Do they not teach women to ride in your kingdom?'

I pursed my lips in response and replied tonelessly, 'No, Maharaj.'

He chuckled. 'Come, walk with us. It will ease your pain.'

'Yes, Maharaj.' As much as I didn't want to be in close proximity to him, I did desperately want to get off the bloody horse. So when a soldier came to help me dismount, I ignored the screaming stiffness in my muscles and slid down, only to find that my knees had turned to jelly. I automatically clutched at the saddle to try and support myself when I felt a firm hand grip my elbow and hold me up. I held my breath.

'You are an endless source of amusement, Tara Bai.'

I gave him a glare under my lashes. 'Thank you, Maharaj.'

Vidyadhara grinned and murmured back, 'Yes Maharaj, no Maharaj, thank you Maharaj … What happened to the ferocious swordswoman of yesterday?'

I bit my lip to hold back a very disrespectful retort. 'She began to value her neck, Maharaj.'

He chuckled – a low rumble. 'Come.'

I breathed again as he stepped away and began to walk a few paces behind him. His touch, as matter-of-fact as it had been, felt disconcerting and I looked at the ground to hide my flushed face.

A shuffling on the side made me look up to see a wiry yogi, dressed in a tiger skin loincloth with most of his body lightly covered in ashes, walking briskly towards the king. He bowed briefly towards Vidyadhara without ceremony, his matter-of-factness testifying to his own power and position. 'Maharaj, I welcome you to this auspicious site.' His voice wasn't loud but exuded intelligence and confidence.

Vidyadhara nodded and said respectfully, 'I trust you are happy with the progress so far, Rajpurohit Sarvadasaji?'

Sarvadasa, personal priest to the king, nodded. 'The visions that the Mahesvara sent us through my dreams are being realized, Maharaj. It will be resplendent, just like the Scorpion Bearer himself.'

Sarvadasa's eyes, as he looked up into Vidyadhara's, had an intensity that reminded me of Kala Devi. Like her, he was also skinny and elderly but moved with a strength and flexibility belied by his size. I found myself wondering if they had other things in common...

'We are pleased to hear that. Where is the chief architect?'

A man dressed in a simple but elegant tunic and a large turban stepped forward and bowed deeply. 'On behalf of all the people working at this site, I welcome Maharaja Dhiraj and thank him for gracing us with his divine presence. We are honoured and overjoyed.'

I mini-rolled my eyes. Didn't Vidyadhara get tired of everyone kissing his ass all the time?

Apparently not. He smiled. 'We are eager to see the progress you have made.'

The chief architect smiled back. 'It would be my honour to show you the site, Maharaj.' He bowed to Vidyadhara and the two of them started off.

Sarvadasa's eyes flickered to mine and held them for a quick instant with a searing gaze, sizing me up. Then, as if deciding I wasn't worthy of notice, he swivelled around and began to follow the king.

I looked about at the sea of men and soldiers who surrounded Puppa and me, and decided the best course of action was to follow Vidyadhara as he had suggested. I caught Puppa's hand and scurried behind him, making sure we stayed a few paces behind.

The chief architect walked the king around the foundation, explaining in a quiet voice the progress they were making. I strained to hear them but was wary of venturing too close. Vidyadhara was right – the confidence I had felt the last time we met was missing. After what had happened with Vidana the previous evening, I felt shaken up. I kept seeing his blurry, intense eyes, smelling his foul breath and inwardly wincing at the memory of his hands squeezing my throat, my breast. My cheek still ached from where he had hit me and I was sure that, if I looked in a mirror, I would see bruises around my neck. My right breast already had black and blue marks where his fingers had dug into it. Yesterday was the first time in my life I had ever been sexually attacked, and I finally understood what women meant when they said they felt violated and unclean. The stench of the moment stayed with you long after you had washed and healed away its tangible remnants.

I took a deep breath and looked around the site again, trying to banish the fear and wake up my archaeologist brain. The foundation stones under the ground were massive. Offerings were strewn around a few of them, obviously from the day before. The priests next to the sacred fire chanted and prayed sleepily, as if they had been there the whole night. I wondered if they kept the fire and chanting going all the time during the construction period, which usually lasted years. I knew that the craftsmen had strict rules of conduct and typically stayed chaste, prayed and meditated before starting work, but this was another level of piousness.

Away from the foundation, at a distance, under wooden sheds and enclosures akin to workshops, were the carvings and spaces where the sculptors worked. I bent down and touched the smooth lines of a dancing apsara, startled for an instant at how enormous it was. High up on the walls, the carvings had seemed smaller than they actually were. It was such a privilege to see this up close, feel its newness. What a pity, I thought, that I couldn't have come here when construction was in full swing and the sculptors were at work.

'Do you like it, Tara Bai?'

I glanced up to see Vidyadhara and the men around him looking at me as I bent down. I stood up quickly. 'Yes, the sculptures are beautiful and so big.'

He nodded. 'They are big because they will sit halfway to the sky, but must still be accessible to the humble pilgrim who would have come a long way to pay homage to the deity.' He cast his eye over the sculpture I had been touching.

I caught my breath as it suddenly hit me that I was standing before Vidyadhara, the very man who had commissioned the much-debated sex carvings on the walls of the Kandariya temple. The only person who could bring to a close the longstanding debate about why such explicit stuff was depicted on the walls of a sacred place. And I wasn't in a position to ask him why he had put them there. What a giant anticlimax.

Then Vidyadhara looked at me with a spark of mischief in his eyes. 'Would you like to see more sculptures?'

I blinked. 'Yes, absolutely! I mean, yes, Maharaj.'

That made him chuckle again. He gestured for me to follow him.

Beyond the site, hidden by trees, there turned out to be a smaller complex completely dedicated to the carvings. There were huts and sheds and ovens and tools. And sculptures, hundreds of them of different sizes and in different stages of creation.

The king walked slowly, carefully looking over the carvings, until he came to a stop under a shed. He waved away the men surrounding him and said in a casual voice, 'Tara Bai, come here.'

I went closer to look and soon realized why he had made the men step away. My jaw dropped. It was the carving I had debated over with the tour guide the other day – the one which featured an upside-down man having sex with a woman while fingering the two attendants who were holding her suspended over him. It was lying flat on the ground, at an angle where I could clearly see the underside of the woman's buttocks. The part that was normally shaded from view when the sculpture was upright on the temple wall. At this angle, I could clearly see the man's erect penis partly sheathed in his partner's vagina.

The attendants' features hadn't been fully carved yet, but the rest lay before me in huge, intricate, shocking detail.

Vidyadhara looked at me carefully and tilted his head in barely disguised amusement. 'What do you think?'

There were many things that could have potentially caught my attention – the delicate detail of the woman's jewelled armband, the coil of her hair that was suspended forever in the process of becoming undone, the layers of intricate necklaces around the man's neck – but I just stared at the space where their bodies joined. Even though I had seen it a hundred times before, it had always been far away, a distant novelty I never had to deal with. *This* was so big and so close it felt overpowering and uncomfortable. 'It's obscene,' I whispered before I could help myself, and then groaned inwardly.

To my surprise, Vidyadhara laughed. 'Why do you think it's obscene?'

I gulped and looked up at his face. He didn't look in the least bit offended. In for a penny … I soldiered on. 'Well, look at what they're doing. Even if you discount the fact that you need to be an acrobat to actually get into that position, how can you do it in front of other people, *with* other people simultaneously? It's a private act, between a couple. Or at least it should be.'

Vidyadhara's smile had got wider as the words tumbled out of my mouth. By the time I'd finished, it was a teasing grin. 'Why should the act be private, Tara Bai?'

Well, duh! 'Because … I don't know. It just should. This is…'

'This is what? Tell me.'

I wanted to slap that grin off his face. 'It's kinky.'

He looked a little confused at that. 'What does "kinky" mean?'

Oh God, I needed to shut up. 'Well, I guess it means out of the ordinary. Something that is not normal or commonplace. Something … deviant.'

Vidyadhara considered me for a moment, the amusement suddenly gone. Then he looked around the complex, said, 'Follow me,' and strode off towards the construction site.

The chief architect, Sarvadasa and the rest of the men scampered after him. I mentally kicked myself and began to follow, dread simmering in my chest. What was I *thinking*? He was the only thing protecting Puppa and me from all the paedophile priests and Vidanas of this world and I had gone and pissed him off.

So I walked up to him, ready to apologize, as he bent down between two large stones that had been carved into cubes. On one stone was a longish, rectangular block sticking out of the centre of one side. Like the stone cube had a penis, basically. The other stone, well, it had a rectangular vagina – a hole exactly the size and shape of the other stone's penis. I knew that this was how most of the Khajuraho temples were constructed – stones that were fit into one another using 'male' and 'female' parts and then stacked to form walls and pillars. In an age when cement and other modern binding materials were absent, this simple, interlocking technique had proven surprisingly stable and long-lasting.

Vidyadhara pointed at the stone and then looked up at me. 'These two stones were built to fit one another and stand with countless other stones just like them. On their own, they are useless. Joined together, they can support a structure that will almost touch the sky. Alone, each of these pairs are just coupled stones. When all the pairs unite as one, they are a tribute to the Mahesvara himself. Is that … kinky?'

I looked at the stones. Only the most perverted of minds would see anything pornographic about the way they would fit together.

'No, it's not.' I looked up at him. 'It's perfectly natural.'

He nodded. 'So was the act you saw depicted in the carving. The only problem, Tara Bai, was in the way you looked at it.' He leaned in and said softly, 'Reminds me of our Turuska friends in the north. They too seem to think our sculptures are obscene. But you said you came from a home-grown kingdom, didn't you, Tara Bai?'

I pressed my lips together. So that's why he had shown that carving to me. 'I do come from a home-grown kingdom, Maharaj. I'm not associated with the Turuskas.'

He smiled. 'We'll find out soon enough, Tara Bai.'

He turned and waved to his men to bring the horses.

Once he had spoken to the chief architect and we were all mounted, Vidyadhara turned his horse towards the crowd of workers and addressed them. 'The Mahesvara has smiled upon you and your families that you are able to contribute to his magnificence. We are grateful for his blessings. Jai Bholenath!' he roared.

'Jai Bholenath!' chorused the workmen back fervently.

He kicked his horse into a gallop and disappeared with his entourage, leaving a thundering cloud of dust in his wake. I had barely pulled my odhna over my head and the bottom half of my face as my own horse leapt forward into the cloud … and the unknown.

12

'He has two wives. The first one is Maharani Satyabhama and the second is Rani Vijaya. The maharani is from Rajputana and they say he loves her even though she's deformed. They say the second one, Rani Vijaya, is young and very beautiful but she can't have a child because…' – Puppa leaned in closer until her soft voice was an even softer whisper in my ear – 'she's cursed.'

I sighed as I splashed the cool stream water on my face, arms and feet. Puppa looked as tired as I did from half a day of hard riding across a mostly uninhabited landscape. Still, that didn't stop her from sharing gossip she'd overheard in the servants' quarters at the thakur's house.

'There could be many reasons why the rani cannot have children. Outside of curses, that is.' I smiled at her wryly.

Puppa shook her head with breathy excitement. 'No, Tara Bai. Maharani Satyabhama is very powerful. The kuwarani's maid said that the king is under her control. Maybe she cursed his second wife so he would always favour her.'

I looked at the temporary camp the soldiers had set up downstream for the king to rest and eat a midday meal. There was a big tent with divans and servants holding large feathered fans. But Vidyadhara chose to sit unceremoniously with his men under the shade of a massive tree while the soldiers watered and fed the horses further downstream. I had grabbed Puppa, told the embarrassed soldiers guarding us that we had 'women's business' and come upstream for some privacy. I guessed they weren't too worried about us running away since we were in the middle of nowhere.

The stream water slid down my parched throat tentatively and I was relieved to find it tasted clean and even a little sweet. 'I thought the maid said he loved the maharani. Why would she be jealous?'

Puppa drank as she spoke. 'Yes, but they've been married since they were children. Their oldest son, the rajkumar, is almost nineteen summers now and he has his own children. Men cannot stay devoted to one woman for that long. It's impossible,' she said, with an absurdly wise look on her face. It reminded me of people who say things like, 'Monogamy is an unnatural physiological and psychological state for the human species,' to sound intellectually provocative at parties.

It also made me a little pensive. I was naturally inclined to treat Puppa as a child, but she had very little of the innocence or immaturity of modern kids. The maid who had dressed me in the thakur's house had said Vidyadhara wasn't young, but he couldn't have been a day older than Hari. If his son was almost nineteen years old, he had to have had him when he was just a teenager. His maharani wouldn't have been older than the young girl whose labour I had helped with yesterday. It was hard to wrap my head around the fact that even though I had saved Puppa from being raped by the priest, she might still end up married and pregnant, perhaps before she became a teenager.

I pushed a tendril of her hair behind her ears and took some small satisfaction from the fact that, at least for now, she was well fed, wearing clean clothing and looked relatively content. I reminded myself that I would have to find a livelihood for her in Kalinjar before I left.

'Did the servants say anything about the kind of person the maharani is?' I asked tentatively. I didn't know much about Satyabhama from history, apart from a plaque or two that had been unearthed with her name on them. I guessed, however, that she wouldn't exactly be thrilled to see her husband bringing home a strange woman when he was supposed to have gone on a religious pilgrimage.

A rustle sounded in the bushes nearby before Puppa had a chance to answer. She screamed just as a soldier popped out of one of them and made a run for it. He had been spying on us!

I stood up and shouted at him, 'You pervert!'

Downstream, I saw Vidyadhara leap up and run towards us, encountering the peeping soldier on the way and catching hold of him roughly by the back of his clothing. He locked the soldier's arms behind his body and marched him back to the spot we were standing.

Vidyadhara threw the shaking man at my feet. 'Tara Bai, he is at your mercy.'

The soldier whimpered, his eyes darting back towards his king. 'Forgive me. It was a mistake.'

I was beyond angry. 'You're not sorry. You're only asking for forgiveness because your king is standing right behind you.

The minute he's not around, you'll be off peeking at other women, you depraved coward.'

Vidyadhara had the smallest of smiles on his face as his eyes raked over me. I suddenly remembered that I had taken my odhna off to wash myself and my thin, scrunched-up sari was probably not providing much coverage. He said in a stern voice that had a hint of laughter in it, 'Should we have him blinded so he can never look at a woman again?'

A part of me really wanted to say yes, but I replied instead, 'He certainly deserves to be blinded.'

The soldier almost buried his forehead in the ground in front of my feet and begged, 'Please, please show mercy! I swear on my mother's life I will never do it again! I swear on my sister!'

I shook my head. Indian men only ever remembered their mothers and sisters when they got caught.

Vidyadhara gazed at me over his soldier's head. 'What do you decide, Tara Bai?' His lips twitched.

The man whimpered again and I sighed. 'I will let him go. This time.'

Vidyadhara looked at me thoughtfully and then kicked the soldier's backside as he said, 'You have been spared. And warned. Go!' The man scrambled down the stream's banks without looking back.

Then he looked at Puppa and commanded softly, 'Get your mistress some food.'

Puppa gave me a quick glance before bowing with folded hands and scampering off in the same direction as the soldier. The camp seemed to suddenly go quiet and I held my breath as I looked into Vidyadhara's contemplative eyes. I couldn't tell what he was thinking but I couldn't mistake the desire I saw there. He had sent Puppa off deliberately, to be alone with me. My eyes widened slightly as I looked into his. The king had saved me from his men, but who would save me from the king?

'I told you, Tara Bai' – his voice was low – 'I don't force women.'

Still, I felt my breaths become shorter as he made no effort to stop looking in my direction. He was standing only steps away and, even if he didn't have any plans to force himself on me, I was overwhelmingly aware of his presence. And the possibility that I might have splashed generous amounts of stream water on the front of my blouse. Cold water. I bent down to pick up my odhna.

'Don't.'

I ignored him and wrapped it around myself like a shawl. Then I looked up at him defiantly.

He cocked his head, his expression unreadable. 'Do you dare disobey me?'

I replied irritatedly, 'If you didn't look at me like that, Maharaj, I wouldn't need to disobey you!'

He smiled. 'Maybe I should be blinded too.'

I lifted my chin. 'Maybe.'

He laughed. 'Maybe I already am.' He turned to walk away. 'You have a beautiful body, Tara Bai. It's a shame you insist on hiding it.'

'I hide it to protect it!'

He turned back to me, his gaze flicking over my indignant expression. 'From whom? You knew I wouldn't touch you. Unless you asked … nicely.'

I glared at him. He gave me a grin and strolled away, back to the camp, just as Puppa came scurrying towards me with an armful of sweet, ghee-laden fresh rotis.

I sat on the ground with a thump and looked down at myself under the odhna. My blouse was not only soaked through in some spots but the drape of my sari was wedged in between my breasts, tightening the blouse and making my taut, peaked nipples strain up against the thin fabric. It looked like a Bollywood item-song costume. Without the built-in bra.

I groaned. If I walked around in the twenty-first century looking like this, I would likely end up in a ditch somewhere and a bunch of politicians would go on TV and say, 'She was asking for it. She should have worn traditional clothes.' The irony was laughable.

I cursed under my breath as Puppa laid the rotis on a cloth. I would need to stay away from Vidyadhara once we got to Kalinjar. Hopefully fade into the crowd until he forgot about me or at least got distracted by all the other women at his disposal.

We ate hungrily and drank again from the stream. Soon, a soldier called for us from below and I gritted my teeth as I climbed stiffy back on my horse. My muscles were already screaming in pain and there was still half the journey left.

However, the second half of the ride was nothing like the first. Vidyadhara was obviously concerned for my safety because, this time, my horse was positioned directly behind his at the front of the contingent, within the circle of his personal guards. One of them held the reins to my horse and Puppa was a few horses behind. Instead of a perpetual cloud of dust in front of me, I was able to actually look around and enjoy the lush, green landscape that surrounded us – forests, streams, hills overflowing with vegetation. At one point, a large herd of deer appeared from nowhere and began to run with us and, for a few moments, I completely forgot my pain and laughed in wonder. The dry and scraggy Bundelkhand I remembered was nothing like this.

I glanced ahead at Vidyadhara, astride his horse. He rode effortlessly, his body swaying to the horse's rhythm. I tried to relax my rigid stance and copy his swaying but was thoroughly distracted by the striking figure he cut on horseback – the generous width of his shoulders, the ripples of his lean muscles as they strained against the riding tunic over his upright back and, if I was perfectly honest with myself, the very suggestive way his hips moved in tandem with his horse's lengthy strides. It finally made sense to me why they got Indian bridegrooms to arrive for weddings on horseback.

Stop checking him out, Tara.

I'm not checking him out, I told myself in a huff. I'm merely making an observation about the origins of Indian wedding rituals.

Yeah, right. The only wedding ritual you're interested in right now is…

I shook my head firmly before averting my gaze towards a hill in the distance.

13

The sun dipped closer to the horizon and I thought I would fall off my horse in exhaustion. Then I saw it. It was unmistakable. A plateau higher than everything else around it, with a fort that looked like it had grown out of the ground at the very top – a gigantic, undulating stone trunk that seemed even bigger and more imposing than its modern version. I couldn't see the north cliff since we were approaching from the southwest, and the high walls were somewhat blocked by a thick jungle that engulfed it on this side, but I assumed we had reached Kalinjar.

Only, the closer we got, the more it looked nothing like the place I had visited. This wasn't a sleepy memorial to a bygone, glorious past. This was a vibrant, thriving, crowded township. The boundaries of the town extended much further than I expected and, within its ramparts, buildings upon buildings that probably housed tens of thousands of people if not more. Villages surrounded the base of the plateau. Fields stretched out around them and they were full of people, cattle and carts. A caravan made its way slowly towards the town some distance away – a long line of carts, cattle and even elephants carrying immense loads on their backs. I blinked – had I not known we were coming here, I wouldn't have recognized it.

As we approached, I heard hundreds of conches blowing in the distance. Vidyadhara gestured with his arm and a group of soldiers galloped ahead of him, past the villages and towards the township at the base of the fort. We slowed down and, after a while, entered one of the villages on the way. A large crowd of people stood in the main square, shouting and cheering for their king. The guards made a tighter circle around Vidyadhara and one of them held an elaborate umbrella over his head as he nudged his horse forward with his legs and waved at them, smiling.

Suddenly, an old woman threw herself, face first, right in front of his horse's path, wailing loudly. One of the other stallions flanking the king's mount reared back and the guards shouted sternly at the woman to get out of the way. Vidyadhara raised his hand to silence them. He urged his horse past the others towards her and said gently, 'Speak. What ails you?'

She crouched at his horse's feet with folded hands and sobbed loudly, 'My granddaughter! Maharaj, my granddaughter!'

Vidyadhara asked, 'What happened to your granddaughter?'

She looked up at him with tears cascading down her cheeks. 'They took her into the fields, Maharaj. Over there!' She pointed to one of the unharvested fields.

'Who?'

'The rajkumar and his men.'

Vidyadhara's face flashed with fury. He shouted to his men and soldiers to remain where they were, quickly turned his horse and set off at a gallop towards the field. A small group of his personal guards followed him, while the rest of us waited in the village, unsure about what to expect. The old woman continued her wailing, sitting on the ground, waving her arms about and throwing her head back, while most of the other villagers just gathered around, watching the spectacle as if they were completely separate from it. I wondered why no one was going over to comfort her.

I told the guard who held my horse's reins that I wanted to dismount. He looked unsure and asked a reluctant, 'Why?' with downcast eyes.

I said I wanted to help the old woman and saw his eyes instantly look up and widen. Then he shook his head emphatically. 'She is of the servant caste. You cannot touch her.'

Irritation washed over me and I looked around, considering for a moment what to do. The old woman didn't look injured in any way. I decided, since the entire village and all the soldiers were watching, perhaps the best course of action was to not draw attention to myself for the moment.

The sound of hooves announced the return of the king and his riders. Three young men on horseback with downcast eyes followed Vidyadhara and a young girl, maybe about thirteen but with particularly well-developed curves, sat behind one of the guards on his horse. She hid her face in one hand and looked like she was crying.

I watched as Vidyadhara commanded the girl to go to her grandmother. The guard helped the girl down from the horse and she ran to her grandmother's side. The old woman looked anything but happy to see her granddaughter and immediately began hitting her relentlessly. I watched in shock as she screamed, 'She's ruined! Her honour is ruined. She has brought shame upon us. Why, oh why, didn't you kill her, Maharaj?' More tears flowed down her face.

Vidyadhara ignored her and glared at one of the young men who was obviously his progeny – a richly dressed teenage version of himself. The boy couldn't have been more than sixteen years old, which probably made him one of the younger brothers to the king's heir whom Puppa had mentioned was nineteen. His father looked at him in contempt and said, 'Get down from your mount and speak for yourself, Rajkumar.'

The rajkumar was red-faced and taut with fury equal to his father's. He grimaced in outrage as he dismounted and went to stand at the centre of the gathering. He looked around – at his friends, at the girl who stood sobbing steps away from him – and, finally, up at his father.

'I did nothing wrong,' he spoke loudly and with authority. 'She came with me willingly.' He stood with his back straight and chin high – a perfect picture of wronged youth.

That made the girl sob louder and the grandmother start lashing out at her again, spitting, 'Whore!' and 'Disgrace!'

Vidyadhara commanded her to stop and addressed the girl, 'Is this true? Did you go willingly? Speak without fear.'

The girl looked beseechingly up at the rajkumar but he kept his eyes focused on his father and ignored her. It was obvious that she had feelings for the boy, even though they clearly weren't returned. She cried harder as she turned to Vidyadhara and stammered out, 'I … I did.'

The son raised his eyebrow at his father almost indistinctly, as if to say 'See? I told you,' but Vidyadhara didn't back down.

'Rajkumar, is there a shortage of women for your pleasure at the palace?'

His son's lips went tight as he railed against the sarcasm. 'No, Maharaj,' he ground out.

'Then why do you choose to dishonour the village women?'

'She was—'

'Quiet!' Vidyadhara looked at his son in disdain. 'It matters little if she was willing or not. Your subjects are not your toys, to be played with without regard. You are responsible for their welfare and, by dishonouring their women, you are bringing dishonour upon the king's position as their protector.'

The rajkumar flushed and he looked down at the horse's hooves, his teenage face torn between outrage at this perceived injustice and shame at the truth of his father's words. He mumbled, 'Forgive me, Maharaj. It won't happen again.'

Vidyadhara nodded. 'Perhaps not. But you will be punished.' He turned to the old woman and said, 'You will receive a generous dowry for your granddaughter. Now, take off your slipper and hit the rajkumar.'

The crowd, the soldiers and even the old woman gasped loudly. The rajkumar's face looked like it was going to spontaneously combust as he stared, unmoving yet shivering, at the ground. His two friends eyed each other in shock and their horses started shifting uneasily. Everyone stared at the king.

Vidyadhara kept looking at the old woman. He said firmly, 'I told you to hit the rajkumar with your slipper. On his head.'

The old woman looked terrified. She folded her hands and crouched on the ground again but Vidyadhara said, 'Your king commands it. Anyone who tries to oppose or punish you for it will face the king's wrath and retribution. Now, do it.'

The rajkumar was breathing heavily, as if barely keeping his anger in check. He flashed his father a glare, walked up to the old woman and lowered his head, waiting. She gulped but took off her slipper with trembling hands and whacked him on the side of his head with it. The crowd gasped again and broke out into loud murmurs, their eyes wide and their open mouths covered with jittery palms.

The rajkumar said nothing as he turned around, bowed low with folded hands in front of his father and then quickly mounted his horse and galloped away at breakneck speed. His friends quickly followed.

Vidyadhara gazed around the crowd. 'Let it be known that no one is above the king's justice. Come and collect your compensation in court,' he said to the old woman.

She bowed shakily and moved away, dragging her still-crying granddaughter with her.

The crowd started cheering as we rode on. We entered the forest through a rock-cut road heavily shielded by tall, fortified ramparts. It was barely wide enough for three horses or one elephant. Higher and higher we climbed until we reached a huge gate – giant, thick wooden doors under a lintel, flanked by towers and embedded with massive metal spikes that looked like they could impale an elephant.

Once inside, we climbed an even steeper road that included even more fortifications on either side. Between the loopholes and undulations high on the walls, I could see narrow ledges, slits, levers and metal links – probably to be used in case the fort was attacked. I remembered reading somewhere that they used to pour hot oil on attacking soldiers and make the road slippery so horses and elephants couldn't walk on it. This fort was no holiday retreat, like so many of its modern counterparts. This was a serious military stronghold.

We entered the town through another series of gates, none of which I recognized. Thousands of people had gathered along the way, on either side of the narrow street and along windows, ledges and rooftops, pushing against each other to see their king. The noise and cheers were deafening. The earthen houses and structures were so close together that they seemed to almost share the same foundations. Water flowed down the middle of the streets and young children skipped over it to run in front of the convoy. Flower petals rained down on Vidyadhara's umbrella from the rooftops as he passed by. Everywhere one looked, there were people with grins on their faces, happy to have their ruler back home. Vidyadhara was obviously wildly popular among his subjects.

We went past a marketplace and my nostrils were hit by the overwhelming smells of roasting nuts and spices, overripe fruit and vegetables and dung. A large water kund was overrun with women filling pots, and people bathing or washing clothes. They all bowed and waved to the king. An elaborate temple stood in a large square around which vendors wandered about selling offerings and trinkets. A cloth vendor sitting on the side of the square looked at me and held up a roll of silken cloth with eager eyes that implied he was open to haggling. I chuckled softly. Some things never changed.

We climbed higher and reached the end of the town where, under another massive gate, I saw a jumble of red vermilion handprints on the walls. My mood, exhilarated after seeing so many happy faces around us, quickly plummeted. The handprints were sati marks – left by women who were on their way to jump into their husbands' funeral pyres. The sheer number of them astounded and repulsed me. And reminded me why I had to get home. Urgently.

Behind the gate waited a welcoming party. At its head was a man on horseback who smiled broadly as Vidyadhara rode towards him. Dressed in a rich but simple tunic, the man was as powerfully built as Vidyadhara, but his face was heavily scarred on the left side. As we got closer, I saw that the scars were actually burn marks. His features were stretched and misshapen because of his injuries, giving him a villainous air that was belied by the warmth in his eyes. As he tried to bow to the king, Vidyadhara came close and slapped him on the back, pulling him into a rough half-hug over the horses' heads.

The man returned the king's affectionate smile before he turned and saw me. He looked back at Vidyadhara with neutral eyes, saying nothing.

Vidyadhara gestured to me. 'Tara Bai. From the kingdom of Chandigarh. She is to be our guest.'

The man looked back at him carefully. 'Chandigarh.'

Vidyadhara nodded back nonchalantly. 'Chandigarh.' Then he glanced at me with a smile. 'Tara Bai, this is Vatsaraja, who is both the senapati and my pratihara. He is worth a thousand men in battle.'

Senapati, head of the army, and pratihara, the king's right-hand man, were two of the most important and powerful positions in a kingdom such as this one. Vatsaraja's influence would be second only to Vidyadhara's. I bowed my head in acknowledgement and Vatsaraja did the same, both trying to suss the other one out.

He said to me matter-of-factly, 'Tara Bai, you are welcome in Kalinjara,' before turning to the king. 'Our maharani awaits your safe return. She requests that she may see for herself that you are unharmed before you retire.'

The smile that crossed Vidyadhara's face at the mention of his queen was genuine. He obviously loved her. 'Then she shall be put at ease immediately.' He turned to me. 'Come, Tara Bai. I will leave you in the safe keeping of the maharani.'

We rode at a brisk pace up the hill beyond the gate. Tall ramparts shielded the view on both sides but I knew we were at the top of the plateau when the ground levelled. The buildings were further away from each other now and most of them were in the same pre-Mughal style as the Khajuraho temples – busy and full of idols and religious imagery with elaborately carved reliefs on wall panels, entrances and pillars. There were soldiers everywhere. We rode past them as they cheered for Vidyadhara from the sidelines.

Finally, deep inside the fort, I caught a glimpse of what looked like a palace, on the banks of a shimmering lake. It was extravagantly peppered with pillars, interconnected towers with countless shikara spires and the kind of detailed and intricate carvings that one found at goddess temples in Khajuraho. Like those temples, it was also incredibly feminine and graceful. I guessed this was the queen's palace.

As we got closer to the main entrance, I was surprised to see women milling about outside. This didn't seem to be anything like the ruins of Rani Mahal in modern Kalinjar. This palace was bigger, airier and had many entrances apart from the main one. Women were going in and out of them, children were playing in the open parkland outside it. Everyone was in full view of the male guards and any other man who happened to walk past. This was a far cry from later centuries where women would be caged into more and more restrictive buildings to the point where it would become impossible for them to be seen by any man outside of their immediate family. I smiled a little to myself at the unexpected but welcome scene.

Just beyond the main entrance, which was covered in red sati marks as with the gate in the town, stood a large group of women with the queen at the head. Her head was covered by a bright, heavily gilded odhna and she held a prayer thali in her hand.

Vidyadhara stopped just before the gigantic entrance and dismounted, striding up to his wife with a small smile on his face. The other men in the contingent also dismounted but stood back. I quickly slid off my horse with the help of the guard, forced my wobbly, aching body to walk towards the group and stood at a moderate distance behind the king.

Maharani Satyabhama, for it must have been her, would probably have noticed me but she gave no indication of it. Her eyes, shaded by the golden edge of her odhna, were smiling up at Vidyadhara. She was a short and plump woman, probably in her mid-thirties, whom no one would have considered beautiful or regal in her bearing. She had dark circles under her eyes and stood with a slight hunch that accentuated her double chin. Yet, there was a certain something about her – an air of quiet, ruthless power, perhaps radiating from the deep-set eyes. You wouldn't want to mess with her.

She bowed low and touched her husband's feet, bringing her hand up to smear the mud from his dirt-encrusted shoes on her head in somewhat extravagant supplication. 'Maharaj, Parameshwar, you are back. The skies have cleared and Savitra, Lord of the Sun, smiles upon us once more.'

Vidyadhara kept smiling silently as she waved the prayer thali in circular motions around his face and pushed the smoke from the diya flame towards him. Then she anointed his forehead with vermilion and bowed again.

He then spoke affectionately, 'I may have brought the sun, Maharani, but I have missed the moon these last three days.'

I had to stop a snort midway in my throat. This man was smooth, I had to give him that. No one would think, from the tender look in his eyes as he gazed upon his wife, that he had been flirting outrageously with me just hours ago. I realized that I was in a different age, when monogamy was a rare and infrequent thing for royals, but I couldn't help feeling a small stab of annoyance.

Vidyadhara half-turned to me and gestured that I step forward. Satyabhama continued to ignore me and look at him as he said, 'This is our guest, Tara Bai, a noblewoman from the kingdom of Chandigarh. We found her lost in Khajuravahaka after being abducted. I will leave her in your care and trust that you will' – he gave Satyabhama an intent look – 'watch over her.'

Satyabhama held his eyes for an instant and then nodded serenely. 'Of course, Maharaj. You need not worry about her well-being.'

She finally looked at me. 'Welcome, Tara Bai. We hope you will feel at home in Rani Bhavan.'

I stared at her expressionless, almost bland face. And felt her eyes jabbing into me.

14

I looked around nervously as I tried to cover my nakedness. The small bathhouse was on the banks of the lake behind Rani Bhavan, one of many attached to the main palace by a corridor. I seemed to be in one of the posher ones, probably because I was supposed to be a high-caste noblewoman. The space was shielded by lattice-like, carved stone walls on three sides. The fourth was open to steps leading down into the lake, with embellished pillars depicting apsaras performing various acts of bathing and shringar, or beautification.

I peered past the pillars to the other side of the lake, absolutely sure that someone on the other end would be enjoying a full frontal view of me at this very moment, but there was nothing in the distance other than a huge, windowless boundary wall. They had obviously thought about this.

Inside the bathhouse, there was an unlit chulha, a traditional stove for heating water, a carved stone bench in the centre and a very large copper vessel that had been filled with water for my bath. I eyed the gleaming copper lota, or mug, in my hand and the bowls of colourful pastes that had been prettily laid out in a tray with flowers, and I chuckled. This was like the medieval equivalent of a 5-star hotel outdoor shower. With less privacy.

I sighed and began to pour water over myself, relieved to finally be able to wash the dust from the ride off my skin. Privacy, as I knew it, was a strictly modern concept. Throughout history, people had bathed, eaten, slept, mated and even defecated in communal environs. I heard a shuffling outside and smiled ruefully. The two young maids sent to help me had looked shocked when I told them I could manage to bathe by myself and they needed to wait outside. The idea that I wanted to undress and apply the pastes on my own body was completely alien to them.

The shuffling noise got louder and I heard footsteps. I turned around to see the queen, Satyabhama, walking inside with a pronounced limp, looking at my body appraisingly and with a tiny bit of amusement. I gasped and tried to cover myself with my hands as she instructed the many women standing behind to bring a stool for her to sit on and ordered the maids back inside.

She turned around to me. 'Tara Bai, there is no need to do it yourself. The servants will bathe you.'

The chastised maids, shamefaced and agitated, quickly ran to my side and began to pour water over my head and scrub me down with brisk, practised strokes. Satyabhama, much to my utter chagrin and surprise, limped over to an elaborately decorated, cushioned stool that had been placed on the side by her attendants and began to watch the proceedings.

I cringed in embarrassment as I felt her gaze and the two sets of hands on my skin but knew better than to argue. If the bloody queen wanted to watch me get rubbed down and washed like a horse in a stable, there was little I could do to stop her. I wondered, at the back of my mind, why she had a limp.

'What is that?' She pointed to my hip.

I looked down and a sliver of apprehension ran through me. I had completely forgotten about my tattoo! The small star-shaped compass on the side of my buttock had been the result of an impulsive night in Manhattan when my college friends and I had smoked large quantities of weed and had deep, meaningful conversations about life while sprawled out in a cupboard-sized apartment. Well, deep and meaningful to us at least. The night had ended with us going to a tattoo parlour and me telling the tattoo artist that my name, Tara, meant a star in Hindi and I didn't know in which direction my life was going. A star-shaped compass on my ass sounded like a good idea at the time. The next morning, I decided I was never smoking weed again.

'It's … it's a birthmark,' I stammered.

She raised her eyebrow.

I improvised. 'It's a mark of my kingdom.' Many tribal communities tattooed themselves and had been doing so for thousands of years. It was the most plausible answer.

Luckily, she didn't push the subject and asked instead, 'Why were you at Khajuravahaka?'

Here goes. 'I was kidnapped by gypsies, as I told the king.' I gulped.

'Why were you dressed in Turuska men's clothing?'

I was surprised word got around that fast, considering there were no women in Vidyadhara's travelling contingent. 'The gypsies made me wear it.'

She considered me for a while. 'Are you a concubine?'

'No! I'm … I'm a maiden.'

That eyebrow went up again. 'At your age? Why?'

I frowned in irritation as the maid's hand swept against my privates. There was no good answer to that. 'I don't know. I just am.'

She paused, as if considering my situation. 'If we were to arrange it, would you want to go back to your kingdom?'

No. Because it didn't exist. I was better off here until I figured things out. 'I have been away a long time. I don't know if I would still be welcome there.'

'Was your maidenhood violated by your kidnappers?'

I looked up and blurted out, 'No!'

She gave me that assessing look again before saying, 'You injured a priest in Khajuravahaka. Harming Brahmans is punishable by death.'

I said through gritted teeth, 'He was trying to rape the devadasi, Puppa.'

'She is only a devadasi.'

I willed myself to be calm. Losing my temper with Satyabhama would only see me locked up in a dungeon somewhere. 'I know. But…' I huffed and started to improvise '… in the kingdom where I come from, devadasis are considered sacred. We believe they are imbibed with,' – oh God, this was really a shot in the dark – 'divine energy and blessings. To sully a devadasi is an insult to the deity whom she serves.'

It was difficult to tell if my rambling had any effect on her at all. This woman could've put a professional poker player to shame.

I pushed on, eager to shield Puppa as best I could. 'Maharaj allowed the devadasi to come here as my servant. I was hoping she could remain under your protection – perhaps as one of your attendants or be given training in a skill.'

'Why can't she continue as your servant? I assume you are staying here if you don't return to your kingdom.'

I gulped again. 'Yes, but … just in case something were to happen to me.'

She smiled a very small smile as she slowly stood up. 'The only thing that will happen to you if you choose to remain here, Tara Bai, is that you will become the king's concubine.'

My eyes widened.

She continued in a matter-of-fact way, 'You are a foreigner but I will expect you to conduct yourself as a noble Rajput woman while you live here. You will follow our customs. And always remember your place. A concubine's position and any power she wields, however beautiful and talented she may be, is temporary. Never forget that, and I will never have reason to think ill of you. Do you understand?'

I lifted my chin and spoke resolutely, 'I am *not* becoming a concubine.'

She smiled again, turned in a slow circle to walk out and then stopped as if a thought had just occurred to her. 'There is to be a gathering and ceremony after moonrise tomorrow in Rang Bhavan. You will attend. Maharaj will want to see you.'

She limped out, followed by all her women. I was left scowling at the two maids scouring my feet with stones.

I exhaled in disgust at my helplessness. The king's concubine? When hell froze over! I asked the women bathing me in a sterner voice than I intended, 'How many concubines live here?'

The maids seemed reluctant to talk so I tried again. 'You may speak without fear. I won't repeat our conversation.'

After a moment, one of the maids mumbled, 'Maharaj keeps only twenty-three concubines in this palace, Tara Bai. The rest are royal women and their attendants. The dancing girls, musicians and courtesans, along with their attendants, live separately in another palace near Rang Mahal. More pleasure women are housed in the town, where most of the court's noblemen house their own concubines as well.'

So, he had two wives, twenty-three concubines and an army of courtesans, dancing girls and pleasure women at his disposal. On top of that, he would also have sexual access to the hundreds, perhaps thousands, of attendants and maids who served all his women. I should think that would be enough for any one man.

The maid glanced up at my frowning face for a quick instant before continuing, 'The old maharaj had eighty-two concubines. Our maharaj is very merciful – most of the women he receives as gifts are married off to husbands of his choosing. He even provides a dowry to ensure they are treated well.'

My head began to reel. 'What if a woman refuses to be a concubine? Or to be married off? Has that ever happened?'

They looked at each other, wide-eyed. 'No one would dare.'

15

It was like something out of a fabulously big-budget Bollywood period film. The main courtyard of Rang Bhavan, the pleasure palace, was awash in firelight and colour. Gold was everywhere – on the walls, pillars, cushions, clothing. A significant amount of it adorned the altar upon which they had placed a decorated idol of a goddess in solid, you guessed it, gold. In front of the altar were offerings and prayer thalis that had been placed before it by the Brahmans who had conducted the prayer ceremony earlier.

To the side sat a troupe of musicians and drummers and, laid out in a horse-shoe pattern right at the very centre of the richly inlaid floor, were divans. The king's divan sat at the head of it all. A covered veranda hugged the huge courtyard on all sides. At a distance behind the king's seat, and on either side of it, were floor mattresses for all the palace women with two divans for the queens – one more elaborate than the other, to highlight Satyabhama's seniority over the other queen, Vijaya.

I looked up at the night sky and saw a bolder moon than I was used to, inexplicably brighter and whiter than it seemed in my time. Around me, seated on the mattresses, were the palace women, each one decked out in blindingly-blingy ghagra skirts, choli blouses and odhnas, their bodies carrying kilos worth of precious stones, gold and natural pearls that were the size of marbles, from the tops of their heads to the tips of their toes. I sat at the back in my relatively unembellished borrowed ghagra, choli and odhna, hoping to lose myself in the sea of faces that surrounded me.

My first night and day in the women's palace had passed in an exhausted haze. I had spent most of the day sleeping in the small, sparse room they had given me and eating whatever food they sent through Puppa.

I had also listened to more gossip than I could remember. Puppa was full of information that she had gathered from lurking in corners and listening to the other women talk.

'Maharanisa,' she had told me with gleaming eyes, 'follows the customs of her maiden home, Rajputana, inside Rani Bhavan.' She lowered her voice. 'She is from a superior clan but her family let her marry Maharaj because he is the most powerful king in the world. He wanted to marry her even though she is deformed.'

I asked, 'What do they mean by deformed? Does it have to do with her limp?'

Puppa nodded. 'One leg is shorter than the other. They say she never lets Maharaj see her limping,' she said conspiratorially before standing up and announcing that she had to leave me unattended for a few hours. One of the young baijilals, a princess, wanted Puppa to hold her odhna while she played.

I smiled at the memory of the anticipation in her eyes. It was a relief to know Puppa was finding her way around and forging relationships. That hopefully meant she'd be fine when I left.

If I left, I reminded myself. I still had no idea how to get back to the twenty-first century.

The musicians started playing as Satyabhama hobbled in, followed by a woman I assumed was the second queen, Vijaya. She was ravishingly beautiful – her glistening chocolate skin, generously lashed eyes, pouty full lips and hourglass curves would have put most modern-day actresses to shame. Not that modern-day actresses had hourglass curves any more.

I blinked as I watched Vijaya glide gracefully to her own divan after settling Satyabhama in hers and then bowing deeply. I couldn't imagine why the king would need twenty-three concubines with a wife like that. She bent over and laughed with her women, sitting around her on mattresses. She couldn't have been more than eighteen years old.

Satyabhama looked over at Vijaya and asked loudly, 'What makes you laugh?'

Vijaya stiffened and the hint of a grimace crossed her face before she looked down at her lap and replied, 'It is nothing, Jija.' She looked slyly under her lashes at Satyabhama and said, 'The women tell me that Maharaj is walking to Rang Bhavan as we speak and he has the gait of a tiger.' Her women giggled.

It was difficult to tell whether she was mocking Satyabhama or I was reading too much into things as usual. Her tone hadn't been taunting but I didn't think it was particularly polite to talk about gait to someone with such a pronounced limp.

Neither did Satyabhama obviously because she looked Vijaya up and down and replied, 'Then let your bearing not be one of a mongoose when he arrives.'

Now it was the turn of the women around the elder queen to snicker softly as Vijaya sat up straighter, her expression seething, and her entourage went quiet.

I heard a soft murmur as two women behind me began to talk to each other.

'The langadi is angry tonight.'

I grimaced inwardly. Langadi was a horribly rude word for someone who was lame.

'The bitch deserved it. She's been acting like a madwoman ever since she heard about Maharaj's new bride, Raja Trilochanpala's daughter.'

Vidyadhara was getting married again? I leaned back a little so I could catch every word.

'She's angry because she won't be able to reign over his nights after the new bride arrives. No hope of a son now. Serves her right!'

'Don't speak in haste. She still has time. The bride is only of ten summers and hasn't even left the palace in Bari yet. Maharaj won't take to her bed until she's older. At least not until her first blood.'

'Then let's pray the bitch doesn't conceive until that happens. She'll be unbearable if she has a son.'

I leaned away from them, closing my eyes briefly and trying not to think about a ten-year-old girl marrying a man in his thirties. It might be perfectly normal for this period, but it was so messed up. Raja Trilochanpala was Vidyadhara's vassal, seated by him on the throne of Kannauj. He would have to pay dues, monetary and political, to his overlord. His daughter was probably part of the package.

'The servants say the new foreigner is beautiful.'

My ears perked up and I moved discreetly back towards them again.

'Enough to distract him?'

'Yes.'

'Interesting ... This should be fun to watch. Once the bitch finds her.'

'Why?'

'Do you know what happens when cold water hits a pot of boiling oil?'

'It explodes.'

'Exactly.'

The woman chuckled. 'I'm sure the langadi will enjoy it.'

'I'm sure she'll be the one throwing the water into the oil!'

They started snickering softly. I turned around and glared at them, giving them a good look at my face.

They gasped and nudged each other, staring at me with panic-stricken eyes as they realized I had heard everything. But before I could say anything to smite their nasty tongues, I felt a light tap on my shoulder.

It was one of Satyabhama's attendants. She whispered in my ear, 'Maharanisa wishes for you to sit with her.'

I gave the medieval mean girls behind me one last glower and got up. The attendant led me to the front and made me sit near Satyabhama's feet, in full view of everyone in the courtyard. Satyabhama looked straight ahead without acknowledging my presence.

I shifted uncomfortably as I felt the eyes of all the palace women on me, their gazes ripe with open curiosity and intrigue. Men – ministers, courtiers and princes – had now started filtering into the courtyard and taking their seats on the divans surrounding the king's in the centre. As they bowed to Satyabhama, I felt their gazes slide downwards discreetly, flicking over the space I occupied without actually looking into my eyes. Thakur Jajuka, Mukhya Mantri Sivanaga and some of the other men who had accompanied Vidyadhara in Khajuravahaka were all present. Thankfully, Vidana wasn't.

I peeked over at Rani Vijaya on the other side of the verandah. She was looking at me too, her eyes clouded and her face shaded by the insecurity visible in beautiful women when presented with a rival for the title of prettiest girl in the room. I felt her gaze scorch over me, sizing up every inch, and felt myself cringing in embarrassment.

I remembered the mean girls and their water and boiling oil analogy. Never, in my entire life, had I considered myself beautiful. My mother was the beautiful one. I spent most of my days digging in, and covered with, mud. What I wanted more than anything was to stand up, inform Satyabhama that I refused to be a pawn in her politics, assure Vijaya that I had no intention of 'distracting' Vidyadhara, find a dark corner and blend into the wall indefinitely.

No such luck. I was front and centre for the moment. Until a succession of conches went off, signalling that the king was entering the palace. Everyone stood up as Vidyadhara strode in, followed by Vatsaraja and a handful of his guards.

My insides thrummed as I took him in. The heavy tunic and crates of jewellery he had worn at the temple, the sturdy yet elaborate clothes he had donned for the journey from

Khajuravahaka to Kalinjara, were gone. In their place was a fine, almost translucent silken tunic that hugged the muscular upper half of his body almost like a second skin while his lower half was loosely draped with a shimmering dhoti of the same material. Despite the few necklaces, wristbands, armbands and earrings he wore and the vertical gash of vermilion on his forehead, he radiated masculinity.

I watched as he lazily cast his eye over the gathering before walking towards Satyabhama. He seemed completely relaxed and at ease despite all the eyes of the courtyard upon him. I supposed this was probably his idea of an intimate gathering.

He stopped in front of her, smiling only slightly as his voice reverberated across the courtyard. 'My spies informed me that the prayer ceremony and tonight's festivities have involved the hand and the keen eye of the maharani of Jejabhukti. In that case, I thought, they will be flawless. Just like the maharani.'

Satyabhama's formal half-smile didn't quite do justice to the extravagance of the compliment, but her eyes sparkled as she bowed, touched his feet and replied, 'If they are flawless, Maharaj, it will be because of the blessings of the Moon God and our Mother Goddess.'

Vidyadhara nodded and turned to look at Vijaya, who bowed low on the opposite side and smiled at him from beneath her lashes. He nodded but didn't go over or say anything to her as he had with Satyabhama. I wondered if that was because of hierarchy or for some other reason. I noted that his eyes lost their softness when he looked over from his dowdy elder wife towards his gorgeous younger wife. Did he hold her inability to conceive against her, like the rest of Rani Bhavan's occupants? Puppa had mentioned that he had eight children from Satyabhama, of which five were boys, so it wasn't as if he didn't have plenty of heirs to his throne. And even if he didn't, infertility was no reason to disrespect any woman.

I huffed inadvertently, on Vijaya's behalf. In the silence that hung around the enclosure, it sounded quite loud and I shifted awkwardly in embarrassment. Vidyadhara's lips twitched and his eyes slid over to mine so briefly that if everyone wasn't staring at him with rapt attention, they would have missed it.

The movement wasn't lost on Satyabhama. She gestured towards me with her hand and said, 'As Maharaj can see, our guest is well. She has decided to remain in Kalinjara for the foreseeable future.'

I held my breath but Vidyadhara only nodded before turning and greeting the men, sitting down and gesturing for everyone else to be seated as well. The musicians started playing and the low rumble of discreet conversations allowed me to retreat into my head and mentally kick myself for my little show of bluster. Now everyone would think I had done it to get his attention. I didn't dare look at Vijaya.

The sound of ghungroos, dancing anklets made with dozens of little bells, made me look up. A line of women walked towards the altar, dressed in dhoti-style saris bound tightly around their waists and odhnas tied around their heads, almost like half-turbans. Each one carried a khanda sword in her hand, which they laid, one by one, in front of the altar as they folded their hands and bowed in supplication. Then they bowed to the king and lined up in front of each other at the very centre of the courtyard. Before I knew what was happening, each leapt towards her 'opponent' and I heard the sharp clang and swish of metal. They started fighting in time to the music.

Talwar baaji, or sword dancing, was a popular tradition among Rajputs all over India even in modern times. I had never seen it performed before but I'd been told that when women did it, they usually didn't do much more than wave the sword around at a safe distance from each other and dance to the music. This, what these women were doing, was not dancing. This was a sort of synchronized fighting – graceful, acrobatic and in perfect harmony with the musicians. Their swords met with as much strength as mine had when I foolishly attacked Vidyadhara with Kala Devi's sword, yet the clanging and hissing of metal upon metal seemed to only add to the music rather than clash with it. The swords must have been heavy but these slightly built women wielded them as if they were made of cardboard. Only the sweat lining their foreheads and the slight grimaces on their faces revealed how much strength, agility and effort went into the dance. Each sound, each leap and somersault, each thrust and parry was perfectly timed and choreographed, yet it felt raw and untamed and full of fury and passion. I was mesmerized.

When it was over, I watched the heaving dancers look over at Vidyadhara and bow deeply. He said something to the woman in front and waved with his hand for his attendant to give her a melon-sized bag of what I presumed must have been gold coins. Considering everything else seemed to be made of gold too. The women bowed again and again and again, their sweat-soaked faces wreathed in smiles as they left, considerably richer than before.

Vidyadhara was equally generous with anyone who spoke to him. At one point, I saw him take off one of his necklaces and hand it over to a younger man who had said something to make him laugh. The younger man, who looked a lot like him, bowed repeatedly just like the women, albeit without grinning. I figured he must be one of Vidyadhara's five sons. He looked older and more serious than the teenager I had seen chastised by Vidyadhara in the village.

'Who's that man speaking to the king?' I asked the woman seated next to me.

'That's Rajkumar Vijaypala, the eldest of Maharaj's sons.'

Vijaypala, the next king, I thought as I looked at his placid expression and formal bearing. He had none of Vidyadhara's magnetism but his eyes seemed kind. Known primarily for being virtuous, Vijaypala would go on to maintain his father's empire but his descendants would slowly lose it, little by little, to invaders until their dynasty died out and remained forgotten for hundreds of years.

More dancers came and went, each one accepting a gift from their king at the end of their performance. Vidyadhara and the men drank, ate and talked throughout it all while the women sat and murmured among themselves. The night air became cooler as the hours passed and I was grateful for the others who sat so closely around me, the combined heat of our bodies compensating for our thin, skimpy clothing.

I looked up at the moon again. It seemed pensive this time, like me. I had no idea what tomorrow would bring or whether I would ever leave this place. But, for the moment, hugged by the primitive yet vital warmth around me, captivated by the pristine beauty of the night sky and the firelit glow of the courtyard, swayed by the hypnotic tunes of the music and the jingles of ghungroos ... for the first time since I woke up on the floor of that temple, I didn't feel terrified, overwhelmed and helpless.

It was a start.

16

Shouts – loud ones – yanked me out of my slumber. I looked around the dark room, registering for the first time in my life how black the night actually is when the only light available comes from the moon.

Feeling my way off my bed and around the small room so I wouldn't trip over Puppa, sleeping on a rollaway bed on the floor, I managed to open the heavy curtain that served as a door and step outside into one of the many covered verandas strewn around Rani Bhavan. This veranda was off one of the courtyards that led to Rani Vijaya's private quarters.

Both the queens had their own, separate wings of Rani Bhavan, complete with their own court, gardens and bathhouses. Favoured concubines had suites of rooms with gardens, princesses and other royal women shared suites depending on their status and everybody else slept dormitory style, indoors and outdoors, depending on where they needed to work when they woke up. The small room, free of embellishments but private, that had been allotted to me showed an uncertainty as to where I fell in the hierarchy of things, as did the simple but expensive pile of clothing that had waited for me on the bed when I returned from bathing on my first day.

I looked around, squinting. Carved pillars, dozens of them, separated the dimly lit veranda from the open-air yard and I slid behind one of them, surprised that no one else had ventured out of their rooms because of the noise. Surely the shouting had woken them up too.

But the veranda seemed to be empty, apart from me and the people in the centre of the courtyard, where the racket was coming from. I peeked from behind the pillar and was shocked to see Rani Vijaya on her knees in front of a half-naked Vidyadhara, clad only in a dhoti and looking extremely irritated.

Vijaya was crying loudly and inconsolably, the drape of her flimsy sleeping-sari sweeping the ground along with her long open hair. Her naked shoulders and breasts heaved with sobs as she crouched at his feet.

'I will kill myself!' she wailed.

This only made him look more irritated as he replied, 'Cease this behaviour. It doesn't suit someone of your stature or do honour to your father's lineage. You know I have as little a choice in this as you do.'

She looked up at him and cried, 'You can say no!'

'You would have me dishonour a king of this realm because of your whim?'

She exhaled in scorn and declared, 'He is only a king because you made him so, because you choose to call him so. He is your vassal, with a battle-weakened army. If you refuse her, he cannot but accept it!'

'I will not put him in that position.' Vidyadhara's reply was firm, causing Vijaya to double up on her wailing.

She stood up and stepped back from him, her nakedness now enhanced by the strained straightness of her back. 'Then you may send your proxy to marry her, Maharaj, but it will need to pass over my dead body.'

Vidyadhara exhaled in muted exasperation. 'Stop this, Vijaya. Why does it matter? You will always have your position and honour as the second queen.'

'But I will not have a son!'

Vidyadhara closed his eyes for an instant. 'I have already told you, we will come together until our union is blessed. Do you doubt my word?'

'She will take you away from me. You will not want me anymore!'

'Enough' – his tone became annoyed – 'of these hysterics. You dishonour your husband by implying that he will not do his duty. Retire now, until you are composed.' He turned his face a fraction towards the shadows behind Vijaya and commanded, 'Help your queen.'

Attendants filtered out of the shadows from behind her and bowed to him before leading a slumped and sobbing Vijaya back towards her quarters. Vidyadhara stayed and watched them until they disappeared around a corner.

For a moment, he just stood and stared. Then, suddenly, he turned his head towards the pillar behind which I was lurking. I jumped back as silently as possible, praying he hadn't seen me. A fraught moment passed. Pressing my forehead against the smooth stone of the pillar, I let out a slow, soft breath before I heard a rustle right behind me. I turned.

He was standing there. With his smile firmly back in place.

I sucked in my breath and stepped back, only to find the traitorous pillar blocking my retreat. I pressed my back against it to create as much distance between us as possible. Vidyadhara's lack of clothing had been disconcerting when he was standing across the yard. Up close, only inches away from my own body and towering over me, it was completely overwhelming.

I concentrated on his face, trying not to let my eyes stray downwards and take in the bends and sinew of his warrior's body. His chest, sprinkled with hair and a slight sheen from a mildly scented oil, exuded heat and strength. I willed myself to stay calm but my quickened breaths told me I was failing miserably.

Vidyadhara felt no similar compunction to focus on my face. He cocked his head as his eyes roamed over my dishevelled state – my thin, rumpled sleeping-sari and blouse, my open hair that tumbled all over the place and sleep-swollen eyes and lips.

'I thought you weren't a spy, Tara Bai,' he murmured in a soft, husky voice.

The deep sound set off involuntary shivers and goosebumps in places I didn't want to acknowledge at that particular moment. I clutched the pillar behind me for support.

'I'm not.'

He smiled again, only this time not entirely with amusement. This smile reflected embers of desire that had begun to burn in his eyes. He was looking at me the same way he had when we stood next to the stream, my body embarrassingly compromised by its nippy water.

'Then why are you spying on me?'

I exhaled. 'I'm not spying. The noise woke me up so I came out to see what it was.'

'By hiding behind a pillar?' His lips twitched and I couldn't help but look at them.

Bad idea because that made him look at mine and sway even closer. I sucked in a breath again and noticed, for the first time, that his breathing wasn't particularly steady either. This was getting out of hand. I had to...

'Tell me, Tara Bai, do you not think others were awoken by our voices? Why don't you see anyone else out here?'

I did wonder that. There were many rooms off this courtyard, full of sleeping women.

'I don't know,' I whispered, shaking my head.

His gaze trailed up to my eyes. 'Because it isn't prudent to spy on your king.'

Of course. The other women must have heard the shouting but had stayed inside. Only I had been stupid enough to satisfy my curiosity.

A sliver of fear coursed through me. 'I … I didn't…'

'Normally' – he continued as if I hadn't spoken – 'I would be very displeased to find an eavesdropper. But you' – his eyes returned to my lips and then raked over me like a cascade of heat – 'I am very pleased to find.'

He leaned in and his hand came up, as if to touch my rumpled hair, when I said in an urgent voice, 'You said you wouldn't touch me!'

He froze in mid-movement. 'What?'

I held my breath. 'At the stream. You said you wouldn't touch me … unless I asked.'

He kept looking at me, unmoving, the desire still raging in his eyes.

'It's your word. You are a man of honour.' I blinked up at his face. I couldn't let him touch me. I didn't trust him. I didn't trust myself.

For a moment, he didn't react, his expression undecipherable. Then his lips broadened into a grin and he gave a soft laugh. 'Well played, Tara Bai.'

He took a small step back and looked at me with an irritating amount of amusement on his face. He thought this was funny?

I glared at him, inexplicably angry at this reaction. 'And you can be assured, I won't ask,' I said. Just to rub it in.

That made him laugh again, 'Maybe you won't. But maybe you will. Let's see if I can't tempt you. Just a little.'

He looked up and reached towards a string of saffron coloured marigold flowers that had been hung on the pillar in preparation for the festivities the previous night. The flowers, bigger and more vibrant than their modern counterparts, were in full bloom and heavy with early morning dewdrops. Vidyadhara plucked one out from between two leaves on the string and considered it.

'This flower is one of my favourites.' He smelled it and then held it under my nose to do the same. I caught a whiff of its bitter scent and grimaced, which made him chuckle. 'Yes, it doesn't smell sweet.' He leaned in closer, inhaled next to my hair and whispered, 'Not as sweet as you.'

I caught my breath. The flower tickled my lips and then my cheek as he grazed it across my skin, taking the scenic route towards my jaw. I felt the dewdrops on my skin, the flower leaving a wet trail wherever it skimmed. My body went into overdrive again. He wasn't touching me, technically. But the effect it was having on me, he might as well have been.

His gaze upon the flower, as he moved it to the curve of my jaw, burnt with intensity. 'But what it lacks in fragrance…' – he brushed it against a particularly sensitive part of my ear and I inhaled sharply through my lips, shivers running down my neck as I watched him, felt his warmth, so close that it invaded my senses – '… it more than makes up for in everything else. Beauty…'

A drop of dew that had been hovering on my jaw decided to give way and slide down my neck. Vidyadhara followed it with his eyes as I felt it go past my collarbone, towards the hollow between my breasts. But, before it could completely disappear into the valley accentuated by my suddenly tight blouse, he pressed the flower against it. His fingers were millimetres away from brushing against the top of my breasts. But they didn't. 'Utility…' He bent down even closer, to the trail of water left by the dewdrop on the base of my neck, and began to blow softly.

I gasped, my neck arching involuntarily as my head fell back to rest against the pillar. I sensed, rather than saw, him smile. The flower was still wedged at the entry of my blouse when, moments later, he raised his face to look at me. His lips hovered just centimetres above mine and I could feel his breath on them. Time stood still. 'And determination.' He smiled as he trailed the flower all the way back up my chest and neck and raised it to his lips.

I watched him kiss the flower that had been pressed on my skin seconds ago, felt the brush of its petals against my own lips and felt my body go a little boneless, readying itself for the touch I knew wouldn't come unless I asked for it.

I clutched the pillar tightly with limp hands, propping myself up with the sheer force of will. This was one battle I was going to win. 'I won't ask.'

He chuckled softly again, but this time the amusement didn't reach his eyes. They were a storm of desire. 'Perhaps not now. But you will. Until then' – he stepped back and I felt unnaturally dismayed at the loss of his presence in my space – 'I will let this humble flower worship you instead.'

He tore out all the tiny saffron petals from the base of the marigold and showered them over my head. As dozens of small petals fluttered all over me, he turned.

'Sleep well, Tara Bai.' And he was gone.

I closed my eyes and slid downwards until I was sitting on the wide base of the pillar, completely drained of strength. My heart was beating so fast I felt like it was going to burst out of my skin. I pressed my hand against my chest and tried to steady my breathing for a few long moments before I looked around, hoping no one had seen us. The last thing I needed was people talking about what happened, especially since everyone already seemed to think it was a foregone conclusion that I would become his concubine.

No such luck. In the shadows, having obviously returned from her quarters, was Vijaya. She stood absolutely still, the folds of her sari gently flapping with the breeze that was always present in this corridor.

I felt the hatred in her eyes pierce me like an arrow.

17

A boy, about six years old, tried to somersault over the mud puddle and fell on his head. He sat up, dazed, in the dirty water and started crying loudly. I watched as a baby elephant ambled over to the child and prodded him gently with its trunk, wrapping the appendage around the child's body to comfort him.

That made me smile. The close bond between the two was as obvious as the one shared between the boy's father and his charge, the baby elephant's mother. The mahut, elephant handler, was scrubbing and washing her broad back in a large pond dedicated to the animals in the fort's stables, while both their offspring played in the mud.

I leaned against the wall I was hiding behind and sighed. Snooping around the fort was probably as bad an idea as snooping on Vidyadhara and Vijaya had been last night, but I couldn't possibly just sit in my room all day and do nothing to get out of this place. Last night, after Vidyadhara had left and I caught Vijaya glaring at me, I bolted back into my room and stayed up the rest of the night wondering what was going to become of me. I had likely made an enemy out of the second most powerful woman in the kingdom. If she really was as crazy as everybody said she was, I was in big trouble.

I glanced around furtively, relieved that nobody had tried to stop me as I walked out of Rani Bhavan and made my way around the fort like a nocturnal animal trying to find its bearings in the daytime, peeking around in the shadows while looking utterly baffled. Hardly anything was the same as the Kalinjar I knew and it made me realize just how many of the buildings had been rebuilt in the centuries after the Chandela dynasty and its distinctive style had died out. I was sure the Neelkanth temple and Kal Bhairava would be around, but had yet to figure out how to get to the north side of the hill. There were so many tall fortifications within the complex that it seemed impossible to even find the external boundary walls, let alone see over them into the countryside beneath the hill. Each palace or palatial building had its own security walls, kunds and outer structures which were surrounded by hubs of activity. There were people and animals everywhere. It was a giant, bustling maze of stone. Which was how, in my aimless wandering, I had somehow stumbled upon the elephant pond.

Two men, whom I knew to be durgadhikaras, policemen, by their signature maroon tunics and turbans walked by and I slid along the wall so they wouldn't see me. There were hardly any women from Rani Bhavan in this part of the fort and I knew they would be suspicious if they saw me. Earlier, I had seen a group of durgadhikaras guarding a mosque with a small dome on top inside which a few men were praying.

These men wore loose pants instead of dhotis, had beards that were groomed differently and looked completely out of place in their surroundings. I guessed they were prisoners of war brought back from the last Turuska battle – most Rajput kings of this age kept some Muslim prisoners alive so they could learn their habits and customs in order to gain the upper hand for the next conflict. It was a pleasant surprise, however, to discover that Vidyadhara had actually allowed his prisoners their own place of worship. It showed respect and an open-mindedness that I hadn't expected.

Then again, I reminded myself, it was a pretty good time for secularism in this part of the world. The Khajuraho complex had temples devoted to Buddhism, Jainism and goddess worship alongside the traditional ones in honour of Shiva and other Hindu gods. Too bad it wouldn't last. One by one, all the kings of this region would charge out of their forts dressed in saffron and their raw valour would be outmatched by the superior military skills and strategies of the Mughals. The kings who surrendered would be forced to become vassals and change their way of life. It would be hundreds of years before the emperor Akbar reintroduced the ideals of secularism.

I kept walking, not really knowing what I was looking for any more. I came across a large gathering of men, women and children in an open ground. Villagers and townsfolk of all classes and castes were loosely lined up in a multitude of queues. They were filing into a covered, stadium-like area that was heavily guarded by soldiers and I followed the crowd to see where they were going.

A guard saw me and his eyes widened. He frantically gestured that I shouldn't walk with the other people and, instead, guided me towards another entry that didn't have a queue. I realized, a few minutes later, that I was entering the king's public court.

Massive pillars held up an overhead structure built along the same aesthetic lines as the Nagara-style temples. Only this structure wasn't to honour a god – it was a showpiece designed to boast the power, prestige and grandeur of the king who presided under its dazzling reliefs. Giant figures, intricately carved and plated with gold, featured in scenes of battle, prayer, courtship and domestic life. A god-like man fought a golden tiger with his bare hands, golden chariots stormed a citadel behind charging elephants, a deity blessed the king, who had golden rays emanating from the overhead sun onto his head. It was quite a statement.

Under the ceiling were more carvings and more gold, along with painted murals dotted with precious and semi-precious stones. The central portion of the court was occupied by gilded divans set in rows opposite each other. Each had seating behind it. At the head of it all, a steep ramp of steps led to a raised stage which had a massive throne, made of solid gold, as the centrepiece and two smaller thrones on either side of it.

I made my way along the path I was sent on by the guard and found myself among a group of noblewomen, sitting at a small distance from the throne behind some of the noblemen. I realized that the court's seating arrangement, all the way back until the very end of the space, was in enclosures – separate ones for different classes and for men and women. The ministers and courtiers obviously sat right in front, around which were the noblemen and women and then, further back, came everybody else. The villagers were right at the back and probably wouldn't even hear what the king said. Next to every pillar and around every enclosure were soldiers with swords. The king's dais was heavily secured by his personal guards.

I sat down on a padded mat and people-watched for what seemed like ages. Musicians sat in one far corner and played while a troupe of female singers sang to the music. The atmosphere was noisy and festive and the air a little stifling with so many people around. The smell of different oils, combined with sweat and collective body heat, made my stomach roll a little.

Finally, the courtiers and ministers came out of a back entrance and took their seats. I was surprised to see Vijaypala walking out with his mother, Satyabhama, and both of them taking the smaller thrones on either side of Vidyadhara's.

I examined Satyabhama carefully, pleasantly surprised that a queen would sit at the head of a court. Her head was uncovered and she was swathed in jewellery studded with precious stones so large they looked almost obscene. The stones and gold on her maang tikka, a jewelled headpiece, alone must have weighed at least a couple of kilos, but you wouldn't have been able to tell from the way she held her head or her regal bearing. Despite her rotund silhouette, she was every inch a queen.

My legs had started to go numb by the time the conches blew to announce the arrival of the king. Everyone in the gathering stood up and one of the courtiers led them in a chant to welcome him into court by reciting his titles, 'Parmesvara Parambhataraka Maharaja Dhiraj ki … jai ho! Kalinjarapati ki … jai ho!' The sound of hundreds of voices reverberated from the curves on the ceiling and became deafening as Vidyadhara, dressed even more resplendently than his wife, entered the court.

He held up his hand and sat on the throne, gesturing that everyone else also be seated. I sat back down and looked intently at his expressionless face and formal demeanour. And tried my best not to recall that just hours ago, the same man had me backed up against a pillar in the dark, running a flower over my heated skin and inundating my senses with his … no, stop. I wasn't going to think about last night. It was a huge mistake to have allowed him to do what he did. I should've moved away. Must. Not. Happen. Again.

Vidyadhara looked at Vatsaraja, standing in front of the platform, and said, 'The court is open. Let the proceedings begin.'

Vatsaraja nodded, bowed and turned to announce, 'Bring forth the petitioners!'

First up was a richly dressed man who was the thakur in charge of one of the southern provinces. He had come to Kalinjara to pay his respects and bring gifts from raids across the borders of Jejabhukti. After he had bowed and presented the gifts, he said loudly, 'It is my honour to bring back to Maharaj riches that are rightfully his.'

Vidyadhara nodded. 'They are accepted with our good wishes.'

The thakur fidgeted. 'Forgive my insolence, Maharaj, but I have prayed for the day you will command me to reclaim the lands that Kalacuri Chandra, the king of the Kalacuri, has usurped from us. Even, if Maharaj and Senapati Vatsarajaji deem it right, to venture deeper into his kingdom. The wealth of the Kalacuri is vast.'

I noticed Thakur Jajuka looking a bit irritated at this, but he kept his mouth shut. Mukhya Mantri Sivanaga, on the other hand, was listening with rapt attention. Vatsaraja, at the mention of his name, kept his face expressionless. The fact that the thakur had asked him for permission along with the king demonstrated exactly how important his position was in Vidyadhara's court.

'Patience, Thakurji. When the time is right.' Vidyadhara's tone was kind but firm. Sivanaga looked disappointed.

The thakur bowed and withdrew.

Vatsaraja then brought forward another well-dressed man who was a tehsildar, a tax collector, for some of the kingdom's lands. He bowed and gave a long-winded account of how all his tehsils, tax districts, were happy to contribute to the kingdom because they were prosperous and peace reigned over the land.

Vidyadhara heard him out and then said with a small smile, 'We are happy to hear that the people are prosperous and live in peace. And that you came all the way here to let us know.'

The man shifted uncomfortably, obviously aware that he had been a bit of a blowhard and replied, 'It is only due to your magnificence and your mercy, Maharaj. Forgive me, Maharaj, but the reason I came here is to ask your advice about a tribe on the edge of one of the areas that fall under my charge.'

Vidyadhara's smile was replaced by a slight frown. 'What is the problem?'

'They are an isolated border tribe, Maharaj. They follow their own gods and refuse ours.'

Vidyadhara stopped frowning. 'That is not unusual. There are many in this land who follow their own gods.'

The man's slightly nasal voice shook slightly as he said, 'Yes, Maharaj. But this tribe has turned away my men many times. They...' – he cleared his throat – '... have refused to pay taxes or recognize the authority of your throne.'

He fell silent and fidgeted nervously as he watched Vidyadhara, as if worried that the king might think him responsible for the problem.

Vidyadhara thought about it for a moment and then spoke to Vijaypala, 'Rajkumar, this is a problem we have faced whenever we have extended our borders. What do you think is the right thing to do in such a situation?'

Vijaypala nodded and replied enthusiastically, 'Maharaj, they must be made to recognize your authority. The preferred way is always through diplomacy but, if they do not relent, they must be compelled through force.'

Vidyadhara smiled. 'They are a border tribe, Rajkumar. If we compel them, they can just cross over into the next kingdom or, worse, help our enemies infiltrate our lands to seek revenge.'

Vijaypala looked less sure of himself now. 'Then, as you have taught me, Maharaj, I shall ask for advice from those with more experience than me. I would like to hear what Mukhya Mantriji has to say.'

Sivanaga stood up and bowed regally, his various odhnas sweeping the floor as he waved his arms for extra flair. 'Thank you, Rajkumar. I am honoured that you seek my advice. These tribals are the worst sort of heathens, with no sense of morality or decency. Their gods are bloodthirsty and licentious, as are their women. I suggest we infiltrate their community and either buy off their leader or forcibly replace him with one of our men. The tribe will not only recognize your authority, Maharaj, but will eventually be converted to follow our superior religion and customs.'

Vidyadhara smiled again but didn't say anything so Vijaypala gestured towards Thakur Jajuka. 'What is your advice, Thakurji?'

Jajuka got up and bowed crisply. 'Thank you, Rajkumar. I believe that trust comes before acceptance. The peaceful cohabitation of all communities, religions and customs is the first step towards building trust. A benevolent approach will lead to happier subjects who will eventually pledge their loyalty to the throne.'

Vijaypala looked at his father, unsure. Vidyadhara nodded at him and addressed the tehsildar. 'You have heard what the court advises. But you, tehsildar, are the only person here who has been in contact with this community. What are your views?'

The tehsildar wasn't expecting to be asked his opinion and stuttered through his answer. 'I … I think the tribal leader is a very strong and principled man, Maharaj. And beloved by his people.'

Vidyadhara nodded. 'A good leader is always beloved by his people. We will invite him to court as our guest and ask him to tell us what is needed in their community to properly integrate them into our realm. Convey the message, tehsildar.'

The man bowed deeply and I looked over at Sivanaga to gauge his reaction. He didn't look happy.

Vatsaraja stepped in front of the platform and spoke to Vidyadhara. 'Maharaj, may I bring forward the ambassador sent by Hamira now?'

The court burst into loud murmurs and I reeled in surprise as I saw Vidyadhara, his face hardening, nod briefly. Hamira? Was Vatsaraja talking about Sultan Mahmud of Ghazni? It couldn't be!

Apparently he was because the bearded nobleman who walked into the court after being announced was dressed in Ghaznavid clothing – pants, front-laced tunic and signature headwear. He was flanked by Vidyadhara's guards and held a scroll which he handed over to Vatsaraja after being compelled by the guards to perform a full bow, one that had him reluctantly crouching on the ground for more than a few moments.

I eyed the scroll with bated breath. Who knew that Sultan Mahmud and Vidyadhara actually had communications with each other before they fought the war. History was being created right before my eyes.

Vatsaraja gave the scroll to Vidyadhara instead of reading it aloud, which I had hoped he would do. I swallowed my disappointment. I'd have given anything to read that scroll.

Vidyadhara pondered over it and then spoke to the messenger with hard eyes and a humourless chuckle, 'Your sultan wishes to extend a hand of friendship, does he? Will he accept Raja Trilochanpala as the rightful king of Kannauj then?'

The ambassador's face was unreadable as he said, 'My sultan wishes to convey to you his admiration for the bravery and skill you displayed almost three winters ago, on the riverbank battlefield. He will not challenge the assassination of Raja Rajyapala of Kannauj and the usurping of his throne by your allies if you accept his hand in friendship and ally your forces with his.'

'Why does the Sultan of Ghazni wish to ally with Jejabhukti?'

The ambassador replied, 'My sultan wishes to head to the lands of your enemy, Bhoja Deva, whose kingdom lies alongside your own. Following which, he invites you to join his campaign against Bhoja Deva's allies, the Kalacuri Chandra and Chola Deva. He wishes the king of Jejabhukti to share the yield from this rich harvest.'

An uproar swept through the court and my own stunned eyes met those of others around me. Bhoja, the king of the neighbouring Paramara kingdom of Malwa, was one of Vidyadhara's oldest enemies and was constantly trying to destabilize and invade Chandela territory. I could almost hear the tick-tocking inside the heads of all the courtiers. If Vidyadhara had the aid of Sultan Mahmud's highly efficient army of raiders, he could defeat the Paramaras, the Kalacuris and potentially even challenge the authority of the great Chola empire, now ruled by the untested son of its illustrious ruler Rajaraja. If they succeeded, Vidyadhara would not only fill his treasury beyond his wildest dreams, but also become the undisputed leader of most of the Indian subcontinent after Sultan Mahmud returned to Ghazni. Then again, could Vidyadhara trust the sultan, his most hated enemy and the man who wanted to destroy his way of life?

Thakur Jajuka stood up and cleared his throat to speak to Vidyadhara above the din. 'Maharaj, perhaps we should take this into the council chambers.'

Vidyadhara remained poker-faced. 'Why bother, Thakurji? Our army and people should have a voice in deciding whether they fight side by side with the Turuskas. Or not.'

There were shouts of support from the crowd at his words, but most of the people around the throne area mirrored Vidyadhara's blank stare. I looked around at their faces and shook my head in confusion. This was not how history went. Or at least not how it was supposed to go. Had something changed? Or was this just an elaborate ruse planned by Sultan Mahmud and events would happen exactly as historians had recorded them?

I began to twist my odhna around in my fingers worriedly. It was unbelievable to me that, as a devout Muslim and brilliant strategist who regularly raided rich kingdoms to line his coffers and consolidate his political power with the age-old ruse of a divine war against 'infidels', the Sultan of Ghazni, idol breaker and temple destroyer, wanted to ally with a Hindu king. But that was also because I knew what happened in the end.

I glanced around. These people had no idea there was a year-long war in their immediate future so they had much less reason to doubt Sultan Mahmud's word and his message. Which reminded me – the ambassador had praised Vidyadhara's bravery and skill in the riverbank battlefield three winters ago. That battle had occurred in the year 1019 CE, which now confirmed that I was in the year 1022 CE and war with the sultan was right around the corner.

Unless … it wasn't? Had *I* inadvertently changed the course of events? I hardly thought so – nothing I had done here so far had been of the slightest consequence. Unless getting the king horny counted as changing history. I shook my head. Wasn't supposed to think about that.

Vidyadhara tilted his head and considered the ambassador. Then he said in an unruffled voice, 'You may return home. I will send a reply with one of my men.'

The ambassador nodded and executed a stiff bow before striding out. The noise of the court wore down into murmurs as Vidyadhara and Vatsaraja carried on with the proceedings as if nothing momentous had occurred.

I felt an overwhelming urge to stand up and tell everyone what I knew. Once again, I had to remind myself that none of these people had any idea what was going to happen so I shouldn't expect them to feel any sense of urgency. But that didn't dampen the panic that was beginning to simmer in my belly.

It was one thing to be reading about wars and carnage in the pages of a history book inside the comfort of my air-conditioned, twenty-first century hotel room. It was entirely different to be stuck right in the middle of it.

18

I threw back the covers and sat up in bed. There was no point trying to sleep. Rays of the late afternoon sunlight peeked in from around the heavy curtain, giving the room a dim, ethereal glow that complemented the very slight chill in the air that preceded the evening. Most of the women in the palace took afternoon naps at this time and the only sounds outside were from the servants as they quietly shuffled about, doing their work.

I rolled onto my stomach and fought down, for the thousandth time in the last week, the butterflies that rose in my belly every time I thought about what had happened in court. I couldn't eat, I couldn't sleep – I was completely overcome by angst and indecision.

Surely, *surely*, I had to do something. I owed it to these people to tell them what I knew. Didn't I?

No, you don't. Not only would they not listen to you, they'd think you were crazy. All you have to think about is getting out of this place before it blows up.

What about Puppa? I was fairly sure I wouldn't be able to take her to my time with me. How could I just abandon her?

She'll be fine. She's already made friends and will likely end up as a servant to one of the princesses.

But what about the ambassador from Ghazni and the potential alliance against the Paramaras? Had history somehow changed?

Unlikely. It's probably a trap.

In that case, shouldn't I *tell* someone?!

Once again, they will think you're crazy. Besides, maybe Vidyadhara already knows it's a trap. If he defeated the sultan of Ghazni in battle twice, he must be pretty smart.

But what if he's not? What if that's the reason Kala Devi sent me back to this time?

Of course. Because snarky archaeologists with a penchant for silly hats would be everybody's first choice for history-saving heroines.

Shut up. Why else would she send me back?

Maybe she had a crush on Hari too.

I groaned softly and got off the bed, the walls of the room closing in around me as I realized that I was no nearer to a decision than I had been days ago. My first instinct, after hearing what I had in court, had been to run. I'd decided to approach Rajpurohit Sarvadasa to see if he could help me. After all, he was a yogi just like Kala Devi, so maybe he would have the same powers. Or, at the very least, he might believe me when I told him I was from the future.

I had asked around and found that, apart from being Vidyadhara's personal priest, Sarvadasa was also the priest and caretaker of the Neelkanth temple. After much navigation, I had finally found my way to the north cliff three days ago and sneaked into the Neelkanth temple when I was sure there were no devotees inside.

I shuddered as I remembered entering the dark, damp cave and finding it empty. Except for a very soft noise coming from behind that door on the side. The same one I had been drawn towards when I had last entered the temple with Hari and the team. The door itself was different but it was in the same place and, this time, it was a tiny bit ajar. I couldn't help myself – I walked right up to it and pushed it open softly, not sure what I would find on the other side.

It had been dark, very dark. But the slight shuffle of my tentative footsteps had echoed down a very long natural tunnel and I guessed it led to the labyrinth of caves and underground reservoirs that lay under the fort, inside the cliff. I had squeezed my body against the low stone wall behind me, not daring to venture too far away from the door.

The sounds were magnified now and I could see a tiny light some way down the tunnel. It sounded like … grunting. Yes, definitely some grunting and shuffling and … my eyes widened as a low moan reverberated against the cavern walls. I inched my way towards the light, not sure what I would find when I got there.

Whatever I may have thought, I definitely did not expect to find Sarvadasa, of all people, bent over the backside of a sari-clad woman, having very vigorous, standing sex with her from behind. I watched, frozen for a moment in surprise and semi-horror, as she clutched the wall of the cave for support and arched her back, moaning and pushing back against him.

A groan from Sarvadasa sent a shiver of revulsion down my spine and I quickly retreated as silently as I could, back into the temple cave. I stood awkwardly in front of the idols for a few moments, not sure of what to do, before deciding I would brazen it out – after all, there was a possibility that Sarvadasa might help me escape. I clutched the heavy temple bell hanging from the ceiling and clanged it loudly. There was no way Sarvadasa wouldn't hear that from inside the cave.

Sure enough, after a few moments, he emerged from behind the door. By this time, I was standing in front of the Neelkanth idol with my hands folded, looking as devotee-like as I possibly could.

Sarvadasa, perfectly unruffled considering what he'd just been doing, looked me up and down with the same intensity as he had at the Kandariya temple site. And a touch of suspicion.

'I've come to pay my respects,' I said in a formal voice, finding it impossible to meet his eyes.

He started chanting automatically, taking me through the motions of prayer much as his descendants had done with our archaeological team when Mr Chauhan had brought us here. I bowed my head, allowing him to sprinkle holy water on me and anoint my forehead after I'd touched it to the idol's feet. He handed me some flowers and a small handful of roasted lentils that had been blessed by the deity.

When he was done, he stopped chanting and looked at me expectantly. This was when I was supposed to make an offering. Except, I had nothing to offer. Even the clothes I was wearing didn't belong to me.

'I have nothing to give except my devotion,' I said, rolling my eyes inwardly at the triteness of it.

He didn't look disappointed. On the contrary, he actually gave a small smirk and replied, 'It is more than most people give. The Mahesvara always gives his blessing to a true and constant devotee.'

It wasn't exactly an opening for further conversation but I was pretty desperate at this point so I carried on talking. 'The ... Mahesvara ... he's very powerful, isn't he?'

Sarvadasa looked at me cautiously. 'Yes.'

'He can do many things that ... we can't understand.'

'Yes. What is your question?'

He didn't beat around the bush, this guy. I took a deep breath. 'There are people who ... are his servants. Who can harness his powers, use them to influence natural forces. I've heard tales of these people.'

He didn't reply. Just kept looking at me, the suspicion back in his gaze.

'Are you ... one of his servants?'

Sarvadasa suddenly looked inexplicably angry. He gave a small sound that sounded almost like a growl and said, 'We must all be his servants. Now, leave.' He waved his hand at me in dismissal, disappeared behind the side door and slammed it shut before I could say anything else.

After that, I hadn't tried to find Sarvadasa again. It was obvious he wasn't inclined to be either friendly or helpful. At least not when I didn't have anything to offer in return. Also, I couldn't get the image of him inside that cavern out of my head. It had been a surprise to find a priest doing the nasty in that way. I mean, I knew that Brahmanical ideas of purity and chastity didn't exactly apply to Shaivite yogis. In fact, the two schools of thought were often at odds with each other when it came to sex. Still, it was a graphic and disturbing image and I didn't particularly feel like running into him again.

Suddenly, my thoughts were interrupted by a rustling outside in the corridor. The curtain in the doorway of my room swished apart to let in an attendant. She looked nervously at my feet and said, 'Maharaj has summoned you, Tara Bai.'

I blinked. 'What?'

She looked up at me and repeated, 'Maharaj has summoned you.'

Oh no. After not seeing or hearing from Vidyadhara since that night a week ago, I figured he must have forgotten about me amidst his more pressing concerns. I fidgeted. 'Where?'

'He is in Rani Bhavan right now. He wishes me to bring you to him.'

I nodded, with not a small amount of trepidation, and followed her down the hallway. As I walked, I automatically adjusted my hair and then chastised myself for caring what I looked like when I met him. It was probably best if I looked as hideous as possible, I thought, even as I smoothed my odhna and tried in vain to regulate my breaths.

She led me down a few hallways and through an anteroom into a luxurious apartment. A sitting area, replete with gilded divans and carved pillars, looked outwards into a large, lush, enclosed garden with its own swing and pond. In the centre of the pond was a gazebo-like island that was connected to the garden by carved stepping stones. Statues of nymphs and animals were surrounded by landscaped flower-laden bushes and freshly watered grass. The chirping of birds filled the air and I heard the faint strains of a lilting string instrument in the distance.

Beyond the sitting chamber was a room with a massive carved bed that also faced the garden and other anterooms that I couldn't pay any attention to because I was so distracted by the person sitting on one of the divans in the sitting area.

It was Vidyadhara. Alone.

The attendant quickly bowed and retreated from the room. I shuffled on my feet and eyed Vidyadhara nervously.

He kept sitting as he asked softly in his deep voice, 'You will not bow to your king, Tara Bai?'

I quickly executed a stilted bow and then waited, standing in front of him. He was dressed relatively simply compared to his court dress, with a light-coloured silken tunic and dhoti. Even then, he overpowered the opulent room with his presence.

He smiled at me and stood up as he said, 'Come, I want to show you around.'

He shepherded me into the garden without touching me but always a hair's breadth away. I only half-listened while he described the flowers and the fish in the pond, the meaning of the statues and the names of the nymphs they depicted. It was indeed a charming garden but I had no idea why he was telling me so much about it.

Then he walked me into the bedroom, saying, 'These are the bedchambers. There is also a prayer room and bathhouse, along with the outer rooms for the servants.'

I looked around at the lavish covers and cushions on the bed, the gilded decor and nodded, completely confused, as I replied, 'I see. It's very nice.'

He turned to me and, once again, I felt the sight of his striking face and broad chest, his nearness, spark up my nerves. 'Do you like these chambers?'

'Um, yes.'

'Good. I have one more thing I want to show you.' He gestured for me to follow him to a large chest on the floor, which he opened. Inside was clothing as fine and rich as any I had seen worn by the two queens. The entire chest was full of ghagras, odhnas and saris of every colour, embroidered and teased with gold and silver thread and precious stones. It was a wardrobe fit for…

I sucked in a breath and looked up at him. He was smiling down at me. 'Do you like what you see?'

'Maharaj, why are you showing me all this?'

His smile grew wider. 'Tell me, does it please you?'

'Yes, it's all beautiful, but…'

'No, wait.' He drew his hand out from behind his back and held out a necklace that dazzled my eyes. It was dripping with emeralds. 'First, let me have permission to put this around your neck.'

I stared at the obscenely sized stones on the necklace, the chest full of clothes, then around the chamber and finally his face. 'Are you trying to *bribe* me?'

He shook his head with a chuckle, not in the least bit offended. 'Bribe is such a crude word, Tara Bai. I'm trying to entice you.' He smiled at me shamelessly.

I glared and took a step back. 'So you think I'm going to fall into your arms in exchange for a bigger bed and some trinkets?'

He grinned. 'If you think these are trinkets, Chandigarh must be a richer kingdom than I thought. My spies tell me you have no jewels or clothing to speak of and you spend your days either hiding in your room or sneaking aimlessly around the fort. Surely you can be better occupied in my arms, Tara Bai,' he added softly.

'First, I'm not sneaking around anywhere.' I tried to hide my surprise that he knew about my movements. 'And second, my body is not for sale. You're the king – you already have hordes of women to keep your arms occupied.'

A tiny flash of irritation sparked in his eyes. 'I'm well aware of the women in my life. And I am not trying to buy your body, Tara Bai, nor am I suggesting anything immoral or indecent. Yes, I've tried to please you, as any man who has ever wanted to spend time with any woman. I'm offering you a position as my companion. The trinkets, as you call them, come with that position.'

I knew I couldn't judge a man of this time by modern standards but I couldn't help myself. 'Well, I'm not the kind of woman who can share a companion with so many others.'

He stared at me for a moment and then cocked his head and said softly, 'Sometimes I don't think you realize you're speaking to a king, Tara Bai.' He took a step closer to me and my heart skipped a beat as he said, 'Maybe it's one of the reasons I find you so intriguing. Tell me something – how can you be unafraid of me and yet so afraid of yourself?'

'W-What?' I stuttered.

He stepped even closer and I resisted the urge to take a step backwards. He stopped an inch away from me and murmured, 'Why do you deny that you want the same things I want? You're a grown, unattached woman who has decided to make Kalinjara her home. What are you afraid of?'

Of losing control. Of being hurt. Of being trapped in the wrong century. Good God, I might even get *pregnant*! 'I'm afraid of nothing. I simply don't want the same things.'

'Lies. Your body tells a different story.'

I couldn't deny that, much as I wanted to. There was no doubt he was a very attractive, compelling man and my body was almost painfully aware of that fact whenever I was near him. 'There is more to a relationship than just … that.'

He smiled an intimate smile and I felt an involuntary tug in my belly as he murmured, 'True. But all those things will come too, in time. Our relationship will be much more than just trinkets or pleasure – you have my word on that. Come, Tara Bai' – he ran his fingers softly along the golden border of the odhna that was draped over my shoulder, never making contact with my skin – 'let me touch you.'

His voice was so beguiling, his presence and gentle tug on my odhna so inviting that, for the tiniest second, I had the urge to simply give in and melt into his solid body. Even someone as grossly under-experienced as I was knew it would be enjoyable. What would it hurt, as long as I was stuck here anyway, to let go a little and … 'No!'

I stepped back, shaking my head slightly to cast the languor out of my fuzzy excuse for a brain. Letting go was the worst idea ever. 'No,' I repeated firmly, more for my benefit than his.

Vidyadhara looked briefly exasperated and I felt a small sliver of apprehension. He wasn't a man used to being denied things, especially by those in his power. Then his smile was back and he exhaled in a rueful acknowledgment of defeat. 'You're a stubborn woman, Tara Bai.'

I exhaled too, suppressing a small stab of disappointment. This way was better for everyone. 'I'll return to my room now.'

'No.'

I looked up at him.

He smiled again. 'You will occupy these chambers from now on. The maharani has provided servants for it. You will also keep the clothes and the necklace. You may not accept my touch as a man, Tara Bai, but it is an affront not to accept a gift from your king.'

'I thought these gifts were simply from a man who wanted to please a woman,' I taunted him despite myself.

He smiled wryly. 'Much as he sometimes rues it, this man is always a king first. Too many depend on him for it to be any different.'

I instantly regretted my words. 'I'm sorry. It must be a heavy burden to carry.'

He shook his head. 'Never a burden. It is a privilege, a divine gift.'

I looked up at his wistful expression and realized this was the first real conversation I had ever had with him. 'May I ask you a question?'

He smiled back. 'You may.'

'The sculptures you showed me at the construction site in Khajuravahaka – why would you put things like that on the walls of a temple?'

He chuckled. 'Ah, I remember you were shocked by them. Perhaps you come from a different kind of place, Tara Bai, where the things that happen between a man and a woman are considered impure. We consider those very things sacred. The Mahesvara manifests in many forms – as a man, as a woman, as a warrior, as a wanderer, as a lover, as an ascetic, as beautiful, as ugly, as clean and as covered in filth. Good and bad, pure and impure, these are all labels created by man, not by God. The Mahesvara sees purity in all things. The most extreme of acts, even the ashes and bones of the dead – they are all his creations equally and therefore they are equally divine. We must, if we aspire to join him on Kailasa, be willing to embrace all things that come from him without judgement.'

He reached out and lightly stroked my odhna again, his eyes never leaving mine. 'The joining of a man and woman is the purest act of all – for it recreates the sacred lingam of the Mahesvara himself, the union of Shiva and Shakti to create balance and oneness in all the worlds. There is no greater act of worship, no greater way to experience the connection with the divine.'

'But why,' I argued, 'must it be a communal act?'

'It isn't always communal. But yes, sometimes it is. So that divine communion may be experienced by all who share in an act of worship.'

Right. That last bit sounded like the mumbo jumbo spouted by hippies or sex gurus in the West. I exhaled. 'I see. Thank you for answering my question.'

His stare became deeper. 'You don't understand. And you won't, until…' He paused, and then smiled as a glimmer entered his eyes.

'Until what?'

He shook his head. 'The time for talking is over, Tara Bai. I must leave now but we will see each other soon.' He stepped away and turned, saying loudly, 'Attend to your mistress.'

Attendants filtered out of the shadows, much to my surprise. Was anybody ever alone in this place, I wondered, as I watched them bow first to Vidyadhara and then, after he left, to me.

A woman who was probably in her forties but looked older because of her weathered skin addressed me first. 'Mistress,

I am Vijamba and I'm the most senior of your servants. I have attended upon Maharanisa for many years and she has entrusted me to serve you.'

Great, I thought to myself, now Satyabhama would know every time I went to pee. I looked at the door Vidyadhara had just exited through and a part of me wished he would come back. Suddenly, he seemed like the only familiar thing in a sea of strangers.

I took a deep breath, adopted my noblewoman voice and told the women to go about their tasks. 'Also,' I said to one of them, 'fetch Puppa. She is my personal attendant.'

If that didn't go down well with Vijamba, she didn't show it. She suggested I sit on the swing in the garden while she pressed my feet. What I really wanted was for her to go away so I could be alone with my thoughts but I allowed her to lead me to the swing anyway. The garden was beautiful in the pre-dusk light and it seemed a shame to shut myself away inside and brood about what all this luxury meant and what Vidyadhara expected in return for it.

Vijamba settled herself at my feet and began to knead them softly. After a few moments, she said, 'I've lived in Rani Bhavan most of my life. I used to attend to one of the old maharaj's concubines before he passed. Once, he bade me to come to him. I used to be quite pretty in my youth, Mistress.'

This was not a conversation I wanted to have. Still, I replied politely, 'I'm sure you were.'

This spurred her on and she smiled with satisfaction. 'Forgive my insolence, Mistress, but there is nothing in the world more satisfying than having the man you love fill you completely and move against you while you watch the ecstasy on his face.'

I choked on my breath and launched into a coughing fit. Vijamba thumped my back gingerly and shouted for someone to bring me water.

After a few minutes of deep breathing and sips of scented water from a delicately carved silver bowl, I sat back on the swing and Vijamba resumed her position at my feet. I eyed her with trepidation.

'Lord Krishna,' she said after a moment of silence and I closed my eyes in dread, 'had many women under his protection, like our maharaj. He loved and pleasured them all equally, never letting any one of them feel neglected or unwanted.'

She had obviously overheard my conversation with Vidyadhara. I sighed in irritation and replied tersely, 'I don't want to discuss this.'

'As you wish, Mistress.'

Just then, Puppa came skipping into the garden, looked around and announced loudly that she liked my new quarters. 'They are not as big or as grand as Baijilal's but they are beautiful!' She beamed. 'Everyone is saying you are now Maharaj's favourite.'

I frowned. 'Favourite?'

'His favourite concubine.'

19

'Why do you wish to leave Rani Bhavan?'

Satyabhama could well have been saying, 'Elephants are grey' for all the inflection or surprise in her tone. She had the most inscrutable expression I'd ever seen on anyone – you never had any idea what she was really thinking.

'Not permanently. I was thinking maybe I could go on a pilgrimage to Khajuravahaka,' I replied with a strained smile.

'You just came from Khajuravahaka.' She sat ramrod straight on the divan in her over-the-top sitting chamber. My plush new chambers were like a hovel compared to hers. At a distance, in her private courtyard, were gathered some of the royal women, making a floor design with coloured pastes.

I fidgeted as I sat on a low stool next to her feet. My cheeks hurt from the tension of holding my smile in place. 'Yes, but I didn't get a chance to pray or make offerings at any of the temples. Besides, Thakur Jajuka's wife invited me to return whenever I liked … so I thought I'd accept her invitation,' I finished weakly.

She considered me languidly before saying, 'Are you not happy with your new lodgings, Tara Bai?'

'No, no, they're very nice,' I replied hurriedly. 'It's just that … I think it's best if I leave for a little while. By staying here, I might create expectations … that I can't fulfil.'

'I see.' She picked up a leaf from a gold box with legs that stood next to the divan and began to chew on it slowly. Slow moments passed before she spoke again, 'Why can't you fulfil those expectations?'

I felt my anger rising. What was she, her husband's pimp? I forced my tone to be civil. 'I mentioned before that I am a maiden. I would like to stay that way. I'm happy to forsake the new lodgings and servants and embark on a pilgrimage so that I might be out of the way and forgotten after some time.'

Satyabhama made a brief sound that I was pretty sure was her version of laughter. 'If you think you will be forgotten, you are mistaken. You will be missed and then you will be brought back immediately. You don't know Maharaj very well, Tara Bai, so let me tell you this.' She raised her eyebrows, her face a little derisive. 'He tolerates your little insolences for now because it entertains him. But he is not a man who forgives disobedience or affronts to his honour.'

'What if I have taken a vow of chastity? Surely he can't expect relations with a woman of God?'

That made Satyabhama emit the sound again. It was definitely laughter. 'If anyone here witnessed the slightest indication that you were a sadhvi, a woman of God, they would have informed Maharaj and he would not have approached you. As it stands, you have shown no interest in any of our rituals or religious observances – you don't fast or pray and you've looked indifferent during most of our ceremonies. You've not only attacked a priest with a sword, you actually attacked the king himself. You are clearly not a woman of God, Tara Bai.'

I hung my head in my hands, my desperation growing. 'Why can't I simply refuse?'

Satyabhama replied, 'You can. My husband has never touched an unwilling woman.'

'But … but he keeps pursuing me!'

She looked at me thoughtfully. 'Perhaps that is because you haven't exactly been pushing him away, have you?'

How did everyone know everything in this damned palace! I felt a flush creep up my cheeks. 'He…'

'He's a very attractive, charming man.' Her eyes were almost compassionate.

I searched her face for a few moments and then asked impulsively, 'Doesn't it bother you that he has other women?'

Satyabhama's eyes flashed for an instant and I immediately regretted my candidness. Then, after a pregnant pause, she spoke in a derisive voice, 'You forget your position, Tara Bai. Maharaj might find your audacity amusing but I do not.'

'I'm sorry.' I looked up at her with genuine remorse. 'I didn't mean to offend you. It was an inappropriate question.'

Her face didn't soften but the anger left it. She waved me away and I got up, remembering to bow just in time. As I was walking out the door, I heard her soft voice.

'What he shares with me, neither you nor any other woman will ever have.'

20

The attendant was dressed in a simple sari, her hair loosely braided down her back. She looked apologetically at my sleepy eyes as I peered at her from the vast expanse that was my bed now. Overhead, a large woven fan rocked back and forth, operated by a resolute attendant who absolutely insisted on sitting outside my bedchamber all night and pulling at its rope. Nothing I could say would deter her from doing what she thought was her job. I got a little guilty every time I felt a waft of air.

'What is it?' I asked, as I absently adjusted the drape of my sleeping-sari to cover my breast cloth. The fabric, so much finer than the saris I had been given before, felt like silk against my skin but also hugged it intimately, not leaving anything to the imagination.

'Forgive me, Tara Bai. Maharaj has summoned you.'

I blinked. 'Now? But it's the middle of the night.'

'Yes. He bade me to fetch you.'

I felt the thump of my heart grow louder in apprehension. What did he want? 'Fetch me where?'

'Maharaj is in Ranisa's chambers.'

He was with Vijaya. Then why on earth was he summoning me? I peered at the attendant's face – I couldn't ask her. I gulped nervously and sat up. 'I'll get dressed.'

The attendant looked even more apologetic. 'Maharaj requests that you come as you are.'

I exclaimed in exasperation under my breath. He was infuriating! Did he really expect to fool around with me in Vijaya's chambers? What the hell was he thinking?

'You haven't exactly been pushing him away, have you?' Satyabhama's words rang in my ears. Well, this was the last straw. Tonight, I would make it perfectly clear that I was not interested in his blatant attempts at seduction. I would stay focused and not let the way my body reacted to him get in the way of doing the right thing. Which was to push him away. No matter how I felt. Or how I knew it would feel. Potentially.

I exclaimed again and threw back the covers in frustration. 'Fine. Let's go.'

The attendant looked a little alarmed by my obvious display of anger but she bowed and led me through the palace into Vijaya's wing. In the antechamber, she handed me over to one of Vijaya's attendants, who bowed low and cast a sly look at my dishevelled clothing.

I straightened my back and stared at her haughtily. These people were not going to intimidate me tonight. 'Where is Maharaj?'

She replied softly, 'Maharaj is with Ranisa. Please come with me.'

She led me through a few chambers towards a courtyard that had been screened off into two halves. On the side of the screen that I could see, Rajpurohit Sarvadasa was conducting a havan, a prayer ceremony, before an altar that was inundated with offerings.

The attendant walked on after bowing to him. He ignored her, loudly chanting mantras that sounded unlike any that I had ever heard. I thought he would ignore me too, but as I passed, his glittering eyes followed me. Even as he kept on chanting and throwing sacred items into the fire without missing a beat.

The attendant led me around the screen and I gasped when I saw what was on the other side. The floor of the open-air courtyard was covered with skulls, flowers, food, earthen water pots all laid out in a grid-like pattern. In the centre of a grid, on a thin mat with plain sheets, was a completely naked Vijaya sitting in an asana, a yoga position, her arms stretched out above her head. Her hands were joined together as if in prayer and she seemed to be chanting something under her breath with intense concentration.

Seeing her like that had taken me by surprise but she wasn't the reason I gasped. Next to the mat, on the floor, Vidyadhara was doing the yogic headstand, sirs-asana. He also seemed to be chanting and meditating. And he was completely naked too.

I stopped in my tracks and began to instinctively back away, looking everywhere but at him. 'I – I can't...'

The attendant smirked at me. Very visibly.

I glared back at her until she tamed her expression into one of barely suppressed glee and then back into standard-issue blandness. She probably couldn't wait to tell Vijaya that I had retreated in shock the moment I had laid eyes on them. They'd probably have a good laugh at my expense.

Well, I wasn't going to give her, or Vijaya, that pleasure. I averted my gaze and strode back into the screened-off space, gesturing at the attendant to lead me. She nodded, walked me to a low divan on the side and gestured for me to sit down.

I planted myself on the divan and stared up into the night sky, my mind a pulpy mess of confusion. What was going on? Why were they doing naked yoga and why the hell was I watching them do it?

I saw that a few attendants, slinking about the veranda surrounding the courtyard, were watching me curiously and sat up straighter. My eyes slid to the scene in front of me as I willed myself to stay calm and pretend I was watching an X-rated film or something. Anything to keep the shock from registering on my face.

I was seated directly behind Vijaya, so she couldn't look at me without turning. Vidyadhara, on the other hand, was faced directly towards me. In complete, full-frontal glory. And, if I was completely honest with myself, he was pretty glorious.

Muscles rippled from every part of his body as they worked to keep him steady in the headstand position. His eyes were closed so I allowed myself to look at his manhood, generously endowed even in a semi-flaccid state. I felt a now-familiar flush creep up from my neck into my face and my heart rate accelerate even as I shifted uncomfortably in embarrassment.

The divan creaked a little from my movement and, suddenly, Vidyadhara opened his eyes. They focused directly on me, piercing me with their intensity, their heat melting into my own eyes for what seemed like an eternity.

My lips fell open and I inhaled deeply as I tried to break the stare. My hand began to fiddle with my sari and I felt intensely aware of the space around me and the senses within me – as I had when he had stood close to me in the veranda the other night. I couldn't look away. It was as if, by opening his eyes, he had tied the two of us with an invisible thread that overcame the distance between us. A thread I felt as keenly as I had felt the marigold flower.

I could hear myself breathing, the incessant drone of Sarvadasa's chanting becoming fainter and fainter with each passing second. Vidyadhara's manhood began to grow and, surprisingly, I couldn't find it in myself to be embarrassed. His eyes stayed locked with mine as he gently and lithely landed his feet on the ground and stood up to face me, unabashed and engorged in arousal. There was nothing leery or suggestive in the way he looked at me, nothing to make me feel in any way ashamed or afraid. There was just the air between us, tangible and electric.

Vijaya stood up and went to him, caressing his arm gently and guiding him towards the mat. He went almost absently, unable to pull his gaze away from me. She seated him cross-legged on the mat and slowly, deliberately, straddled his lap, taking his manhood inside her and wrapping her legs around his waist.

I gasped as I saw her body close around him, saw the two of them connected in that way. My eyes widened and I felt a powerful urge to look away, to refuse to be a part of this, but his eyes wouldn't let me.

Vijaya hugged him and rocked gently, putting her hand on his cheek, trying to turn his face. Make him look at her. He caught her wrist and pulled it down, refusing to look away from me. She began to move against him, her lithe body sliding against his with a precision that showcased her own strength and agility.

I felt, rather than saw, his hands caress her automatically. My body responded in the same way hers did. Tremors ran down my spine and I felt a primal pull deep in my belly as I arched my back ever so slightly, weak and energized at the same time. The part of me that wanted to put a stop to this, that wanted to get up and leave, became increasingly enfeebled with each passing moment.

I didn't want to leave. I wanted his eyes to stay on mine, I wanted to feel what he – what every part of him – was doing. His hands slid to her breasts, caressing and pinching them, and I felt my own breasts pebble and strain against my clothing. I grasped the sheets on the divan under me for support as I felt another sharp tug of pleasure in my womb that left me breathing as heavily as he was.

Suddenly, he got up on his knees, carrying a still-straddled Vijaya effortlessly. Laying her down on her back and holding her hips against him, he started driving his manhood into her rhythmically, never for a second taking his eyes away from mine. Willing me to feel what he was doing.

I grasped the sheets tighter, instinctively pressing myself down through the sari against the heel of my foot that lay underneath. The sheath between my legs began to throb insistently as I watched him fan out the fingers of his hand on her belly and dip his thumb into the place where they were connected.

Vijaya gasped and let out a moan as he teased her with his thumb, thrusting relentlessly while holding her steady with his other hand. I bit my lower lip as I began to move my hips a fraction each time he did, over and over until the throbbing became almost frenzied and a slow burn began to simmer through me. Moments passed – maybe it was minutes or maybe hours – as our eyes danced with each other. Him silently, and me struggling to breathe.

Suddenly, the tension that had been pushing me higher and higher gave way and my body was wracked by an exquisite spasm. I squeezed my eyes shut, threw my head back and exclaimed as I felt the walls of my sheath slam together, contracting wildly to release a sea of pleasure into every inch of my body. Again and again, like relentless waves crashing against the side of a cliff. I fisted my hands on the sheets and felt it wash over me, giving myself to it completely until it subsided into a pleasant hum of sensation. I sank back and tried to compose my laboured breathing, utterly spent.

'Tara.'

I opened my eyes and looked at him. He looked a little drained too and I realized he had just experienced the same thing I did.

'Now do you understand?' His voice was deeper, huskier than usual.

I wanted to say I did, but my gaze inadvertently slid down to Vijaya. She had turned her head and was looking at me.

If hell existed, it was in her eyes.

21

The dragonfly circled above the algae that floated just under the surface of the lotus-clad pond. Deeper beneath the surface, I saw the outline of a fish. Watching. Waiting.

'Fly away,' I whispered to the dragonfly, as if it could understand me.

It dived instead, only to be instantly swallowed by the fish that leapt out of the water with enviable precision. I sighed and sat back on the rock, looking around me at the wooded park next to Rani Bhavan. The dragonfly wasn't the only one making bad choices these days.

I should have left before it got out of hand.

You had one of the most intense experiences of your life and are officially not an orgasm virgin any more.

But at what cost? How could I reconcile what happened to me with the pain in Vijaya's eyes?

He put that pain there, not you. You did nothing wrong.

I stayed.

I sighed again, picking up a pebble from the ground and aimlessly throwing it into the water. Close by, a group of children squealed as they ran around trying to catch each other. This park was their territory. I had begun coming here for respite from the constant stream of attendants in my chambers. I liked to think I was alone with my thoughts here, even though I knew that I was being watched constantly.

A rustling and the tinkle of jewellery made me look up and my stomach sank in dread. Vijaya and her entourage were walking straight towards me. Behind them, Vijamba and two of my attendants followed with fearful looks on their faces.

I exhaled slowly and stood up, facing her with my shoulders pushed back. I knew this moment would come. Since that night, I had wondered constantly when she would confront me, what she would say to me.

She was fully decked out today, the look on her face more that of a predator than a jilted lover. She stopped a few feet away and looked me up and down with deliberate disdain. 'The foreigner wears none of the jewellery he gives her,' she said to her attendants in a loud, derisive voice. 'Maybe she thinks they're not good enough for her. Maybe she imagines herself a queen. Vijamba, tell your mistress that there is a big difference between a wife and a whore.'

I didn't want to return the venom in her words. I wouldn't wish what she must be going through on anyone, no matter how much I disliked them. 'Your quarrel is not with me, Ranisa. I didn't know what was going to happen.'

She laughed bitterly, stepped closer and sneered, 'And yet you sat there, writhing and moaning like a common prostitute off the street.' I could feel the anger radiating out of her, as if she was barely holding herself back. 'You think I don't know what game you're playing? Stringing him along with your wiles, playing the pretty innocent whenever he's near. You're nothing but a spy, gathering information for our enemies.'

'I'm not a spy and I want nothing to do with him.'

'*Liar*!' she shrieked at me and lunged unexpectedly, her arms outstretched towards my face. I put my hands up to defend myself even as she was quickly caught and pulled back by her attendants. The looks on their faces and the expert way they restrained her suggested they had done this before.

'Ranisa,' one of them whispered urgently towards her, 'he will be furious if you leave a mark on her.'

She struggled against them and cried out uncontrollably, 'You think he will protect you forever? Hah! He will have his way and tire of you in a fortnight. Then you'd better watch out!'

Bile rose in my throat as visions of me being stabbed in my sleep or poisoned through my food flashed through my mind. I reacted instinctively. 'You'd better think carefully about your own position before you think about mine, Ranisa. If he treats you like this now, imagine how difficult your life would be if he knew you had tried to harm me.'

'You bitch!' she snarled at me with the kind of rage that definitely seemed beyond the realm of normal. 'Make no mistake, I will make you pay for that night. I'll make you regret the day you were born.'

'I keep telling you,' I replied, struggling to keep my voice calm in the face of her fury, 'I have no quarrel with you. It was not my intention to participate or to hurt you that night. Maharaj sent for me.'

But she was beyond the point of even registering my words. Tears flowed freely down her face and she was shaking as she leaned towards me with a grimace on her face. 'You will pay,' she spat before turning and walking off.

I watched her leave and took a wobbly step back towards the rock I'd been sitting on, suddenly realizing I was shaking too. Vijamba and the other women rushed to help me sit down.

Vijamba's hand began to rub my back in a comforting way. 'She is like that sometimes, Mistress. Cannot have a child, that one, so she takes it out on everybody else.'

I looked back at her. 'So she threatens the king's concubines like that regularly?'

Vijamba shifted before saying, 'Not exactly. Maharaj has never had a favourite before.' She looked at me and smiled as she tried to knead the tension out of my shoulders. 'They say he asks about you every day. It is the first time he has done that since he married Maharanisa as a boy.'

I hung my head in my hands and groaned. What he should be doing, instead of asking about me and stirring up conflicts in Rani Bhavan, was worrying about the sultan of Ghazni's impending attack. Now I had gone and made an enemy of his queen. Forget getting back to the twenty-first century, I may not even survive her vengeance long enough to try.

'He doesn't love her, Mistress. Never did, not even in the beginning. He still goes to her because she is childless. His heart is kind and she knows it.'

I replied in annoyance, 'That's no excuse for what he did.'

Vijamba tutted, instinctively disapproving of any words against her king. 'It's about time he did something, Mistress. She has terrorized Rani Bhavan for too long. Even taunted

Maharanisa with her vile tongue. Now that you're here, maybe she will be put in her place.'

I shook my head. 'I don't want –'

'He is the king.' Vijamba's voice took on a surprisingly firm tone. 'If he loves you, he will protect you. There is nothing she can do if you make him fall in love with you. There have been many times in history when a concubine has taken precedence over a queen.'

Make Vidyadhara love me? I laughed without humour. 'I thought he loved the maharani.'

Vijamba's eyes shaded in caution and I remembered that she was Satyabhama's woman. Still, she looked at the ground and said in a soft murmur, 'There are many kinds of love, Mistress.'

Then she looked back up and said gently, 'Accept him. It will make everything easier. Let go, and you will be happier.'

I stared at her. *'It's better to let go and leave yourself open to all that comes your way. Hurt might come, but so will possibility.'* Kala Devi's words rang in my ears. Is this what she was talking about? Was it my destiny to be here, to be with Vidyadhara? Was I just flailing against an irresistible tide? It was too much to comprehend. What about my life? My family, my career? How could I let it all go? All this while, I had thought the reason I was here was because Kala Devi was out of her mind. But what if this was meant to be?

I remembered Vidyadhara's eyes as he had looked at me that night. Did my future lie with him? He was a man of his time and, like every other king in the history of the world, there would always be many women in his life. But there had also been many kings in history who had loved only one woman despite being married to many. Could Vidyadhara and I make a relationship work, or would I spend the rest of my life fending off the likes of Vijaya?

It was as though Vijamba could read my thoughts. She said, 'You need time to think about this, Mistress. No hurry. Come, we will take you back to rest.'

I barely remembered walking through the palace with them, barely registered her helping me into bed. I was too busy trying to figure out my future.

Did my future belong in the past?

22

My chambers felt quieter, as if everyone around me was giving me the space I needed to think. The days passed with frustrating regularity but I was no closer to knowing what I was supposed to do – or even what I wanted to do.

One morning, I resolved to stop hiding and venture out. If I was going to stay, I might as well start getting involved in palace life. I walked into the main courtyard, where the women of the palace met to socialize, gossip and occupy themselves with non-menial tasks. A troupe of female musicians was playing folk music that sounded upbeat and even a little raunchy. A few royal women sat and sang along while a few danced, giggling, in the middle of the yard. Some of the others sat by the pillars of the encircling veranda, smiling at the antics of the dancers and making garlands out of marigold flowers for an upcoming celebration or festival. Which seemed to occur every second day.

I tentatively made my way towards the garland-making group, not sure how they would react to me. They ended up being unexpectedly warm and welcoming, sitting me down and giving me my own garland to prepare. Puppa ran back and forth for supplies, beaming. Sitting above the rest of us on a divan, the king's daughter-in-law and Vijaypala's wife, Bhuvana Devi, smiled and told me about the evening's festivities in between yelling instructions to her maids and children. She was already a few months pregnant with another baby and she glowed with happy hormones. I realized from their behaviour exactly how unpopular Vijaya was among the palace women – while no one mentioned it specifically, I could tell they were all rooting for me in some kind of imaginary two-women contest of 'who gets the king'.

I wasn't in any mood to analyse or resist it. I laughed along with them at the antics of the younger girls and crowded with them in interest when a vendor of knick-knacks and curiosities entered the courtyard to sell her wares.

She was a short, stocky woman who looked weather-beaten and hardy, dressed in loose pants, a long tunic and a thick odhna that had been untidily draped. The scent of clove oil was strong around her as she crooned to the palace women to come closer and look at what she had for sale from foreign lands all over the world. She opened the large cloth bags that she had carried in with the help of the servants and out came carpets, bales of cloth, spices, weapons and odds and ends that the women couldn't identify.

I could barely control my excitement as I inched closer and asked if I could touch some of them.

The woman looked at my interested expression and slyly crooked a beckoning finger at me. 'You're a curious one. What will you find today, I wonder? Will it be this small dagger made of gold? It's too soft a metal to be used for anything other than decorating a waist. Still, it can slit skin as easily as a metal one and looks deadly enough to deter any unwanted attention.'

I shook my head politely. Instead, I sifted through the objects carefully, holding them up and examining their details with a practised eye. My breath caught when I spotted a quill and an ink pot that were obviously European. The feather looked ragged from age and wear and the ink pot, a dented and rusty metal one, looked as though all the ink would have dried up.

'It is not new, I will admit,' came the vendor's voice silkily. 'But it comes from lands far, far beyond the kingdom of Hamira. From his enemies on the other side of his empire. Their people are tall, with skin the colour of milk and hair the colour of the sun at midday. During winter, their ground gets covered with frozen rain and it is so cold that they must cover even their noses when they step outside for fear it will freeze and fall off.' She leaned back and said loudly for the benefit of her rapt listeners on the other side, 'It is so cold, they don't bathe either.'

Some of the women scrunched up their noses and one of them, an attendant of Bhuvana Devi's, exclaimed, 'For the entire winter?'

The vendor grinned and I noticed she was missing several teeth. 'Not a single washing until spring.'

'Even the men?'

'Yes.'

The attendant pondered over that for a moment and then asked, 'Don't they smell?'

The vendor's grin turned mischievous. 'Yes. But when a man is given a choice between smelling like a rotting onion or having the sword between his legs freeze and fall off, he'll choose the smell.'

The women collectively burst into peals of laughter. I couldn't help but laugh along, shaking my head wryly as I thought about how much more I could tell these women about people and places they would never see or experience. Too bad I couldn't do that without putting myself in danger.

The vendor turned to me again and pointed at the quill and ink pot. 'I can have that in working condition if you buy it. It will take me mere moments to restore it for you.'

I fingered them and sighed. 'I don't have any coin to pay you with, unfortunately.'

She was unrelenting. 'You needn't pay with coin. What have you to barter?'

I thought about the gifts Vidyadhara had given me. Gifts that didn't feel like they were mine to give or barter away. 'Nothing. I'll pass, thank you.' I turned the heavy feather in my fingers one last time and determinedly put it back on her cloth.

Bhuvana Devi, who had been watching this exchange, now spoke, 'Tara Bai, what would you do with those items?'

I looked at her and smiled. 'Write with them. They're meant for writing.'

A look of shock went around the group with the women looking at each other meaningfully.

Bhuvana Devi frowned at me. 'You can write?'

Too late, I realized my mistake. Women were not educated in this time. Writing was a rare skill, restricted mostly to Brahman and Kayastha men. Even the king himself might know only the basics of writing, with everything written down for him from a young age. I knew Vidyadhara wasn't illiterate because I had seen him read the scroll in court, but many kings were known to be. It wasn't unusual.

I stumbled out my reply. 'I … er, yes. No, I meant … only very little.'

Bhuvana Devi spoke to the vendor, 'I will buy this for Tara Bai. Restore it now so it may be used.'

I protested but she was adamant. The vendor sharpened and cleaned the quill deftly before pouring a pungent liquid into the ink pot slowly and shaking it, to loosen the dried ink. Bhuvana Devi sent an attendant to fetch some palm leaf paper while we waited.

When the ink was ready, Bhuvana Devi set the palm leaf in front of me and indicated that I should write something. A crowd had gathered around us and even the vendor leaned over in curiosity.

'What should I write?' I asked tentatively.

Bhuvana Devi smiled. 'Whatever you know.'

After some thought, I decided the safest bet was to make the symbol for Om. I dipped the quill in the ink pot and began writing. When the nib touched the leaf and the shape began to form, I could hear some gasps from the onlookers. When I was done, I looked up to find half of them gazing at me in awe and the other half with suspicion.

Bhuvana Devi smiled and said, 'More. What else can you write?'

I wrote my name and then I wrote 'Bhuvana Devi' in Hindi, amidst much oohing and ahhing from everyone. Finally, she said, 'Tell me, Tara Bai. In your kingdom, are all women given this kind of education?'

I replied, 'Most of them, yes. Except for the very poor.'

'Why do they teach women writing when it can be of no practical use in their lives?'

I took a deep breath. 'Women may not be comparable to men in terms of brute strength but they are as capable as men when it comes to intellect and understanding. If given a chance, women can do many of the same jobs that men can and do it as well as them.'

'Why would they want to?'

I chuckled, a part of me barely believing I was trying to explain feminism to a woman from the eleventh century. 'So that a woman does not have to depend on a man. So that women can live in a fairer society where they are given the same standing as men.'

A few of the women tittered and I remembered that the concepts of equality, human rights and liberty are modern ones and far too radical for this time. I quickly said, 'When a woman is educated, she is able to help her husband make good decisions and take better care of her family's health. She is also better able to run a household when her husband is absent … like when he goes off to fight wars.'

That obviously resonated with Bhuvana Devi because she nodded and smiled. Just as she was about to speak again, a guard strode into the courtyard. He was dressed in court regalia. The king, he announced loudly, had summoned me to court. Immediately.

A slight sliver of unease went down my back as the crowd around me quickly dispersed. Still, fortified by the memory of the look in Vidyadhara's eyes that night, I nodded and stood up quickly. Rushing to my chambers to get ready, I slipped on the emerald necklace he had gifted me before following the guard.

The court was in full swing and Vidyadhara, Vijaypala and Satyabhama were sitting in their formal regalia on their thrones. The guard had handed me over to a soldier who led me up the aisle towards the king. Around me sat all the princes, ministers and courtiers, and behind them sat all the noblemen and women.

As I approached Vidyadhara's dais, however, I began to feel a buzz of apprehension. No one smiled or acknowledged me in any way. Vidyadhara's face was as stiff and formal as it had been the other day in court but, underneath it, I sensed he was furious about something. Satyabhama and Vijaypala just stared at me without expression.

That was when I noticed a man standing on the side, between two soldiers. He was fair-complexioned with light eyes and had a nobleman's air about him. His thick woollen clothes identified him as being from somewhere in the north, where the climate was colder. He looked at me with recognition and a relieved smile that looked a little exaggerated. I had no idea who he was.

I came to a stop in front of the dais and bowed to Vidyadhara as I was expected to. His eyes were dark with anger as he addressed me in a formal tone, 'Tara Bai, you have been summoned to court because this man has come forward to claim you. He says he is your husband. Is this true?' He pointed towards the light-eyed man.

I blinked in confusion, not registering what he said for a moment. Then, as the full force of his words hit me, I staggered back and said, 'What? No!' I turned to look at the man in complete bafflement. 'I've never seen him before!'

The man straightened to his full height, maybe an inch or two above mine, and actually had the gall to smile at me intimately, almost affectionately. 'Tara, don't be angry with me anymore. I forgive you for running away. Let us go home.'

'Home?' I ejaculated in horror. 'What the hell are you talking about? I've never met you in my life and I've certainly never been married.' I turned to Vidyadhara and said loudly, 'He's lying!'

The man shook his head at me in apparent resignation and then turned to Vidyadhara. 'Maharaj, I'm telling the truth. My wife's words come from anger. She ran away from me last winter with a band of gypsies and I have been looking for her ever since.'

My eyes widened. 'You bloody liar! Who are you and what do you want from me?'

He replied, 'I want you to come back home.'

I forced myself to calm down and not panic. Yelling at him would make me sound hysterical and give him the upper hand. This was a trick – clearly someone had set me up. As much as I wanted to charge at him and scratch his eyes out, I had to be the reasonable one here. I had to make all of them believe me. If they let this man take me, it would be catastrophic. If he didn't kill me first, he'd probably make me wish I was dead.

'Maharaj' – my voice wobbled a bit but I looked into Vidyadhara's eyes and willed him to listen without anger – 'whatever else I may have said, I did not lie to you about being a maiden. This man is a stranger to me. I don't know why he's pretending to be my husband but please' – my eyes welled up – 'believe me. I have no husband and I did not run away but was taken against my will from my home. These are the truest words I have ever spoken. I have trusted your word at all times. Please trust mine.'

Vidyadhara's face was a mask and his eyes still dark as ever. He spoke to the man, 'Do you have proof that this woman is your wife?'

'Yes, Maharaj,' the man replied easily, fiddling with some parchment in his hands. 'I have brought our marriage record to show you.'

I shot back, 'You brought a piece of parchment? Those can be bought for a measly trifle. It means nothing!'

'You will be quiet, Tara Bai.' Vidyadhara didn't look at me as he spoke. Instead, he gestured towards the parchment, which was handed to him by Vatsaraja. He looked over it carefully for a few moments and then said in a calm but chilling voice, 'According to this, you both have been married for the last fourteen summers. Are there any children?'

The man spoke quickly, 'No, Maharaj. That was one of the reasons our union was unhappy. My wife is barren.'

'He's lying!' I shouted.

Vidyadhara put up his hand for silence. 'Are there any witnesses who can testify to your marriage?'

The stranger replied, 'My brother who accompanies me can swear that he was present at our wedding, Maharaj. He also shares our family residence so he can vouch for our marital relations.'

I felt my life unravelling before my eyes. This was a cruel joke. 'Please, Maharaj. These are all lies. Someone is trying to get rid of me. Don't believe him.'

Vidyadhara didn't look at me but the stranger did. I swear I saw a glimmer of victory in his eyes. 'Tara, I know I haven't been the best of husbands but you have taken this far enough.'

'Who's paying you to do this?' I choked out through my tears.

'Nonsense! You are my wife and I have every right to claim you.' He turned his back on me and bowed again to Vidyadhara. 'Maharaj, I have provided proof and a witness. She is a loose-tongued woman who has already admitted to lying to you in the past. It is quite clear-cut – I await with impatience to take what belongs to me back to my home.'

'Maharaj,' came Satyabhama's soft voice. 'May I ask this man a question?' I peered up at her, my eyes desperate.

Vidyadhara nodded, the anger still blazing in his eyes. Satyabhama asked the man, 'You say you are her husband.'

'I am.'

'You have had marital relations with her for fourteen summers.'

The man nodded. 'I have.'

Satyabhama continued calmly, 'In that case, you must know about the mark on her body.'

A murmur began to go around the court and Vatsaraja put his hand up for silence. The stranger clearly wasn't expecting this because he was quiet for a moment. I exhaled – my tattoo! Any husband of fourteen years should know about a tattoo on his wife's ass. I saw a glimmer of hope shine through the blackness as Satyabhama repeated, 'Do you know this mark?'

He shifted a tiny bit on his feet. 'Yes.'

Satyabhama nodded. 'You may tell the court on which part of her body it lies.'

I quickly wrapped my odhna around me so he couldn't see my upper body. The ghagra skirt already covered my hips and legs. This was my only chance of escape.

The man didn't speak for a moment, but I saw his fingers clasp each other nervously behind his back as he turned his head to look at me. I glared back, adjusting my odhna tighter around my shoulders. His eyes fell to my fingers as he said, 'Her shoulder.'

I heaved a slow, silent breath of relief. Satyabhama's expression didn't change. 'And what is the shape of this mark?'

The fingers grew even tighter behind his back as the moments passed. 'It is odd-shaped.'

Satyabhama looked over at Vidyadhara and said softly, 'The mark is neither odd-shaped nor is it on her shoulder, Maharaj. This man is lying.'

The court erupted with noise and Vidyadhara's expression grew even more furious. Only this time, thank God, it wasn't directed towards me. The stranger fell to his knees and stammered, 'Maharaj, m-mercy! A messenger from the palace paid us and g-gave instructions. We are just travelling merchants. We meant no harm to her.'

'Your actions show otherwise!' Vidyadhara's deep voice rang out decisively. 'You will be executed along with your companions. Your wares will be gifted to Tara Bai, to make amends for the distress you have caused her. Take him away.'

Soldiers came and caught the man just as he turned on his knees towards me and begged me to intercede on his behalf. He would have done me no harm, he screamed desperately as they carried him away.

I stood shivering with relief and shock. That was a close call and a reminder of exactly how precarious my position was in this place. Vidyadhara looked at me, his face still formal but his eyes diffused. 'You may return to your chambers, Tara Bai.'

I stumbled visibly as I walked out. I had to do something – I couldn't let that happen to me again. Puppa met me at the entrance of Rani Bhavan. She had tears streaked all over her face but her eyes bulged with anger.

'It was Rani Vijaya who arranged it.'

23

My knuckles ached as I hung tightly onto the elaborately gilded and carved side-bar of the howdah, a wide seat saddled on elephants. Above me was a canopy embroidered with gold and silver and, beneath me, effortlessly carrying the cushioned platform we sat on, was one of the largest elephants I had ever seen in my life. I looked downwards and immediately regretted it as I felt a tiny wave of vertigo. We were way above the ground and swaying from side to side along with the elephant's gait.

By 'we' I meant me and Vidyadhara, who was sitting on the divan-like howdah with me. He sat just far enough to avoid touching me and just close enough to make my body hum in anticipation. It had been his idea for me to go hunting with him. Yesterday, an attendant had brought in a new set of clothes for me, complete with a tray full of matching jewellery for seemingly every part of my body. She told me that the king had requested I join him for a hunt and it would please him greatly if I wore his gifts, as I had done in court.

The style of the jewels had made me smile as I had fingered them. Their stones were set in delicate patterns with understated lines and were much more suited to my taste than the chunky stuff worn by everyone else. He had obviously thought about what I would like. Perhaps it was his way of apologizing for what had happened in court.

I had spent two days holed up in my chambers after that incident, trying to get over it. The executed merchant's wares, a caravan full of spices, cloth and perfumed oils, had arrived at Rani Bhavan the next day. I'd asked for them to be distributed to the needy. I wanted nothing to do with them.

I also realized that Vijamba had spoken a harsh truth when she said that Vidyadhara had to be the one to protect me. Much as it rankled that my life, my safety and welfare would be dependent on a man – any man, no matter how I felt about him – I had to be pragmatic about it. I was living in a different age now. If I wanted to survive, I needed to play by its rules.

So, I accepted his invitation and, after my bath in the morning, donned the clothes and jewels he had gifted me. I even allowed Vijamba and her women to apply kohl to my eyes and rub my cheeks and lips with a paste that left a mild colour when it washed off. I looked into the metal mirror in my chambers and could barely recognize myself.

Neither, it seemed, could Vidyadhara. He had stopped in his tracks and stared for a few moments when he entered my chambers to pick me up. Then he chuckled and said, 'You look beautiful,' before ushering me outside to where at least a hundred men, hunters on horseback and foot, soldiers and servants, were waiting. With an elephant carrying a royal canopy.

'You have recovered from that incident in court?' he asked as we passed through the town and towards the dense jungle that cascaded down the hill.

'Yes, I have.'

He nodded. 'Good. I hope today will be more pleasant. Shall I shoot a deer for your evening meal? Or would you prefer a more substantial trophy, like a tiger?' he asked with a smile.

I stared back at him in horror. 'No!'

He looked nonplussed at my expression. 'Why not?'

'Because … because I don't like to kill things.'

A spark of humour entered his eyes. 'You are on a hunt, Tara Bai.'

I sighed. I was the product of a generation that had nearly seen the tiger and many species of deer wiped out of existence. But, without the benefit of hindsight, I couldn't expect him to understand. 'Not a deer or a tiger. I would feel terrible killing animals of such grace and beauty.'

He smiled. 'In that case, we shall hunt fowl or boar. Even you, Tara Bai, cannot accuse a boar of being beautiful.'

I smiled back at him and felt tingly at the look I got in response. 'Can I ask you something that's been on my mind?'

'I would be very interested to know what's on your mind.'

I took a deep breath. 'The message you got from … Hamira.' I tried to gauge his reaction but his expression didn't change. 'Do you really believe that he means to ally with you?'

He cocked his head and peered back at me, his eyes watchful but his tone light. 'Why do you ask?'

'I don't mean to pry and I'm sorry if this is one of those things I'm not supposed to ask a king, but I just wondered what your thoughts were.'

'My thoughts on this matter, Tara Bai' – his lips twitched – 'are best left inside me. What are your thoughts? You wouldn't have asked if you didn't have them.'

I exhaled with relief. 'I just don't think he's telling the truth. I think it's a trap.'

He shrugged lightly. 'It's possible. Only time will tell. You needn't worry about anything.'

'I think you should be ready for an attack.'

That made him grin. 'Kalinjara is always ready for an attack. Now, you may rest easy while I shoot your measly fowl. They're in the trees ahead.'

He said very little to me for the next hour as he brought down a number of wild fowl with arrows shot out of a bow that looked too heavy to carry, let alone shoot with. Once in a while, he pointed out a deer in the distance with a teasing look that I couldn't help but smile at. Unexpectedly, I found myself laughing out loud more than a few times at something he'd say. When he wasn't being a king, Vidyadhara was actually fun to be around.

As the sun crested the sky, his men set up a luxurious forest camp for our meal and began to cook it downhill. We dismounted and he led me to an ancient tree at some distance from the camp, its base naturally canopied against the midday heat by its thick foliage. A light breeze complemented the chirping sounds of the forest. He sat me down on a huge tree root that stuck out of the ground.

'I hope you don't mind the lack of fanfare,' he said.

I watched him lounge on the root and thought aloud, 'You don't care for fanfare. Even when you travelled from Khajuravahaka, you rode ahead while the rest of your party came in a more comfortable convoy. You'd rather sit here, under a tree, than on the soft divan in your tent.'

'I'm a warrior. Soft beds aren't good for me,' he quipped. He took off the sword hanging from his cummerbund and leaned it against the tree in an obvious gesture of relaxation. His tunic stretched with the movement and I remembered how it had moulded itself to his contours every time he had held up the bow to shoot arrows from the elephant.

I felt heat rush to my face and got up, turning my cheeks away so he wouldn't see it. Unfortunately, I collided with a low-hanging branch and a bunch of my hair got caught in its leaves. I wore it in a loose bun on the nape of my neck every day, much against Vijamba's wish to oil it and plait it back tightly. The bun unravelled and my hair fell loose as I pulled lightly. I felt the tug against my scalp, but some strands at the top were tangled up and I couldn't turn my head.

Vidyadhara kept looking at me without moving, an impish look in his eyes. 'Need help?'

The moment lay suspended, waiting for a conclusion. If I asked him for help, he'd have to touch my hair. Was that tacit agreement to touch the rest of me? More importantly, did I want him to?

He sighed and said matter-of-factly, 'Your face speaks louder than words, you know.'

I swallowed and closed my eyes for a brief moment. I was done fighting. 'Could you help me, please?'

He got up slowly and came over. Then, as if each strand of my hair was made of gold, he slowly untangled them one by one. I was turned away from him but I could feel the warmth of his body behind me. When he was done, he stood still, unmoving, as I turned back to face him.

'Thank you,' I whispered. And then I put my hand on his arm that still held the branch, touching him for the first time since we'd left Khajuravahaka. Under the fabric of his tunic, his body felt like warm stone.

I'm not sure what reaction I was expecting. A part of me thought he might grab me out of sheer impatience, or even laugh because he had finally got his way.

Instead, he just kept standing, with my hand on his arm. Looking at me with a spark in his eyes. Then he took my hand in his own. I felt his fingers caress mine. 'Tara,' he murmured. 'She taunts me from afar and acts so prim when I come near. She won't let me touch her, yet allows me to give her pleasure with my eyes.'

He laughed softly when I rolled my eyes at him and then reached over and ran a finger down from the side of my eye to my jaw. The finger came to a stop under my chin, which it pushed up gently but firmly. He whispered, 'Will she allow me to give her pleasure with my body?'

My breaths became shallow and my heart a sledgehammer as I peered up at him. This man knew I wanted him as much as he wanted me. Yet, he held back. My reservations fell away. 'Yes.'

His eyes darkened with unabashed desire. He pulled my hand gently and sat back down on the giant root until I was sitting sideways on his lap. I felt his solid sinew against my body, his warm breath close to mine and my limbs turned molten.

His fingers made their way down my neck as I closed my eyes and let my head fall back a little to give him better access. Heat spread in waves across my body. He gently began to stroke my neck. 'She quivers with my touch but her own is as hesitant as the deer she won't allow me to kill.' His lips brushed my ear as he whispered, 'Do you know the best way to make a deer trust you?'

My eyes fluttered open and I gulped. 'How?'

His hand moved from my neck back up to my face and his fingers brushed against my lips, at first lightly and then more insistently.

'You have to go very slowly and be very gentle,' he murmured as his finger ran back and forth over my lower lip. 'Did you know deer love to be stroked?'

I felt his other hand on the curve of my waist, stroking the bare skin beneath the drape of my odhna. Slowly and gently. I arched against him slightly, my fingers on his shoulders tugging him closer.

I inhaled as he ran one wicked finger along the border of my tie-up blouse, just below my breast. Then gasped when it brushed through the fabric across my nipple once, twice … insistently. I swayed towards him but he held back, his hands relentlessly stroking me.

I brought my own hands to his chest and toyed for a second with the ties on the side of his tunic. Then, in a moment of pure impulsiveness, I pulled them loose. The front of his tunic fell open, revealing an expanse of hot, muscular chest and I couldn't help run my hand over it.

He smiled, his eyes blazing with desire. 'My turn,' he said, as he deftly pulled open the tie at the back of my blouse. My breasts, free from their restraint, fell towards him as he divested me of my choli and odhna. He looked, turning their peaks taut with his gaze, but didn't touch. Instead, he brought his eyes back to mine and murmured, 'Beautiful,' before his lips swept mine into a fiery kiss.

I felt small stabs from the precious stones in my necklace as his naked chest pressed into mine but I didn't care. I wrapped my arms around him, ran my hands through his hair, over his back and revelled in the games our lips played. Our tongues duelled in much the same way our swords had the first time we ever met. Just like then, I was completely disarmed. Only this time, I liked it. A lot.

I felt his hand cupping my breast and pulled away momentarily, gasping for air. I arched against him again, impatient for more as he ran his thumb over my nipple, back and forth, again and again until it throbbed and extended outwards almost desperately. Then he rolled and pinched it between his thumb and finger and I huffed, with both pleasure and impatience, as his lips returned to mine.

'Please,' I whispered and felt his smile against my mouth. He lowered his head, kissing my neck and shoulders, unhurriedly and thoroughly, as if he had all the time in the world. I writhed against him, egging him on until he finally took my nipple in his mouth, nuzzling before pulling it between his lips and teeth. I moaned softly as I looked down, watching him stoke the fire in my body with half-lidded eyes.

Suddenly, a sharp movement in the trees some distance away caught my peripheral vision. I opened my eyes lazily and looked over Vidyadhara's head, expecting to see a bird or a monkey or a squirrel hopping between branches. Instead, what I saw froze the blood in my veins.

A small man crouched on the branches of a tall tree. He was quite far away but I could make out the lines of his white dhoti and skin against the green of the foliage around him. In his arms, he held a bow, taut with a drawn arrow that was just about to take flight.

Directly towards Vidyadhara's back.

I screamed.

What happened next must have taken only seconds. But it felt like I had stepped out of my body and was watching the whole thing like a spectator, in slow motion.

Vidyadhara pushed me onto the ground and, wrapping me tightly in his arms, began to roll on the forest floor as arrow after arrow landed on the ground, sometimes centimetres away from our bodies. He shouted something loudly as he rolled, but I couldn't make out what he said because of my own screams. Fear, raw and debilitating, coursed through me every time I saw an arrow pierce the ground. I thought I'd had a number of brushes with death since Kala Devi had sent me here. Now I realized what it truly meant to stare death in the face.

Finally, Vidyadhara rolled us behind a large tree and pressed me against the trunk just as another arrow hit the other side of the tree. The archer couldn't reach us anymore. I heard shouts and the sounds of men, hundreds of them, running through the forest. Dozens of them charged past us as I huddled against the tree trunk, shielded from view by his embrace.

'Stay here.' Vidyadhara swiftly took off his tunic and draped it over me before running in the direction of the archer.

I squeezed the tunic against my chest and pressed into the tree, shaking with shock. More shouting and sounds of a struggle came from the distance, but I was unable to process any of it. I knew I should probably be doing something to help myself but I was petrified into immobility.

Vidyadhara came running back to me with my choli and odhna. 'Put these back on. You're safe now, don't worry. We have him.'

Gently but quickly, he helped me with my clothes and shrugged on his own, saying, 'We need to get back so he can be questioned before someone tries to kill him. Or he tries to kill himself.'

I nodded, incapable of speech and barely even registering his words. When we were done and ready to leave, he put his hands on my shoulders and gazed into my eyes. 'We will talk later. You saved your king's life today. It won't be forgotten.'

He crushed his lips against mine for the smallest of seconds and then we were off, back in the direction of the palace.

24

It had been many hours since the attack but I was still shaking. I turned my head on the pillow and stared out into the garden, bathed in moonlight, the water in the pond shimmering with ripples created by the creatures that lived in and around it. The pleasure pavilion at the centre of the pond must have held much promise for the previous occupant of these chambers, but it had no appeal for me at the moment.

I cast off the covers and stopped for a moment as I heard the very light jingle of the anklets I still wore. The sound was as common as air around here, with every palace woman tinkling a tiny bit as she walked. The sound marked me as one of them. I reached over and snapped them off. Then I removed, slowly and deliberately, the rest of the jewellery I had donned in the morning – from my waist, neck, arms and head.

Silently, I stepped off my massive bed and into the garden. An attendant stirred from a roll-out bed on the floor of the veranda and asked sleepily, 'Mistress?'

'Shh…, go back to sleep,' I told her firmly.

I looked up at the moon, bright and sympathetic. It looked down upon a harsh world. A world so raw it went beyond what most modern people could fathom. A world where laws and their enforcement, courts, treasuries, everything to do with the state all came under the purview of one man. A man whom hundreds of thousands, perhaps millions, of people depended on to keep order in their lives. A man who had almost been killed today.

Involuntary shudders ran down my spine for the thousandth time today. I had been extremely lucky so far. I had remained unscathed in a place where people routinely played games with other people's lives. But I had a sinking suspicion that my luck had almost run out. If Vidyadhara had been killed today, I might have been forced to climb into a funeral pyre along with his wives and concubines. I might have actually become the most reactionary, regressive thing I could possibly conceive of as a modern Indian woman – a sati.

That's why I was still shaking.

How could I live like this? How could I have it hanging over my head for the rest of my life? Even if I had the most perfect of relationships with Vidyadhara, even if I managed to successfully navigate the landmines that were the other women in this palace, even if I managed to create a life and family for myself and survive the absence of twenty-first century healthcare and conveniences, I would never be able to get away from the fact that one day, sometime within the next two decades, Vidyadhara would die and his son, Vijaypala would become king. And I would be burnt alive.

A light breeze played with my hair, checking the surge of panic I had at the thought. Was I overthinking it? What if I went back to my own time and got run over by a car, leaving me to endure an agonizing death over weeks and months? I shook my head in frustration. Death wasn't the point – no one could decide when or how they died. But sati, that went against everything I believed in. I just had to keep trying to get back to my own time. I owed it to my future self.

I fiddled with my sleeping-sari. Maybe Sarvadasa would agree to help me if I confided in him. I had nothing substantial to bribe him with but surely, as a yogi, he would be obliged to help. Or he might know of someone who could. Maybe even lead me to Kala Devi. After all, she did say she was from this time. Maybe she was out there somewhere and Sarvadasa could lead me to her. I had to ask him. It was my one and only shot at getting back.

And what better time to start than right now. Vijamba had mentioned that he lived near the Neelkanth temple but no one knew where. I thought about the tunnel leading into the catacombs from the door inside the cave. It was the kind of living space that seemed suited to a yogi. The history and myth of the temple, the rock idol and the religious fervour of these people would dissuade anyone from opening the door inside the cave. It would be one of the most private places in the fort.

I looked around to make sure all the attendants were asleep and went back to my room. The underside of my bed covering was a lining of a soft, dark-coloured cotton. I wrapped it around myself and covered my head, praying that I'd blend into the darkness outside.

I ducked into the hallways and slid out of Rani Bhavan through one of the many side entrances used by the servants. The guards were thankfully asleep and their lamp had been allowed to burn out. I slunk through the shadows the entire time during the long trek to the side of the north cliff where the Neelkanth temple cave hugged the rock.

The temple cave was shadowy, lit by a single fire lamp, the distant echoes of dripping water adding drama to its ghostly air. I tiptoed to the side door and slipped into it. The cavern inside was pitch-black. I left the door ajar to let a tiny bit of light in and felt my way down the tunnel. I could hear voices, whispers almost, and I followed the sound, deciding to see who Sarvadasa was with before revealing myself. I didn't want anyone else to know I was here. When I could make out what was being said, I stopped and listened.

'You worry needlessly, Rajpurohit,' said an unfamiliar voice.

Sarvadasa's voice sounded peeved. 'It is my place to be worried. I am the one who shall face the king's wrath if you fail again. What kind of idiots work for you? That archer didn't even bother to hide himself!'

I stopped breathing for a few shocked moments. My heart started thumping so loudly I was worried they might hear it.

'We will not fail again. My sultan has been sending troops and supplies secretly to his vassals under the guise of merchant caravans. He has already started marching his army to take Gwalior. After that, he will come to take Kalinjara and teach your cocksure king a lesson.'

Sarvadasa asked, 'How many men do you need to slip into the fort through the catacombs?'

A tiny gasp escaped my lips. I froze, expecting them to be alerted to my presence. But, after a mere moment, the man's voice replied.

'Not many. About six. Just enough to disable defences and open the gates. It is important, however, that they are not intercepted when you bring them through the caves. Who else has access to them?'

'Senapati Vatsaraja has a secret group of soldiers and civilians who operate the underground network. Their identities are known only to him and the king. It is protected at all times. But don't worry, I've been roaming these caves since I was a boy when my father was in charge of the temple. I'll be able to steal your men past the soldiers.'

The man replied, 'That is good. And your king does not suspect anything? What has he told his advisors after the incident?'

Sarvadasa's reply was abrupt. 'I am not privy to his private conversations. But I do know he is suspicious. There have been no obvious signs he is preparing, but that doesn't mean he isn't. He knows Kalinjara is in no real danger as long as the underground network, its tunnels and reservoirs are safe. And he trusts those who are familiar with it. Including me.'

'Can the sultan of Ghazni trust you, Rajpurohit?'

Sarvadasa said sarcastically, 'Your sultan doesn't have a choice but to trust me.'

There was a pause. Then the man replied, 'You should know that my sultan is not a man to be trifled with.'

Sarvadasa's tone was derisive. 'They say your sultan likes nothing better than trifling. In pleasure chambers. With other men.'

'I should cut off your tongue for that. Maybe I will, after all this is over and Kalinjara bows down to Ghazni.'

'You could try. If you survive it.' Sarvadasa's tone was dismissive.

I looked back at the dim temple light shining through the door in the distance and decided I had heard enough. Any second now, they were going to discover me and I wouldn't live to see sunrise. I had to get out of there fast.

I crept back to the door, grateful for the echoes of dripping water that shielded the very slight shuffle of my hurried steps. Once I was out of the temple cave, I made a mad dash back to Rani Bhavan. Many questions assaulted me on the way back, but I waited until I was safely ensconced in my chambers before I gulped back my exhausted gasps and thought about what I'd heard.

Sarvadasa was a traitor!

And my hunch was right – the message from the sultan of Ghazni had been a ruse. He had no intention of allying with Vidyadhara against the Paramaras and their allies. He was coming to seek his revenge, to unseat Vidyadhara just as Vidyadhara had unseated the Sultan's vassal, Rajyapala. It was going to happen just as history said it did.

Except for the bit where the king's traitorous rajpurohit would compromise the security of the fort by sneaking in Ghaznavid soldiers.

I pressed my fingers against my head and furiously tried to recall every detail of my knowledge about the sultan's attempt to take Kalinjara. Sultan Mahmud had attacked King Kirtiraja of Gwalior, Vidyadhara's vassal, on his trek across the subcontinent. For four days, he laid siege to Gwalior Fort until Kirtiraja offered a tribute and sent him on his way. The sultan had then marched to Kalinjara and laid siege, failing to take the fort in the first few battles. After that, he had encircled and camped around the hill for a year until, finally, he had come to an agreement with Vidyadhara, exchanged gifts and gone home. By that time, his own resources were running low and his army was tired. He never returned to Kalinjara.

So, I thought, what had really saved Kalinjara during that year, when all supplies to the fort had been cut off by the Ghaznavid army, was the underground catacombs and reservoirs. They had allowed the fort's residents to stay watered and fed, and allowed Vidyadhara's men free movement around the area without Sultan Mahmud's knowledge. This played a critical part in the upcoming conflict. Which, if the sultan had already started marching towards Gwalior, was a very short time away.

I hung my head in my hands. So where did Sarvadasa come into all this? If he helped the Ghaznavid army breach the underground network, the fort would almost certainly be taken. Unless the men were intercepted by Vatsaraja's soldiers on their way and killed. Did that happen? I didn't know. History books were never this specific, not when talking about events that had occurred a thousand years in the past.

What I did know was that if the fort was taken, hundreds of thousands of people would lose their lives. Sultan Mahmud would also ransack the kingdom and destroy its temples. He would probably level the Khajuraho temples to the ground. Without them, a crucial part of our history would be lost forever. Archaeologists would be digging up bits of rubble instead of magnificent intact temples.

I had to do something.

'*Time is a wheel … Sometimes, it is possible to fold the wheel … I only do it when there is a purpose*,' Kala Devi had said to me. What was her purpose? Why had I been sent back? What was important enough for a yogini like her to consider bending the wheel of time?

Did I have to save the Khajuraho temples?

If so, how? I had already saved Vidyadhara's life. Should I now tell him about what I'd heard Sarvadasa say? Would he believe my word against a man he had known his entire life?

If he didn't, where would that leave me? And if he did, and Sarvadasa was killed or put away, who would be left to help me get back to the future?

Nobody. I'd be left here. Waiting to become a sati someday.

On the other hand, if I didn't tell anyone and Sarvadasa helped me somehow to go through time, then nobody would stop him … and the war would wipe out the Khajuraho temples, kill all the men and make the women who lived on and around this hill, all of them, commit mass sati, or jauhar, by jumping into a communal funeral pyre. Satyabhama, pregnant Bhuvana Devi, Puppa, Vijamba … everyone. Everyone who had taken me in and given me a home. Given me their trust and protection.

It was me or them.

I laughed a little hysterically. I couldn't help it. A billion people in the country and Kala Devi had chosen me to take this on. I could've done something with my life. I could've been a successful archaeologist, maybe even mustered up the guts to flirt with Hari one day. I laughed again. Hari and all my issues with him seemed so far away, so trivial. Now I was busy deciding if it was worth sacrificing my future for the future of an entire civilization.

Oh, who was I kidding? There was no decision to make. Kala Devi had sent me here for a very good reason.

She knew I would do the right thing.

25

Her dark brown eyes bored into me as usual, making me fidget on the stool at her feet, where I was seated. She had said nothing for the last few minutes, ever since I spilled the beans on the conversation I overheard between Sarvadasa and the man from Ghazni in the cave.

I'm not sure what reaction I expected when I went to Satyabhama's chambers and told her. I'd certainly thought that there would be more of a sense of urgency. But she stayed as unruffled as ever, considering me with her gaze in the same detached manner with which she had saved my life in court.

Which reminded me. 'I also wanted to thank you for what you did for me in court that day. I don't know what would have happened if that man had taken me away.'

She nodded dismissively before saying, 'What were you doing in the temple at night?'

I exhaled. That was a question I was prepared for. 'I wanted to speak to Sarvadasa.'

'Why didn't you request to meet him in your rooms? Or go to him during the day?'

I replied, 'I wanted to speak privately with him about performing a prayer ceremony for me. There have been a few dangerous situations of late and I want to cleanse myself of evil spirits. I didn't want my attendants to gossip about it in the palace.' I was banking on her believing that a secret havan was worth the nocturnal trek to the Neelkanth temple. She was the most diligently pious person I had ever met, constantly compelling the women of the palace to conduct fasts, prayers, ceremonies and rituals for the smallest of occasions. If anyone was going to believe that I wanted a ceremony to rid myself of evil spirits, it would be Satyabhama.

She did. 'Have you recounted the conversation exactly as you heard it, Tara Bai? Think carefully. Have you added your own words to it when you told me?'

I shook my head. 'There is no doubt in what he said or implied. The sultan of Ghazni is heading to Gwalior with an invading army as we speak. He will attack their fort and then he will come here and attack Kalinjara. The rajpurohit will lead a small group of his men through the underground cave network and these men will disarm the fort and open the gates for the sultan's army. I have recounted the conversation exactly as I heard it.'

I paused for a moment and then continued, 'Maharaj ... he told me that Kalinjara is always prepared for an attack. But if the catacombs are breached...' I trailed off, unsure of how to continue.

She raised one brow and asked, 'You have discussed the fort's defences with Maharaj?'

'No,' I said quickly. 'I just asked him a few questions when we went hunting yesterday. He doesn't know this information yet. Will you tell him?'

She looked carefully at me again before saying, 'Tara Bai, you have accused the rajpurohit of being a traitor. This is no small claim. He is one of Maharaj's most trusted men. Do you have proof?'

'I understand it's a big claim and know the risks. I've only told you because it's the right thing to do. I bear Sarvadasa no grudge and I wasn't planning to hear what I did. There is no way for me to have proof,' I replied.

'Proof is necessary if you want people to believe you,' she said softly. 'Luckily, it can be obtained when needed.' She lowered her voice. 'Who else knows about this?'

'No one. I have told only you.'

'Good.' She nodded. 'This is what you will do.'

I listened carefully as she spoke in a soft murmur, making sure no one could overhear her. Afterwards, I left for my chambers and spent the rest of the day there. At some point, Vidyadhara's personal guards carried in a huge wooden chest and my attendants opened it with much excitement to reveal swaths and swaths of the finest cloth in every colour, embroidered with golden thread. Underneath the fabric lay intricately carved ivory implements, mirrors, gilded slippers and a smaller chest full of jewellery. Vijamba fingered a pendant with a glistening ruby as big as her nose and grinned coyly as she murmured, 'Maharaj must be very pleased indeed.' Puppa modelled a bolt of heavy cloth, dragging it across the floor carelessly until she was chastised by one of the older women.

Hours later, a few more guards arrived, this time with a small tame deer. They left it in the garden and said they would pick it up before nightfall. Puppa giggled gleefully as we fed the deer leaves and gently petted its spotted back as it grazed.

I laughed along, some of her excitement rubbing off on me, but couldn't get rid of a sense of foreboding that kept me glancing towards one particular corner of my sitting room all evening. It was a large space, holding two divans, and lay underneath wide undulating arches that extended beyond the walls of my chambers.

That night, when I was sure everyone had gone to sleep, I walked over to the corner and sat on one of the divans. Silence, except for the chirping of nocturnal life and the quiet snores of my attendants in the adjoining rooms, enveloped me. I looked up at the ceiling arches and listened for some more time.

All I could hear were my own breaths. I sighed. And prayed Satyabhama's plan would work.

The next day, I sent Vijamba to deliver a message to Sarvadasa, requesting him to conduct a cleansing havan in my chambers. He sent back word that he would come to my rooms just before sunset and gave Vijamba a list of things to collect for the prayer ceremony. The rest of the day was spent setting up a space for the event, which I insisted should be conducted in the corner under the arches. My attendants set up pillars wrapped with flower garlands and a base for the sacrificial fire, adorning the space with spiced wood, fruit, flowers, ghee, sweets, cloth, incense and silver utensils and implements. While all this was going on I paced nervously in the garden.

I had worn my full concubine regalia this morning. My hair, neck, ears, arms, waist and feet were adorned with gold and rubies – the nose-sized pendant hung between my breasts.

Vijamba had painted intricate designs on my feet and hands with red colour and my eyes were blackened with a generous dollop of kohl. I still refused to oil my hair, but Vijamba was more than satisfied when she stepped back and examined me. 'You look radiant, Mistress,' she said proudly.

I felt anything but radiant. My nerves were jangled and butterflies in my belly ensured I could barely eat the mid-morning meal that was laid out in front of me. But, I sternly told myself, it was critical that I played my part perfectly. The lives of everyone around, my own life, depended on my performance today.

As the sun began to recede, I heard a murmur of excitement from the women in the sitting room. To my surprise, Vidyadhara strode in and said firmly, 'Leave us.'

My attendants scurried away as he joined me in my bedchamber, where I was trying to distract myself from worrying by fiddling with the gifts he had sent the day before.

He smiled down at the heavy, gold-embroidered cloth I was fingering and murmured, 'Does it please you?'

I stood up and bowed and felt his hands on my shoulders, pulling me up. He caressed my skin as I replied, 'It does, Maharaj.'

Our eyes met and a shot of desire sizzled through me. He pulled me to him and then, unexpectedly and unceremoniously, lifted me up and dropped me on the bed. I shrieked and then laughed as he lay down next to me, his face looming over mine.

'I had hoped to be spending a very enjoyable evening with you in this bed, Tara Bai. But you've thought up of something more important, haven't you?' His voice was a whisper against my neck as he slowly, deliberately, parted my legs and slid his length up against the apex of them. He was hard as a rock.

'She told you?' I whispered and gasped at the same time, nervousness overshadowing the rippling frissons of pleasure that were streaking upwards from where our bodies touched.

I felt his thumb stroking my waist. 'She did.' His eyes, although sparkling with his usual humour and languor, were unreadable. I couldn't tell if he believed I was telling the truth or not.

'Do you believe me?'

His lips nuzzled mine. 'I don't disbelieve you.' He bit my lower lip gently.

I nudged his face back up so I could look at him. 'I'll prove it to you.'

He chuckled and shook his head slightly. 'Life is never going to be boring with you, isn't it?'

I was too uneasy to continue in this vein. I put my hands on his chest and pushed lightly. 'Go, please. He'll be here at sundown. He mustn't see you here.'

Vidyadhara looked into my eyes carefully for a moment before getting up and pulling me to my feet. 'I will return later.'

I nodded worriedly as I watched him leave. Our familiarity, his trust in me, assuming he had any, had been hard-won. I could potentially be throwing it all away. It was not a good thought with which to start the evening's proceedings.

26

He poured the ghee into a bowl after melting it over the fire. The spicy smell of incense filled my nostrils and the fumes, wafting my way due to an inconvenient breeze, made my eyes water.

Still, I took a deep breath and sat down next to Sarvadasa on the floor. The divans had been removed from the corner to make space for the sacred havan fire and I had a quick final glance up at the ceiling and around the room to make sure things were set up correctly.

Sarvadasa hadn't said much since he arrived, except for huffing a bit at the apparently haphazard way my attendants had set up the offerings. He had then started rearranging everything and was now getting ready to start the evening's proceedings.

I turned towards the surrounding attendants and servants who had gathered around to participate. 'Go. All of you, please go away. This will be a private ceremony.'

Their eyes widened in surprise and not a little bit of disapproval. Havans were not usually private affairs. Vijamba attempted a discreet comeback. 'But, Mistress, what if Rajpurohitji needs anything for the prayer?'

'I will get it for him. Now I wish to meditate. Leave the room, all of you.' My voice sounded uncharacteristically imperious and I felt slightly ashamed of it.

They filed out. When the last one had left the room, Sarvadasa raised his piercing eyes at me and regarded me carefully for what seemed like a long time. Then he sneered and said, 'Let's start your *meditation*, Tara Bai. What do you want?' as he went about setting up the last of the offerings for the fire.

I reeled a little at his blunt words. He wasn't a fool. I'd have to tread carefully. 'I wish to cleanse myself of evil spirits,' I replied in what I hoped wasn't a shaky voice. His wiry, tiger skin-clad body was covered in markings and smelled strongly of burnt wood and the sticky-sweet scent of ganja.

His stare bore into me. 'Who are you?'

'W-What?'

'Who are you?' he repeated. 'Where did you come from?'

'I'm Tara Singh from Chandigarh.'

He grunted a disbelieving laugh. 'You are a fool if you think anyone believes that story. Who sent you here?'

I felt my anger rising. 'Nobody sent me. I was kidnapped!'

The truth of that statement must have shown in my eyes because he replied, 'By whom?'

I stared back at him, torn by indecision. For a moment, just for a moment, I abandoned my original plan and decided to throw it out there. 'Kala Devi.'

He inhaled sharply and his eyes widened in utter shock. A silver spoon fell from his fingers with a clink.

Oh God. 'You know her,' I whispered, more a statement than a question.

He looked back with almost scared eyes, as if Kala Devi were some kind of monster out of a horror movie who would appear out of nowhere and pounce on him if he made the wrong move.

I couldn't stop myself from asking, 'Do you … do you know where she is?' My mind went into overdrive. Was there a chance, a real chance, he could take me to her?

He was recovering from the shock. 'I might.'

Here it was. This was my chance to abandon my plan to trap him into a confession and take back my life, my future. It would probably be the last, the only, chance I ever got. I looked at his penetrating, secret-laden eyes and heard the thud of my jittery heart against the walls of my chest, debating furiously with myself.

I closed my eyes and took a deep, shuddering breath. When I opened them, I had made up my mind. 'I heard you talking to the Ghaznavid man.'

There, it was done. No going back now. I squashed the heartache that ripped through me and tried to focus on the task at hand. There would be a lifetime after this moment to mourn the loss of everything, and everyone, I'd just given up.

A mask fell over Sarvadasa's face. He was, once again, simply the rajpurohit, concerned with moving the prayer proceedings along before the auspicious sunset time had passed. He gestured for me to pass him a small silver pot near my feet as he said, 'The evil spirits in your chambers have obviously also possessed your mind. We will conduct a series of havans to evict them.'

I stared at his face and murmured, 'We are alone. You may speak freely.'

'Every day a different havan for a different kind of evil. You will need to fast during the day and only eat at certain times during the night … I will leave instructions with your attendants.'

I suppressed my irritation and said, 'I know what you plan to do. Sneaking those soldiers inside through the catacombs. Maybe I can help.' I arched one eyebrow at him in an attempt to act coy.

His expression turned ugly for the briefest of seconds but then the neutral mask was back on. 'Let us start now. Before you descend into madness.' He began to stoke the sacred fire into life and chant loudly.

'I could help you, or' – I stared at him intently – 'I could tell Maharaj what I heard.'

His voice faltered a little but he carried on chanting. I took a deep breath, my desperation growing by the second. 'I'll make a deal with you. I'll help you get the soldiers inside and, when you escape, I go along. You deliver me to Kala Devi in return.'

He sneered a little, implying I couldn't possibly be of any help to him. I racked my brains and pushed on. 'Senapati Vatsaraja's wife and I are close.' This was a lie. She lived in a house outside the palace and her visits were limited to the chambers of royal family members, not concubines. 'She told me that the senapati loves the sweetmeats made in Rani Bhavan's kitchens.'

He looked up at me. His hands and voice continued to perform the rituals and chants, but he seemed to be sizing me up. I held his gaze, my eyes confident. Poison was a well-known and effective political tool, employed throughout the ages by everyone, in every denomination, with a high degree of success. I knew the idea of poisoning Vatsaraja would be a tempting one. A sudden loss of leadership would result in temporary chaos in the army, a situation that would provide the ideal opportunity for an enemy to slink past security.

I watched as he threw incense-laden woodchips into the fire without looking. I could see the indecision in his eyes. And I knew the moment he decided to play it safe by looking away from me to chant even louder. I exhaled in frustration, stretched out my hand involuntarily and touched his arm. 'Rajpurohitji—'

He shrieked like an animal and drew back from me as if my touch had torched him. 'You filthy whore!' he raged at me in disgust. 'You would defile a man of God with your unholy touch!'

That was the last straw. I lost my temper. 'Seriously? You're talking about getting defiled because I touched your arm? And your vigorous bouts of sex in the caves beyond your temple, right next door to your deities, don't defile you? You're like the king of those caves, aren't you? No one knows what the hell you do in there or who you do it with. Well, I know. I know everything. There's no point pretending with me anymore, Sarvadasa. You decide if you want me as a friend or as an enemy. We can have a mutually beneficial arrangement or I could sabotage your plans. You choose.'

His hand closed around my neck and squeezed as he dropped all shred of pretence and locked his vicious eyes with mine. 'You will die before you sabotage my plans, you bitch.'

What was it with these medieval men and the choking? 'I might,' I gasped back quickly, my blood surging even as my breaths struggled, 'but it won't bode well for you. Do you think they will still trust you if they find Maharaj's favourite concubine dead? You need their trust. Without it, you can do nothing.'

He bared his teeth at me, almost as if he wanted to bite a chunk of my throat off. My eyes widened but I held my ground. Finally, his grip on my throat loosened and he backed off, breathing heavily and looking down towards the sacred fire. After a few endless moments, he whispered, 'You want me to take you to Kala Devi.'

'Yes,' I whispered back. 'You will need to escape after you bring in the soldiers. Take me to her. You will never see me again after that.'

'And in return for this favour?'

'I will help you succeed in your endeavour,' I replied, 'by not telling anyone what I know and even, if necessary, arranging for the senapati to be … incapacitated.'

He stayed silent, staring at me as if trying to decide whether he could trust me.

I spoke again, willing him to reveal himself. 'I'm miserable here. He will discard me when his desire fades and I will be at the mercy of my enemies. I want to go home and Kala Devi is the only person who can send me back. Please, Rajpurohitji, let us help each other.'

He blinked once and I realized that it was the first time I had ever seen him blink. Then he whispered, 'Alright.'

'You will help me?'

He nodded. 'I will. You will stay silent, Tara Bai. Not even your closest attendants must know. There are spies everywhere and you are watched constantly. I will send word if I need your help.'

I breathed quickly. 'When will we leave? You said the sultan is already on his way to Gwalior.'

He jerked his head in irritation. 'All I know is that they will send a group of men ahead of the army. The rest will require your patience.'

I whispered so as not to break the spell, 'So the ambassador, the alliance with Jejabhukti, was a ruse. They mean to take the fort.'

Sarvadasa blinked again, a whisper of a smile touching his lips. 'Yes. But we, Tara Bai, will be long gone before that happens.'

I let out a long, exhausted breath. It was done. I had made him confess. And Vidyadhara, Satyabhama and others, sitting at the other end of the secret whispering arch that connected this corner of my chambers to another room close by, had just heard everything he said. I had initially been shocked when Satyabhama told me that all the conversations I ever shared with anyone in and around this corner were routinely eavesdropped upon. But I had to admire how, in an age before microphones and spy cams, they had managed to build into their structures such effective spying techniques merely by manipulating acoustics through architecture and mathematics. It was so simple and yet so brilliant.

As I watched Sarvadasa go about the prayer ceremony as if our conversation had never happened, my mind receded into a suspended state, numbing itself for the moment in order to internalize the magnitude of what had just happened. I barely registered Vatsaraja barging into the room with soldiers and arresting Sarvadasa for being a traitor. I leapt away on pure instinct from a howling and crazed Sarvadasa before he could grab me. I watched as Vatsaraja put a fist into his face and told him he would relish keeping him on the verge of death for as long as possible, until he begged to die.

I saw Vidyadhara walk into the room and regard Sarvadasa, restrained by soldiers, with utter disgust. 'You have dishonoured your family and the memory of your father. You will answer to your ancestors, Sarvadasa. Soon.'

They took him away and Vatsaraja followed, after giving Vidyadhara a pointed look in the eye. Vidyadhara nodded and then turned to me. We were alone again.

'Who is Kala Devi?'

27

I remembered one late night, in college, when I was in the dorm room I shared with my roommate, Sejal, who came from a very conservative Gujarati family. She was out with her boyfriend Mark and I was studying when Sejal's parents walked into the room unexpectedly. They had no idea she was seeing anyone or that she was probably in Mark's dorm room at that very moment, doing very un-Gujarati things with him. I made something up about Sejal researching a paper in the library even though I knew the library had closed two hours ago. I saw, from the tortured look in their eyes, that they didn't believe me. I was a terrible liar.

And yet, I had been lying non-stop since I came to Jejabhukti. I had told so many, in fact, that I didn't even remember most of them now. And obviously my talent for duplicity hadn't improved over the years because hardly anyone believed my tales about Chandigarh or gypsies. If I was going to make a life for myself here in this fort, with Vidyadhara, I needed to stop lying.

I looked over at him, standing ramrod straight across the room from me, a watchful expression on his face. His eyes burnt with unanswered questions. I wanted to wipe away his doubts and make him look at me as he'd done in the forest. I wanted him to know that the choice hadn't been easy, but I had chosen him, his people and their way of life. I was committed now. For better or worse.

'Will you come with me to the garden?' I asked softly, gesturing to what I now thought of as my 'spy corner'.

He nodded and followed me out into the garden, far enough from the corner that I was sure we wouldn't be overheard. I turned and took a deep breath. 'Kala Devi is an old woman whom I suspect might be a yogi. A very powerful yogi.'

I watched as he processed that. Then he asked, 'And she kidnapped you?'

'Yes.'

'From where?'

I hesitated. 'From … the place I was in before.' I looked down, unsure how to continue.

He stepped closer and nudged my chin up with his fingers until I met his eyes again. 'Where was that?'

'You won't understand,' I whispered.

'Try me,' he replied in a low, soft voice that invited me to melt into him and just tell him everything. Let him fix it for me. As if he could.

'You'll think I'm mad.'

'No, I won't. I've spent enough time with you, Tara, to know you're not mad. Trust me with the truth.'

I sighed. 'It's a place one can only reach with yogic powers.'

His forehead creased in a slight frown. 'Another world?'

'Yes.'

He kept looking at me, saying nothing.

I shook my head and continued, 'Look, I don't expect you to understand. You can't. Even *I* don't understand how or why she sent me. I've stopped trying to figure it out – there's no one here who can answer my questions. The important thing is that you understand I'm not a danger to you or your people. Not a spy, not a thief and no longer a liar. Just a woman who, for whatever reason, was taken from her home and left in your kingdom.'

'Sarvadasa offered to take you to this Kala Devi, so she could send you back home. And you still proved him a traitor. Why?'

I looked up at him and huffed. 'Because letting him go would mean that Kalinjara would fall to the Sultan of Ghazni. I couldn't let that happen to all of you.'

He smiled but stayed silent.

I continued, 'I don't even know if finding Kala Devi will be of any use. She might refuse to help me or she may be incapable of it. I don't want to torture my mind with questions for the rest of my life. All I know is that I'm here now. To stay by your side. If you'll have me.'

His hand came up to my face again. 'One last question and then I will tell you my decision.'

I nodded.

'Are you ever going to tell me about ... this place you come from?'

I shook my head slowly. 'I don't think that's a good idea. I'm going to ask you to trust me instead. Will you?'

He smiled again and bent his head to brush his lips against mine. 'Kalinjara and its king are greatly indebted to you, Tara Bai of Chandigarh,' he whispered. 'You have saved them on two separate occasions. You deserve to have whatever you wish.'

I felt tingles run down my back as his fingers stroked my jaw and his other hand snaked around my waist. I swayed towards him. 'Stop. I can't concentrate when you do that.'

He grinned. 'Then don't.' His lips met mine in a searing kiss.

Moments later, when all I really wanted him to do was take me to the bedchamber and put me out of my misery, he raised his head. 'I will be honoured to have such a courageous woman by my side.'

Another quick kiss and he gently stepped back. 'But now it seems we will have war sooner than we expected, so I must leave you for the moment. And pray for the day, hopefully very soon in the future, when I won't have to.'

I nodded shakily. He probably had less than a fortnight before the sultan of Ghazni's army was within sight of the fort. There would be a lot to do in the meantime.

'I'll be waiting, Maharaj.' I smiled up at him.

He returned my smile with an impish one of his own. 'You say "Maharaj" with the least deference I have ever heard. Maybe, after all this is over, we can find another name for you to use when we're alone.'

I rolled my eyes. 'Do all your women have private names for you?'

He shook his head and said gently, 'No one ever forgets I am their king, Tara. Except you.' He nudged a strand of hair off my face and stared into my eyes. 'You're the only one who makes me forget too.'

He brushed his lips against my forehead and turned. I watched as he strode out of the garden and sighed involuntarily. It was hard to see him leave. And it was only going to get more difficult and complicated from now on. I took a deep breath as I looked around my chambers. This was my home now.

I felt a tear sting my eye but, before I could indulge it, I saw Satyabhama limp in through the entryway into my sitting area. She only had two women in attendance, a departure from her usual entourage.

I walked towards her and bowed, just as she said, 'Well done. That was a clever performance.'

I smiled. 'You heard everything.'

She nodded. 'I did. We are in your debt once again, Tara Bai.'

I shook my head. 'It was nothing, Maharanisa.'

She stared at me intently for several long moments and then said, 'Come with me. I want to show you something.'

She mumbled something to one of her attendants who quickly bowed and scurried off. Then she gestured for me to follow her. We walked at an excruciatingly slow pace, her entourage joining us in the hallway outside my chambers. Her maids walked ahead, lighting the way with fire lamps, carrying her sitting stool in case she felt tired and holding an elaborate umbrella over her head when we ventured into the open-air courtyards of the palace. Finally, at the palace entrance, we stopped and waited as guards carrying two palanquins laid them on the ground before us.

Satyabhama turned to me. 'Be seated.' While she was being helped into one of the palanquins, she instructed two of her female attendants to follow her on foot while the others remained behind. A contingent of guards promptly surrounded her as she was lifted into the air.

Puzzled, I sat down inside the second palaquin and hung on as four guards lifted me up and began to walk down the stone path at a brisk pace. Darkness had begun to envelop the landscape as we turned towards a part of the fort I was unfamiliar with. There were fewer buildings and more trees in this area. The stone path was less maintained and the guards stepped over undergrowth that surged upwards from between large blocks of stone. The low light, combined with dim shadows cast over the ground by the trees and the overall feel of neglect created an eeriness which made my hair stand on end. Where on earth were we going?

We arrived at a large stone gate, much like the gates I had passed when I first entered the fort. But this one was less elaborately carved, with a raw starkness about it. Carved on its sides were single figures, hundreds of them, each standing with closed eyes and folded hands in its own frame. They were all women.

A frisson of fear ran down my back and then, as we passed through the gate, my blood froze. Red vermilion in the shape of hands was smeared all over the inside of the gateway. More lone figures stared back at me from beneath the stains. Beyond the gateway was a single building facing a large, overgrown field. It was a temple. A sati temple. This was the fort's shamshan bhumi, the cremation ground.

Satyabhama's palanquin was set down and she gestured for me to come to her. I walked over as she said, 'It is inauspicious for us women to come here, Tara Bai. But necessary, once in a while, to remind us of what we fight for.'

Completely spooked by my surroundings and shivering slightly with the mental images crashing through my brain, I barely registered her meaning.

'Tomorrow we will start building a very large platform on the side of this field.' Satyabhama looked at me intently, her eyes blazing with a spark I had never seen before even as her expression stayed neutral. 'It will stand over a giant pyre. We will pray every day that we do not have to light this particular pyre. For, when we do, every single woman and child in Kalinjara will walk into it. Tens of thousands of them.'

I felt a wave of nausea rise up my throat and threaten to overwhelm me. I wheezed for air, fighting to control myself, to push the wave back inside me. It didn't work. I ran to the side, away from the women, and heaved into the grass. Everything I had been holding inside, all my pent-up regret, rage, fear and despair came out in gasping, wrenching sobs. I cried for everything I had lost, for the people I would never see again. For myself. I curled into my knees and cried like I had never cried before. Loudly and completely.

I felt the brush of a gentle hand on the back of my neck and looked up through blurry eyes and shuddering gulps to find Satyabhama smiling at me. It was the first time she had ever done that. 'I'm … I'm sorry,' I stammered.

'It's all right, Tara Bai. You have been brave enough for one evening.' She gestured for me to stand and one of her attendants hurried towards me with a cloth to wipe my face.

After I had calmed down, she continued, 'I brought you here to explain to you that what you did was not nothing. You saved the lives of not only the women in the palace but of all the women and children in the town and surrounding villages. This is why we are in your debt.'

I looked down, unable to reply. I hadn't even thought about the townspeople or the villagers.

Satyabhama nudged up my chin with a quick touch of her finger. 'Ask for something and it shall be yours.'

I shook my head. 'I was only doing the right thing, Maharanisa.'

'Nevertheless, you shall ask for a reward. Anything.'

I looked back at her. She couldn't do anything for me that would matter. So, I said the only thing that came to mind. 'The devadasi Puppa. If anything were to ever happen to me in the future…'

Satyabhama nodded. 'She will be provided for. And when the time comes, I will see to it that she is married to a man of substance. You have my word, Tara Bai.'

'Thank you.'

She said, 'And now let us return so we can inform Rani Vijaya about the evening's proceedings. She will want to thank you personally.'

I frowned, unable to imagine any situation where Vijaya would want to thank me. 'Why?'

'Maharaj will be sending word to Gwalior Fort immediately that they should expect an attack. It is Rani Vijaya's maika, her maiden home. She will be very grateful.' Satyabhama smiled wryly. 'You might even be the first woman in the palace to make a friend of her.'

28

I never really appreciated how much less hectic and noisy life was here, compared to in the twenty-first century, until I suddenly felt the chaos hit me like a truck.

Overnight, the already-bustling town that sat around the fort went into turbo-charged overdrive. Hordes of families with their bags and baggage, stocks of food, bullock carts and cattle, some even carrying construction material, started filtering into the fort. Merchants carrying giant vats of oil and grain, ammunition and animals, began to camp outside the fort's entryway, lining up to sell their goods to the army. No one was interested in silk or spices any more. Those vendors had packed up, shuttered their stalls and left – they would return when peacetime guaranteed good business.

A few days ago, I had been walking in the park outside the palace with Vijamba when I saw a line of elephants pulling giant, cauldron-like vessels on wheels.

'They boil oil in them and pour it on enemy soldiers. It makes their horses slip on the stone. They also shoot fire arrows into the oil and set the enemy aflame,' Vijamba had said in response to my confused expression.

I had shuddered and kept silent. She then proceeded to tell me how the jewellers in town had been recruited to forge weapons along with the blacksmiths and all boys over the age of seven were busy sharpening weapons for the army. The priests had apparently commenced fasting along with a yagna, a prayer ceremony, which would continue day and night until the enemy was defeated.

I almost chuckled to myself when I heard that, despite the apprehension coursing through my veins. Sultan Mahmud's siege of Kalinjara had gone on for a year, according to history. Those were going to be very hungry and sleepy priests by the end of it.

In the palace too, there was a bustle and an invisible strain of tension that had not been there before. Satyabhama had called a gathering of all the royal women and attendants in the main courtyard the day after our visit to the cremation ground. The mention of war had brought on much crying and shrieking among the women. Bhuvana Devi, now further along in her pregnancy, fainted at the realization that her husband would be leading the defence of the fort along with Vidyadhara and Vatsaraja.

Rani Vijaya, who had been informed by us the night before, stood and stared ahead stoically when Satyabhama made the announcement. Despite our earlier acrimony, Vijaya even managed to nod a greeting towards me, much to my surprise. There hadn't been much of a reaction when we told her that Vidyadhara was sending word to Gwalior Fort about the impending attack. She had only muttered a few formal, stilted words of gratitude for my help.

The next day, I had walked into my chambers to find a thick gold armlet on my bed, a gift that Vijamba said had been delivered by Vijaya's attendant only moments earlier. Vijamba refused to let me touch it and insisted on taking the gleaming ornament 'for cleaning', which I'm pretty certain was code for 'test it for poison'. She obviously didn't believe that leopards were capable of changing their spots. The armlet turned out to be benign, and I was utterly relieved that Vijaya seemed to have made her peace with me.

A couple of activity-filled weeks later, completely out of the blue, in a caravan longer than a few Indian Railway trains attached end to end and far more elaborate, showed up Vidyadhara's wife number three. The bride, already married to him by proxy, was carried into the fort in a huge bridal palanquin of solid gold, accompanied by large contingents of horses and elephants and a few thousand soldiers. Not to mention endless carriages full of gifts, jewellery, cloth, sweets and spices. She was only eleven years old.

I stood back and watched from the edges of the crowd as Satyabhama formally welcomed her into Rani Bhavan and received the gifts sent by her father. As put off as I was with the obscene amount of wealth that the bride had brought as her dowry, I was even more furious when Vidyadhara made a brief appearance in the main courtyard of Rani Bhavan to greet her ceremoniously at her new home. In between the intense formality of the rituals and people and prayers involved, he treated her like the child she was, but it turned my stomach to know that one day, when she was deemed old enough, he would have sex with her even though she was younger than two of his own daughters.

I felt a pang inside as I watched him smile at her in a patient, distracted way. The girl was nervous and fidgety and kept glancing at an older woman who stood next to her for guidance, probably her attendant. Most of the time, she kept her eyes firmly on her own lap and allowed the people around her to move her arms and feet as they required for the ceremonies. Finally, she crouched at the feet of all three – Vidyadhara, Satyabhama and Vijaya – before being led away to the chambers that had been rather hastily prepared for her. I watched Satyabhama's and Vijaya's reactions carefully – neither of them showed the girl any warmth and stood stiffy while she touched her forehead to their toes, murmuring the ritual blessing that they were required to utter. There would be time later to size her up and see what kind of influence she would have on the atmosphere in the palace.

Vidyadhara caught my eye after the ceremony was over and nodded at me. Instantly, Vijamba was at my side, ushering me back to my chambers and whispering, 'Maharaj wishes to speak to you.'

I, on the other hand, was in no mood to speak to him.

'She's a child!' was the first thing that came out of my mouth when he walked into my sitting room.

He dismissed my attendants and looked at me warily. 'Yes. She will spend the rest of her formative years here, under the maharani's guidance.'

He tried to take me into his arms, but I backed away and said angrily, 'You'll … you and her…' – I closed my eyes in disgust – '…you know what I mean.' I couldn't bring myself to say it.

'Not now. Not for a very long time,' he replied.

'But you will.'

Vidyadhara looked at me and said carefully, 'She is the new rani, Tara. You know that. The marriage has joined our kingdom with her father's and is a matter of honour for both families. This is the way things are done. You must accept that.'

Except that I couldn't. I peered at him, standing a few paces away from me. His handsomeness was marred the tiniest bit by dark shadows under his eyes but his energy, his magnetism, was still as compelling as ever. It was impossible not to be drawn to him, drawn into him. And yet, he was a man of his time. Before I ever met him, before I knew him outside of history books, I had casually labelled him a Rajput liberal. And, I guess he was, relatively. But he was still a man of his time.

And, despite being a woman of *my* time, I had no choice but to accept that.

I sighed. No one said this was going to be easy. 'Fine. I understand,' I said, unable to keep an indignant note out of my voice.

Normally, he would have smiled and teased me out of my anger, but the strain that was evident on his face provoked a different reaction this time. 'No, you don't, but you must try, Tara. As long as you understand that I am king and my duty will always have to come first, you will be happy. Listen to me.' He stepped closer and bent his head towards me. 'We received word from Gwalior earlier today. The sultan of Ghazni conceded defeat and his army has begun to march again. The fort stands.' He grinned.

Technically, King Kirtiraja of Gwalior had conceded and paid a large tribute to the sultan, but I figured they would position it as a victory among themselves for obvious reasons. I smiled back despite myself. 'That's wonderful.'

'I wanted to tell you myself.' He began to put his arms around me and I felt my heart rate accelerating in spite of everything as my body stood flush against his. 'My doe with the heart of a tiger.'

'That means they're coming towards us now.'

'Yes.' He leaned his forehead against mine. 'We will prevail, don't worry. I have faced him twice before and Kalinjara is impregnable. Thanks to you.' He smiled again.

'Is Rajpurohit Sarvadasa dead?'

His eyes went dark. 'No, it's not that simple. He is a man of God. But he is as good as dead.'

His arms tightened and his smile was one of ruefulness. 'Tara … what I wouldn't give for a few carefree hours with you. We must pray for a quick resolution, like Gwalior.'

I sighed. He had no idea that he had a year-long fight coming up. I wished I could tell him but that might change the outcome. I was done messing with history. 'I will hope for that' – I cleared my throat mischievously – 'Maharaj.'

He grinned back. 'Insolent woman.' His arms tightened even more and he began to nuzzle my neck. 'I want you so much.'

Just as my hands went up and around his neck, he pulled back. 'Not like this. There is much to do. Wait for me here, in Rani Bhavan. I want you to stop wandering around the fort by yourself. It's not safe and I cannot spare the people to keep an eye on you. Understood?'

'Have I been spied upon everywhere, all the time?'

He smiled. 'Will you obey me, you disrespectful, irresistible nymph?'

Nobody had ever called me a nymph before. My lips twitched. 'Yes, Maharaj.'

Of course not.

29

I was thinking about Hari. Sitting on my swing and drying my washed hair in the morning sun, with Vijamba and my attendants pottering about and fussing over me as usual, I found my thoughts wandering back to a time when life wasn't nearly as complicated or perilous.

I chuckled ruefully. What would my future have looked like if I had flirted with Hari that day in the ruins of Rani Mahal? If I had smiled at him, encouraged him? He might have asked me out on a date, we might have begun a relationship. He might have kissed me and it might have been like the millions of times I imagined his lips on mine. We might even have gotten married one day and I could've worked on archaeological digs with him around the world. I wouldn't have had to share him with anyone. I wouldn't have had to sit around aimlessly, fearing for his life and my own around the clock.

I ran my fingers through my hair absently. Everyone probably thought I was dead right now. Enough time had passed for them to have given up hope of finding me. My parents and family would be in mourning, my friends would shed a few tears and move on with their lives. And Hari would probably walk down the aisle with Sarah or someone like her. They'd live in a giant, fenceless house in upstate New York with a forest in the backyard and have little biracial babies who would run around excavation sites playing havoc with the samples and crew. But no one would mind because the racially mixed kids are always the cutest. Maybe Hari would wonder, once in a while, what happened to me – a small faded question mark, lost in the larger text of his life.

I shook my head to clear away my maudlin thoughts. There was absolutely no point in thinking about things like that. This was my thorny bed of roses now and, even though I never chose it, I was going to make the best of it.

'Tara Bai! Tara Bai!' Puppa came running into the garden, panting to catch her breath. Vijamba looked reprovingly at her – she almost never remembered to call me 'Mistress'.

'What is it?' I asked.

Puppa glanced around, suddenly aware of all the women around her. Her eyes darted to mine. 'Come with me!'

I wanted to ask her where, but I saw the urgent look in her eyes and realized she didn't want the others to know. So I nodded and stood up.

Vijamba immediately piped up, 'Mistress, you will not leave the palace? There are foreign soldiers all over the fort.'

By 'foreign' she meant they were from neighbouring, allied kingdoms. Most of whom spoke the same languages and had the same customs and religious practices. Funny how our sense of identity is so intertwined with such fluid and intangible things as borders. 'I won't,' I replied, and followed Puppa into the hallway.

But we did indeed leave the palace through a side entrance. Puppa's eyes were alight with a mixture of fear and excitement as she kept looking back at me, urging me to follow her quickly without asking questions. We weaved through alleys behind buildings and back lanes, avoiding all the main roads and paths. She navigated our route with the confidence of an expert and I realized Puppa had been much busier than I thought since we arrived at the fort.

Finally, when my breaths began to get laboured, she ducked behind a building and gestured for me to follow her through a small side entrance. It led directly to a steep, dimly lit and irregular staircase. We climbed, and then climbed some more. I struggled to catch my breath and felt a cramp coming into my side. 'W-Where,' I wheezed, 'are we going?'

'Almost there,' she mumbled back.

Suddenly, we came upon a small door and emerged onto what seemed like the parapet of a tower. A tower taller than any of the buildings around it with a 360-degree, bird's-eye view of the fort and the lands beyond it. I gasped and laughed with surprise and elation, turning my head this way and that like a child who'd just entered Disneyland. Then I was stunned into silence.

It was the Ghaznavid army.

It was like watching a hive of bees or a shoal of small fish. Tens of thousands of separate parts and yet it moved like one giant beast. Like an enormous dragon with a tail that was longer than its body and with powerful arms and legs that clawed out of its massive trunk, all moving sinuously together with the grace of a serpent. At the dragon's nose rode a contingent with raised flags bearing their sultan's emblem, the heavily guarded head shielding their emperor's own horse somewhere inside. The vast body of the dragon was a cavalry, the size of which seemed impossibly disproportionate to the rest of the army. At the dragon's flanks ambled a smaller, but significant number of war elephants and, behind them, trailing into a long tail, was what looked like the infantry, porters and their equipment.

I watched as the dragon started to break up and fan out in formation, beginning to widen as they approached the hill on which stood Kalinjara. Sultan Mahmud's military skills were legendary and his vast army, with men and beasts numbering in the hundreds of thousands, moved with the practised choreography of performers.

'May the Mahesvara save us,' murmured Puppa, her face etched with terror that was probably mirrored in my own face.

'Don't worry,' I whispered back. 'He will.' It would be Okay, I told myself repeatedly.

Then, for the first time in my life, I prayed.

The next few days went by in a whirl. The palace was full of unfamiliar people, walking around looking busy. Food and water were strictly rationed. Every corner seemed to contain a group of women talking in fearful murmurs. There were distant, unidentifiable sounds carried by the wind – rumbling, screaming and banging – sounds of the fort's army setting up their defences and the sultan's army setting up camp around the hill. Once in a while, a loud roar of men would send the palace women into crying or fainting spells. There were fathers, husbands, brothers and sons in every woman's prayers. Satyabhama was fasting and keeping a near-constant vigil for her husband and sons in the small temple she had adjoining her chambers. Attendants scurried in and out of her palace wing, carrying instructions for everyone else to follow. I almost envied the purposefulness with which she approached each day. All I could do was pace different parts of the palace and wait. For the storm to start.

And it did. Distant booms and blasts punctuated the air, which seemed heavier and dustier. We were too far inside the fort for any of the projectiles flung over the ramparts to reach us but we could sense the ground shaking as they struck other structures, feel the vibrations of thunderous roaring that tens of thousands of men made when they were trying to strike fear into the hearts of an entire population. It was terrifying. Like hiding in a building as bombs fall from the sky, wreaking destruction all around while you wait for the one that's meant for you.

I huddled with Puppa and the rest of my attendants in my chambers while we listened, the smell of burning wood and flesh wafting past us. Vijamba tried to keep up a show of normality – she made me sit on my swing and rubbed oil into my feet, as if pretending there wasn't a war going on around us would somehow make it go away.

Then, one day, the parkland outside Rani Bhavan caught fire. We rushed out en masse with blankets and pots of water and tried our best to stifle the blazing brush. Luckily, the trees were old, their thick trunks and mature branches not easily set alight by a fire ball. As I held a wet cloth against my face and beat the flames with my other hand, I spotted a large, twin-barbed arrow shank lying in the grass. Its point and barbs were large and sharp, its shank as long as a knife, typical of long-range fire arrows used by the Turks. I picked it up quickly and knotted it into my odhna, thinking I would examine it later.

That was when I heard Vijamba whisper urgently in my ear, 'Mistress, come back into your chambers at once!'

I shook my head. 'No, we need to put out the fire before it spreads.'

'Mistress,' she said with panicky eyes, 'I must get you to safety. Rajpurohit...'

I stopped and turned towards her. 'What about him?'

'He's escaped.'

No! My head reeled. If he got out, it would be disastrous! 'Does Maharaj know?'

'Yes, there are soldiers scouring the fort. But there are many secret passageways, Mistress. We must take you to safety.'

Sarvadasa would know all the secret passageways. The soldiers would be no match for him. I needed to do something! I gave my wool blanket to Vijamba, 'You help with the fire. I'll go back inside by myself.'

'I'll come with—'

'No,' I replied sharply. 'They need as many hands as possible over here, otherwise the fire will spread to Rani Bhavan. You will obey me!' Vijamba's eyes widened at my tone, harsher than I had ever used before, and she nodded reluctantly.

The minute her head was turned, I began to run in the direction of the Neelkanth temple. I had no idea what I was going to do if I actually found him. But I would be damned if I just sat around and waited for him to have the hundreds of thousands of people holed up in the fort butchered by the Ghaznavid army. I withdrew the arrow shank from the folds of my odhna. It wasn't much of a weapon but I felt slightly safer with it next to my skin.

The roads of the fort were in utter chaos. Fire arrows streaked whistling paths across the sky, landing in clumps of bush and setting them ablaze or bouncing off buildings. The smell of burning was overpowering, the noise deafening. I heard men screaming and willed myself to be calm. I told myself to move along close to the walls to avoid getting lanced by a piece of flying metal.

Suddenly, my ghagra skirt got caught on the side of a cart that was lying abandoned on the side of the road. I swore and bent down to quickly untangle it.

'What do we have here?'

I froze. Sarvadasa's soft murmur had come from the outbuilding just behind the cart. Before I could stand up, I felt a vice-like grip on my upper arm and I was yanked up like a rag doll. I heard a long rip as my skirt tore away from the cart.

'It's the bitch who gave me away,' his voice said softly, close to my ear.

I turned to look at him and was horrified into silence for a moment. Branded across his forehead was the word 'shakharandra', the Sanskrit word for a man who has betrayed his faith. Worse than a traitor. The rest of his face was covered with patches of melted skin, as if boiling oil had been dripped on it. He had been blinded in one eye. There was a gaping, cauterized hole where his eye socket should have been.

I gasped as I looked further down. He was covered with a filthy odhna that was stuck to the large, melted patches all over his chest, arms and back. His tiger-skin loincloth looked battered and blackened with dried urine and excrement, and he had lost whatever little flesh he had on his bones. Vidyadhara had said he was as good as dead – he certainly looked, and smelled, like death.

But his one eye shone back at me with the kind of hatred that is only possible when a person has stood at death's door and has nothing left to lose. His fingers bit into my skin viciously, his strength completely at odds with his debilitated appearance. I glared back at him and tried to shake him off, but my struggling was completely ineffectual.

'Today's my lucky day, it seems,' he snarled as he pulled me quickly towards the outbuilding. 'Not only am I going to escape and live to cut the senapati's eye out of his face like he did mine, but I'm going to punish the whore who was responsible for it.'

Too late did I realize that I should've brought people with me to help. I hadn't found him, he had found me.

I screamed with every ounce of strength I had, digging my heels in the ground to try to stop him from dragging me. When that didn't work, I remembered I had the arrowhead in my hand.

I stabbed at the hand holding my arm and heard him exclaim in pain as the arrow's point broke skin and drew blood. His fingers released their hold and I glanced around wildly, looking for soldiers, before I broke into a run.

I hadn't got far though, when he caught up and yanked my odhna from behind. I pulled free of it and kept running, trying desperately to find other people, screaming my head off.

I felt his hand wrap around my mouth from behind and was yanked to an abrupt stop as his other arm went around my body, trapping my arms. He spun me around and hit me across my face. The world began to spin and my jaw went numb. I felt the arrowhead grabbed out of my hand before I dimly registered his hands coming up again to restrain my arms and pull me half off my feet.

I struggled against him uselessly as he began to drag me back to the outbuilding. Somewhere, at the back of my mind,

I wondered how such an emaciated-looking man could possibly be this strong. Then I remembered he wasn't a regular Brahman but a yogi. If Brahmans were plump, pampered and squeamish house cats, yogis were their feral cousins.

As we cornered the outbuilding, from the side of my eye, I saw my odhna fluttering to the ground in the middle of the road. I hoped someone would find it quickly. The building was deserted and Sarvadasa pushed me through a small door into a dark, dank hallway. In the small, enclosed space, my nostrils were suddenly filled with the reek of him. He smelled like the worst sort of decay and I couldn't help but gag as he shoved my head and body underneath a stone staircase.

The space beneath the stairs was empty and I wondered for a moment if he was going to kill and leave me there. But then, he touched a joint between two stones on the wall and I heard a thump. Sarvadasa pushed at the stones using his entire body weight and, to my shock and horror, it fell back. There was a tiny room behind the wall.

'No!' I resisted as he stepped inside before me, keeping a tight hold on my arms behind my back. There wasn't even enough room for the two of us to comfortably stand inside the hidden chamber. Then I followed his eyes to the floor. There was a trapdoor there.

'No!' I screamed louder. I knew, without needing to be told, that the trapdoor led to the catacombs under the ground.

I felt the point of the arrowhead, the one that had been wrenched out of my hand, pressed against my throat and almost laughed at the irony. I had not only been stupid enough to go chasing after Sarvadasa without protection but had also supplied him with a weapon.

'You'll go down quietly, whore. Unless you want a hole in your neck,' he hissed at me. Then he positioned me at the top of the trapdoor, let go of my arms and bore down on my shoulders until my feet felt a ladder beneath them. My chest throbbed in fear as the point pressed into my skin. For a moment, I thought of jumping off the ladder and making a dash for it, but it was very dark and I had no idea how far down the ladder went. I could end up breaking my back, or worse.

'Don't even think about jumping. You'll never be able to find your way out. Many fools have tried to navigate this labyrinth – they either fall into one of the wells and drown or die of starvation in a deep trench.' Sarvadasa's voice echoed a little as he descended the ladder after me and promptly jumped off before I could. It seemed the bottom wasn't that far after all.

'They'll come after you,' I mumbled warily, my eyes still trying to adjust to the darkness as I stepped off the ladder into what felt like a catacomb. The air felt heavy and wet and smelled mouldy.

'By then both of us would be long gone, my beauty. At least you will. I'll be coming back.' He laughed as he pulled me roughly into a narrow natural tunnel in the rock. His easy knowledge of the way around the tunnels terrified me.

'You're still going to bring the enemy soldiers in, aren't you?' My eyes widened as I tried to shake him off again.

He slammed my back into the wall of the tunnel, his face coming only inches away so his good eye could stare into mine, 'Yes, I'm still going to bring the enemy soldiers in, Tara Bai. Or whatever your name really is. I'm going to bring them in, watch them drive their swords into every body that still draws breath, and laugh. And then I'm going to give the senapati a taste of his own medicine. That thought is the only thing that's kept me alive since your little enactment that night.'

'What're you going to do with me?' I whispered.

His face took on a lecherous expression and I felt my insides roll in revulsion. His hand came up to my chin and I felt his filthy fingers cup it and then squeeze into the flesh of my cheeks, pushing my head back against the rock. 'I heard the sultan's army couldn't take Gwalior Fort. They must be very disheartened after such a long march. The soldiers would've been away from their women for a long time. I'm sure they wouldn't mind a few minutes each with the king's favourite concubine.'

He laughed, plumped my cheeks with his fingers and continued, 'Do you know what happens to a woman after she's been taken by a hundred men?' His face came closer, his foul breath fanning my gasps. 'After ten, the most spirited of women break and begin to beg for mercy. After thirty, they beg for death. Slowly, but certainly, their life force ebbs out along with their tears and the blood from between their legs. Don't worry, after fifty men, you probably won't even feel it anymore.'

Ice, cold and thick, crept its way from my stomach into every part of me at his words. I began to shake involuntarily.

'Scared, aren't you?' He smiled, 'You should have thought of that before you took me on. Now you will pay the price.' He started pulling me again.

We slowly moved through the network of caves. Despite the darkness, Sarvadasa moved with the confidence of one who had been roaming these pathways his entire life. He stepped carefully over crevices and rock formations that were covered in slippery moss. Water dripped on us from invisible cracks overhead. Some caves and tunnels were only about a foot wide and others required us to bend and crawl.

I tried to regulate my breath when I felt the rock close in around me in the dark but panic kept bubbling through. I had nowhere to run. Every time we passed a trench or a well, I thought about breaking free and jumping in. One part of me thought that would be a better way to die than to go with him and be raped till death but another part of me hadn't given up hope that someone would find us. Surely, Vatsaraja would be looking down here for Sarvadasa. Surely, Vijamba or Puppa would noticc that I wasn't in the palace. If I could just slow him down, keep him talking, maybe I could delay matters until help arrived. I couldn't give up yet.

Finally, we entered a large natural cavern. I could hear water and I realized that one end of the cavern fell away into a steep, sheer drop below which was a water reservoir, black and murky. The floor of the cavern was rocky and uneven.

I twisted my ankle purposely against a stone on the ground and fell into a heap. 'Ahhh!' I exclaimed. 'It's broken! My ankle's broken!' It wasn't the best performance I had ever given but it was the best I could come up with in the circumstances.

Sarvadasa shook me roughly and yanked me up. 'You think I care? Walk!'

'I can't!' I shrieked and fell down again. 'I can't stand up.' I was taking a gamble that he was too weakened by his imprisonment and torture to physically carry me himself.

I felt the arrowhead pressing into my throat again and laughed derisively. 'Go ahead. Kill me now. I'd rather have my throat slit than go out there with you.'

He pressed it harder against my skin and I winced in pain as he said, 'Aha, she finally begins to comprehend her fate. You had it so easy, didn't you?' He kept coming closer and I kept shifting away from him on the ground. 'From the moment you mysteriously appeared in Khajuravahaka, everyone has been dancing to your tune. All because he desired you. But now your days of taking the easy way are over.' He removed the arrowhead from my neck and slammed his hand against the side of my head.

'Get up!' he screeched in an unnaturally high-pitched voice. Then he shook me. 'Get up, bitch!'

I scrambled up against the wall of the cavern, as far away as possible from him. My head was reeling from the blow but my mind stayed sharp for the moment. 'I haven't had it easy. You have. You lived a life of comfort as one of the king's most trusted men. Why would you betray him? What can the sultan give you that Maharaj cannot? Money? Power? You already had plenty of both!'

I could make out his surprised expression even in the dark. He straightened and sneered. 'Look how confidently the word "Maharaj" slips from your mouth. You already consider yourself his mouthpiece, don't you?'

'Why did you do it?' I whispered.

He couldn't resist. 'Why did I do it? Why? Because your precious Maharaj is doomed. His way of life is doomed. The kingdoms, all of them, they're falling like flies circling above a roasting pit. Every year, Hamira comes marching with his army and returns to Ghazni with gold and people to commit to slavery. Every year. And yet, the kings can't stop squabbling among themselves, can't look beyond their own noses, can't stop their drinking and womanizing long enough to see the writing on the wall.'

His one eye blazed at me in the dark as he began to pace the ground. 'We think we're better than them. We think we have the gods on our side, the power of righteousness within our swords. We think we can pray our way out of it. We think honour will save the day. What a joke! We send out a hundred thousand men to be slaughtered by thirty thousand Turuska cavalry. They move in unison, like the wind, their curved swords slashing in formation. Our men, with all their honour and divine blessings, are sliced through like wild pigs. This happens every year in a different part of the Bharatiya subcontinent!'

He began to wave his hands about and I felt a small glimmer of hope as I realized he was in the middle of a rant that had been supressed for too long to stay inside him any longer. With any luck, I could keep him at it for long enough for Vatsaraja's men to find us.

'Do you know, they formed a united league many moons ago? All the kings, allies and foes, decided to come together to do away with Hamira once and for all. I went with them, to help them try to organize their armies into some sort of cohesive force. The councils spent day after day pandering to each king's demands, flattering them, cajoling them while they puffed out their chests like peacocks and looked down their noses at each other. In the end, on the battlefield, they each went their separate way, unable to agree on even the most basic of strategies. And what happened? Their armies were decimated. The last time your precious maharaj faced the sultan on the riverbank, he had to abandon his cause and return to Kalinjara, preferring to fight another day rather than lose his men. Fools, all of them!'

Sarvadasa shook his head. 'We have to face it. We're on the losing side. Kalinjara will fall, like the rest of them. If not now, then eventually. But I…', he came closer to peer into my face again '… I always survive, Tara Bai. I made sure I was on the winning side. Until you came along and tried to thwart my plans. Unsuccessfully, by the way. I will still carry them out.'

I cried out, 'Hundreds of thousands of innocent people will die! Women and children!'

'They will die anyway. Either by their own hand or by Hamira's. He will not bother taking too many slaves this far away from his empire. He'll just take the riches and kill anyone who stands in his way. It is what any invader would do.'

I shook my head. 'He'll destroy the temples at Khajuravahaka. Doesn't that mean anything to you? Hundreds of years of effort, the coming together of faiths, the art and sculptures—'

Sarvadasa laughed in surprise. 'You care about the *temples*? Those piles of stone don't mean anything. They're just another golden goose for the king and his fat mukhya mantri. A clever ruse to entice the people to part with their coin. Faith is just another means of controlling people, Tara Bai. To keep them from thinking for themselves.' He laughed again before continuing. 'You think Hamira fights for his faith? You think he despises our faith? He cares for nothing but the riches he gathers and the power he can buy with them. Their war against infidels keeps his soldiers in line, keeps them fighting even after they fall. Faith is the whip and man is the horse.'

'How can you say that? You're a man of God!'

'God is a creation of man. Priesthood is just a profession' – he ran his finger down my cheek and I pulled away in disgust – 'much like being a concubine. You profess to love something for a living.'

He bared his teeth, some of which were broken, and stood up. Strolling over to the sheer drop into the well, he said, 'Speaking of love, you are sitting in one of the more well-known parts of the underground labyrinth. This spot was where a pair of young lovers in ancient times jumped to their death because their families would not allow them to be married. They were from different castes, you see. This particular well is unique because it is completely enclosed by a smooth vertical rock and fed through small cracks barely wide enough for a rodent to pass through. There is no way out – even the most powerful of swimmers will eventually tire and drown. I could push you in right now but I'm not feeling generous enough to grant you an easy death.'

He pulled me to my feet and held me upright. 'I know your ankle is not hurt, Tara Bai. If you come with me, perhaps Hamira will have mercy on you and take you for himself. If you insist on lying down here, perhaps I can give you a taste of what you can expect with the soldiers.'

He began to pull at my skirt and I screamed, fighting him with everything I had. Suddenly, I heard footsteps. Sarvadasa froze for a quick instant before doubling his efforts to drag me away, but I fell to the floor and screamed again.

'Tara!' It was Vidyadhara's voice.

'I'm here!' I had never felt so relieved in my entire life.

The relief lasted for a mere moment before I was hauled to my feet once again and the arrowhead pressed tightly against my throat. There was a flicker of firelight from one of the tunnels and then the cavern filled with light as Vidyadhara, Vatsaraja and a contingent of heavily armed guards filled the space.

I saw a spark of relief in Vidyadhara's eyes before they shaded over and turned to Sarvadasa, who now stood behind me with one arm draped across my body and the other holding the arrow against my throat. Vidyadhara raised his hand a fraction and the men around him stopped and stayed poised, ready to strike at his command.

After a moment of taking in the situation, he said in a voice tinged with mockery, 'You're getting careless, old man. You left her odhna lying on the road.'

Sarvadasa's tone held some of the same mockery as he replied, 'Came yourself, did you? This whore must be special to you.' He visibly increased the arrow's pressure.

I said hurriedly, 'He's going to escape and lead the soldiers inside, according to his original plan.' I winced as the sharp point dug even deeper into my skin, almost breaking it.

Vatsaraja fidgeted but Vidyadhara gestured for him to wait. Then he said, 'The entry points are well guarded. Any enemy that you may lead inside will be dealt with swiftly.'

Sarvadasa laughed. 'So confident, as always. There are entries you and your men have no idea of. I have been cultivating them for decades, waiting for the right moment. Your guards don't stand a chance.'

Vidyadhara looked at him and, for a brief moment, his eyes reflected betrayal instead of careful control. 'Why?'

Sarvadasa glared at him and taunted, 'Because unlike you, I am always on the winning side.'

Vidyadhara's eyes turned angry. 'We will be victorious.'

'For how long?' Sarvadasa shot back. 'Your father's only redeeming quality was that he died early. Your sons are pampered fools. Unless it submits to Hamira, Jejabhukti is doomed. I won't go down with you.'

'You will go down, Sarvadasa. Your soul will answer to the Mahesvara for your actions.'

That made Sarvadasa laugh again. 'I will leave the Mahesvara here in this land, along with your charred remains, and escape, thanks to this little whore here. And I will grow a beard and wear their clothes and chant the name of their god whenever they're looking. My scars will mark me as a convert to their faith and they will reward me with riches. And I will think of you sometimes – the last of your ilk with any true honour. But your honour won't save you, fool. It will kill you.'

Vidyadhara blinked impatiently, inching forward as he said, 'Hand her over and I will grant you a quick death.'

'No,' Sarvadasa replied silkily as he shuffled backwards until we stood with the sheer drop into the well at our backs. 'You will give me your word that you'll let me walk out of here unharmed. In return, I will give you the woman. Otherwise, I will drive this arrow into her neck and throw her into the well. We both know you won't be able to get her out.'

'If you do that, you'll be worse than dead.'

Sarvadasa sneered. 'Yes, but your favourite concubine, the one who saved your life and the lives of your subjects, to whom you owe a debt of honour, will be forever entombed under your very nose. You would have failed to protect her.'

Vatsaraja's eyes had been carefully studying the cavern while the other two had been talking. Vidyadhara now looked at him for a brief moment and Vatsaraja shook his head.

Sarvadasa continued in a taunting voice, 'It's useless to try to take her. Give me your word, Maharaj. Once you give it, she is yours.'

'No!' I looked at Vidyadhara. 'If you let him walk out, he'll bring in the enemy.'

'Quiet, Tara,' replied Vidyadhara softly, not looking at me.

'Maharaj, please.' I willed him to look at me, and he did. I held his gaze and said slowly, deliberately, 'Listen to me. Don't let him go. Kalinjara will not fall. As long as he doesn't bring them in, it will not fall.'

I could see the slight confusion in Vidyadhara's face as he tried to understand what I was saying. But then he said softly, 'We won't let him bring them in.'

'If you let him go now, he will!'

'Trust me, Tara.'

Vatsaraja fidgeted and mumbled, 'Maharaj—'

'Quiet,' commanded Vidyadhara. 'Tara Bai has protected Jejabhukti twice. Now it is our turn to protect her.'

Sarvadasa smiled. 'Such devotion to a mere concubine…'

I shook my head. 'Don't do it, please…'

Vatsaraja took a small step forward and said again, 'Maharaj—'

Vidyadhara put up his hand and silenced everyone. 'I give you my word…'

'No!' I screamed.

'… that you may leave here unharmed if you hand over Tara Bai safely.'

I stared at him, stunned. I wasn't the only one. I don't think anyone in the cavern had expected him to actually allow Sarvadasa to walk out alive. He had no way of guaranteeing that the wily old yogi wouldn't find his way back inside the fort with enemy soldiers. If he sealed off the underground network, he would be sealing off the fort from essential supplies and information. And if Sarvadasa had been cultivating new entry points for decades, he would almost certainly not use the ones Vidyadhara was keeping guarded. It was suicide and Vatsaraja knew it from the way he was looking at his king.

I looked into Vidyadhara's eyes and whispered, 'Please don't do this.'

'It is done.' Sarvadasa laughed. He removed the point of the arrow from my neck and his arm fell away from me. 'His word is inviolable. Once given, even he cannot take it back. You're an even bigger fool than I thought,' he said to Vidyadhara. 'You just gave away your kingdom, your throne, your wives and children, and the wives and children of every man who believes you to be the Mahesvara's divine representative in this world. For what? For a woman. This is why your kind will eventually kneel to Hamira.'

'You wouldn't understand, you traitor.' Vidyadhara shook his head. 'Honour, fidelity, justice, love, faith – these are things people like you don't value. But these are the very things we fight for. Without them, we defend nothing but mud and rock. If I left her to die by your hand, I would be no better than you.' He gestured towards a tunnel. 'Now get out. We will show you, and Hamira, how we defend our own.'

Vidyadhara turned to me and held out his hand. 'Come to me, Tara.'

I could feel my heart slam against my ribcage. His words had such conviction, and yet, Sarvadasa was right. Vidyadhara's way of life would soon come to an end. Their forts would fall and they would become vassals. Women would be covered up and shut away inside harems. The faiths that had once coexisted peacefully within the golden gates of Khajuravahaka would turn against one another. Invaders would look upon the erotic sculptures on temple walls and demolish them for being obscene. Vidyadhara wouldn't live to see it but his impregnable Kalinjara would also fall and be rebuilt in the same style as the invaders he was fighting against right now. It would happen. Eventually.

But not now. It was too soon. This wasn't the way history was supposed to go. Suddenly, my purpose became clear. I realized, finally, why I had been sent here by Kala Devi. Not to change history. But to ensure that history stayed the same. To ensure that the people of Kalinjara and the temples of Khajuraho lived to see another day.

I turned to look at Sarvadasa and then turned back to Vidyadhara. I smiled at him. 'Thank you. For everything.'

His expression changed and became watchful. 'Tara…'

'I can't let you do it, I'm sorry.'

His eyes widened. 'No.'

Before anyone could react, I turned and slammed into Sarvadasa with all the strength I had, taking him by surprise and pushing both of us over the edge of the ridge. Into the well.

'Tara, no!' Vidyadhara lunged forward towards me, trying unsuccessfully to grab any part of my body he could reach. He was too late.

I heard Sarvadasa scream.

I saw Vidyadhara's anguished face fall further and further away. Until I couldn't see it any more.

The water hit my back, hard, and then swallowed me into its dense, dark depths for a few panic-stricken moments before

I instinctively pulled myself up to the surface and gasped for air. It was pitch-dark.

A hand caught my shoulder and pulled me under. I struggled with it and shook it off for a moment before it returned. Then, two hands clutched at my shoulders and dragged me underwater. Sarvadasa was pulling me down with him. My lungs screamed for air and I desperately tried to claw my way to the surface. But, in the darkness, I couldn't tell which way the surface was any more.

This was it. I felt the water pressing into my head and spinning around me. I let go and closed my eyes. Gave myself to the blackness.

30

It came out in a rush from my nose and throat, burning its way through my windpipe. I coughed and wheezed and retched until most of the water was out of my system and I could feel precious air fill my lungs instead. I took long drags of it until my racing heart slowed to a manageable pace.

That was when I realized I was lying face down on a floor. And the air I was breathing smelled of fresh, pungent cow dung.

My eyes flew open. I was in a cowshed. One cow stood at the end of it, chewing a mouthful of dried grass and regarding me contemplatively. She mooed.

I scrambled up to my feet, my limbs feeling heavy and my back and head hurting as if someone had hit me with a cricket bat. I was soaking wet, still in the skimpy choli blouse and ghagra skirt I had been wearing when I jumped into the well. My slippers had fallen off my feet and I was barefoot. I ran my hands over my face and body. Despite feeling pretty beaten up, I was still in one piece. I was alive!

I smiled shakily and looked around, expecting to see Vijamba or Puppa or even Vidyadhara somewhere close by. I needed to ask them how they had gotten me out of the well. Suddenly, something on the floor caught my eye.

It was my purse. And my Indiana Jones hat.

My breath caught. I backed away towards the opening of the cowshed, stumbling my way outside into the open, my eyes squinting from the harsh sunlight. I was in a village. There were huts. And, parked outside a few of the huts, were bicycles. Overhead were power lines and the air felt heavy and dusty.

'Oh God,' I whispered. I looked back at the cowshed and recognized it as the one Kala Devi had taken me to before sending me back a thousand years. Only there was no hut next to it this time. And no sign of Kala Devi.

I ran back inside and knelt on the floor next to my purse. The one I thought she had stolen. Rummaging inside, I found all the things I had left behind that day, which now seemed so long ago I could barely recall it. My wallet, my watch, my tampons … my phone!

I picked it up with shaking fingers. Automatically, I pressed the button to switch it on. The screen sprang to life and I looked at the date on it.

I was back in the twenty-first century. On the same day I had left it.

I sat on the floor with a thump. It hadn't been a dream. It couldn't have been – I was still wearing the clothes I had put on this morning. Still wearing the bangles, toe rings and anklets that Vijamba insisted I keep on all the time to ward off evil spirits and indicate I was a 'married' woman. No, it had been real. The people, the places, the war…

The war!

What happened after I left?

I pressed more buttons on the phone, desperately trying to unlock it, but I couldn't remember the password. Exhaling in frustration and upset at myself for forgetting, I pressed the Emergency Call button on the screen. Hari's mobile number popped up.

I stared at it for a moment. Hari, the team, the dig at Khajuraho … it all came rushing back to me. I pressed the call button.

The phone rang twice before I heard Hari's voice. It sounded worried. 'Tara?'

'Hari,' I murmured in a rasping voice. My throat hadn't cleared completely of water yet and it hurt a bit to talk.

'Where are you? Everyone's been searching for hours. Your phone's been switched off. Are you Okay?'

Was I Okay? I wasn't sure yet. 'I don't know. The war – Hari, I need to know what happened…'

'Tara, where are you?'

'I don't know.'

I could hear him exhale. Then he said, 'Okay, are your location services on?'

I couldn't wrap my confused mind around that. 'I don't know.'

'Tara, listen to me. Stay where you are. I'm tracking your phone. I'm coming to get you, Okay?'

I nodded, relieved to not have to do anything for the moment. 'Okay.'

He hung up. I leaned back against the mud wall in exhaustion and closed my eyes. Tears began to pour out of them automatically. Thoughts flitted in and out of my head at ridiculous speeds, all tangled up. I had only been missing for a few hours. What I had experienced for months in the year 1022 CE had amounted to less than a day in the present. No one had mourned me after all. I had been ready to die in that cavern. Vidyadhara and Puppa, all of them, would believe that I died.

I blinked out more tears as another thought hit me. Had I succeeded in saving everyone? Khajuraho – was it still standing? All this while, Kala Devi had known I would come back. And she hadn't told me. I should hate her even more for what she put me through. And yet, I didn't. I couldn't hate her at all. I didn't know what to feel at this moment – relief because I was safe or anguish for those I left behind.

I sat on the floor, lost in my thoughts and soaking the mud beneath me with my sodden clothes until I heard a car honking and Hari's voice shouting my name. I stood up, gathered my bag and my hat and walked out unsteadily.

Hari was standing next to a cluster of huts, dressed in his usual T-shirt and cargo pants with heavy hiking boots much like those I wore when I had woken up in Khajuravahaka. It was a shock to see a person dressed in modern clothing. I called out to him hoarsely, 'Hari!'

He turned and looked at me, his eyes widening in astonishment. They raked down my body and I realized, for the first time, how out of place and indecent I must look in my medieval clothes. And to top it off, they were wet. In the past, this would have bothered me and I would've probably tried to cover up in embarrassment. But now I surprised myself by ignoring his confused and shocked expression as he walked up to me.

'Are you all right? What happened?' he asked incredulously.

'Hari, I need to ask you something,' I said, shaking my head at his question.

'Tara—'

'Hami … Sultan Mahmud of Ghazni – when he came to conquer Kalinjar, what happened?'

He looked at me as if I had gone crazy.

'Please,' I implored, trying to look as calm and sane as was possible under the circumstances. 'When he failed to overthrow Gwalior and came to Kalinjar, during the time of King Vidyadhara in the year 1022 CE – what happened?'

Hari's eyes moved over my face worriedly. Probably deciding that the best way to deal with me was by playing along, he replied, 'He kept up the campaign for a year, until Vidyadhara offered him elephants and a poem and he gifted Vidyadhara control of his conquered forts in return. Then he went back to Ghazni. Tara, what is this about?'

'And Vidyadhara, the people of Kalinjar – they survived?'

'Yes. Vidyadhara ruled for at least another decade or more.'

'And Khajuraho?'

'What about it?'

I blinked. 'Do the temples stand?'

Hari frowned, 'Tara, do you have a concussion?'

'Why?'

'You were just at the temple complex this morning, when you disappeared.'

I couldn't help myself – I laughed. Not a little laugh either, but a big, completely hysterical one. Hari probably thought I'd lost my mind.

If he did, he didn't say it. He took a deep breath and began to shepherd me to his car. 'Never mind, let's get back to the hotel. You can tell me what happened later. Are you hurt?'

'No.'

'Good.' He nodded. 'Sit in the car. I might have a jacket in the back for you until we get to the hotel.'

'Why do I need a jacket?'

His eyes skimmed over my chest before rushing back to my face. 'To cover up.'

I met his look with questioning eyes. 'Do you have a problem with what I'm wearing?'

He blinked and shook his head. 'What … no, I just think it'll be better for you not to walk into town like that. For your own safety.'

I was too tired to argue. I let him seat me in his car and drape his jacket over my shoulders.

He got into the driver's seat and looked over at me carefully. 'After you rest at the hotel, can you please tell me what happened? I may need to call the police.'

I shook my head. 'No need to get them involved. I'll tell you, but first I need to ask you for a favour.'

He nodded. 'Of course.'

'You won't refuse?'

'No, what is it?'

'Could you please take me to Kalinjar?'

31

Hari convinced me to wait until the next morning to go to Kalinjar. He walked me to my hotel room, where Sumithra and Gopa were waiting for me, frantic that they hadn't been able to get in touch with me for several hours.

As I stood just inside the door, a little dazed, Sumithra poked at my limbs to check for injury. 'Please tell me some psycho bandit didn't kidnap you and make you dance for him dressed as a village girl like they do in those old Hindi movies. You haven't been raped, have you?' Her eyes were as wide as saucers with worry.

'Shut up, Sumithra,' Gopa snapped uncharacteristically as she handed me a clean pair of pyjamas and a T-shirt from the cupboard in my room and shepherded me into the bathroom to have a shower.

I locked the bathroom door automatically and leaned against it, looking around at the sink, western-style toilet bowl and showerhead. Then, with an involuntary chuckle, I walked towards the shower and turned the tap on. Instantly, the water started flowing into the cubicle. I turned it off and on a few times and then held up my lavender-scented shower gel to my nose, my mind churning back to the numerous times I had bathed out in the open, two attendants scrubbing my body using pastes made with lentils and spices, fruit, vegetables and herbs. I fingered my deodorant and body lotion on the sink countertop and then ran my hands over the skin on my arms – Vijamba's potions had kept it supple and healthy, but nowhere near the artificial smoothness provided by modern toiletries.

After my shower, I ran my hands along the clothes Gopa had handed me, once so familiar and now so foreign, as if they belonged to someone else. And perhaps they did. The woman who had worn them earlier was nothing like the woman who stared back at me from the vanity mirror above the sink. This was a different person. Slightly weathered but much stronger for it. Less certain about her opinions but much surer of herself. A woman who had learnt what was important, what was not, and how little time each of us have to figure it all out. A woman who had faced the end of her life, only for it to be given back to her. She didn't know exactly what she wanted to do with it yet, but she knew she didn't want to waste it. Not a single second.

After much fussing and a dinner that felt over-spiced and heavy, Gopa and Sumithra put me to bed and left. The noisy hum of the air conditioner didn't do much to assuage the feeling of loneliness that enveloped me as I thought about the women who had slept around my bed chamber every night for months.

I thought about Vidyadhara. The look on his face as I had fallen away from him. I squeezed my eyes tighter to try to banish the image from my mind. But then it was replaced by another, equally tormenting, one. Of his eyes, as they had hovered over mine, playful and dark with desire. How his lips felt on mine, the feel of his hands as they roamed over me, the embracing weight of his body on mine. I would never see him again.

He would think me dead. Would he mourn me? Or would he be too preoccupied with war? Probably the latter. And then, by the time the war was over, he would have three wives and a palace full of concubines to distract him from the fact that he had once cared about me. As I cared about him. As tricky and difficult as it would've been, I had accepted and embraced a life with him. When I thought I had no other choice…

I sighed into the darkness. Now that my life wasn't hanging by a thread any more, I would have time to figure out my feelings, I supposed. I let the emotional and physical exhaustion of the day press me into slumber.

The next morning, Hari forced me to eat a slice of toast, despite my protests. My body had got used to eating only two meals a day. After a quick team meeting, he announced he was taking me to Kalinjar, much to everyone's surprise. When Sumithra offered to come along, he said with a pointed look, 'No, I'll take Tara. I'd like to talk to her on the drive.' Everyone had nodded in a frowning, worried way – they were treating me with kid gloves.

As we drove by the temple complex I smiled slightly to myself, feeling a connection, an affection for it that I had never felt before. This despite the fact that I had almost killed a priest somewhere in that complex. Almost got myself killed as well.

'Tara, are you ready to tell me what happened?' Hari's deep voice rumbled softly in the cool comfort of the car.

I took a deep breath and got a whiff of the cologne he always wore. I looked over at him and watched for a moment as he navigated the town's heavy traffic. His presence, his smell, his voice – they felt familiar, comforting. I exhaled.

'Did I ever tell you about Kala Devi?'

He shook his head. 'No.'

I took another deep breath. 'She's an old lady I met a few weeks ago. I kept running into her around town. Well, turns out she knows how to hypnotize people. She took me to that village.'

'And?'

I sighed. I couldn't tell him the truth without him thinking I had lost my marbles. I'd have to lie again – hopefully for the last time. 'And, nothing. I had no idea what I was doing or where I was going. When I came around, I was dressed in those clothes. We talked for a while. Then she left and I called you.'

'Why were your clothes wet?'

I blinked. 'Er, I fell into the cowshed's water tank. Happened when I was hypnotized.'

Hari paused for a second, shooting me an awkward glance. He said, 'Tara, were you … violated in any way? I mean, maybe you don't know if something happened, but…'

'No.' I shook my head firmly. 'I would know if something happened, don't worry. I feel fine. She's just a batty old lady who wanted to play dress-up. Let's forget about it and move on.'

'You sure? You can write a police report. They can arrest her.'

'I'm sure.' Not only would Kala Devi be untraceable, but I wasn't angry with her anymore. I didn't exactly love her for what she did or how she did it, but I understood why. It had been for the right reasons and I couldn't bring myself to hate her for that.

I smiled at Hari. 'Really, I'm Okay.'

He smiled back briefly before turning his eyes back to the road. Then he put his hand on mine and squeezed it. 'I'm glad you're Okay.'

I surprised myself when I squeezed back. 'Thanks for driving me.'

'You're welcome. Why are we going to Kalinjar, by the way?'

'I want to check something out … that Kala Devi told me.' Okay, so maybe *this* lie would be the last.

He didn't question me again for the rest of the drive. Instead, he told me about his other archaeological projects and soon had me laughing with anecdotes about dig crews that went on drunken sprees and lost artefacts, affairs between crew members and close calls with government inspectors who threatened to close down excavations if the artefacts dug up didn't tow the political line of the day. For the first time since I got back, I didn't feel like I'd been shot out of a cannon and landed on the moon.

We got to Kalinjar and it took me a while to get my bearings. Nothing was as I remembered it from just the day before. Only the Neelkanth temple still stood and I didn't want to go near it, images of Sarvadasa still vivid in my head.

Instead, we entered the part of the catacombs that was still accessible through the official entrance. They weren't open to the public so Hari had to contact Mr Chauhan from the ASI to pull some strings and allow us inside. An elderly man, probably in his seventies, accompanied us down into the tunnels. As we followed his slow, deliberate steps, I looked around at the widened pathways, complete with railings, safety planks and light bulbs. Warning signs hung where the rock was considered unstable or the passage too narrow or the ceiling too low. It made me let out a humourless chuckle – what on earth was I doing, reliving the nightmare journey through these catacombs with Sarvadasa? Although much had changed, including the smell and look of the place, it still had an eerie, lifeless feel to it.

Miraculously, we found our way to the cavern. I didn't know why I wanted to come here but I felt inexplicably drawn to it. This was the place where I'd decided to take my own life. Where I'd jumped to what I thought would be my death. Now, on the other side of that decision, I couldn't make sense of my desire to come to this cavern except that, maybe, a part of me had indeed died here and I wanted to pay homage to it.

I walked slowly to the drop into the well. The water was long gone and most of the hole had been filled with rock and rubble. There was a railing preventing anyone from going too close to the edge – a fact that almost brought the tears pooling in my eyes out on my cheeks.

I turned to say something to Hari when a niche in the wall of the cavern caught my eye. I walked closer to it. It was a carving that had been cut out of the natural rock.

I asked the elderly man for the torch he had carried with him in case the lights went out in the catacombs and shone it on the carving.

It was a single apsara, a nymph, standing in a rock-cut frame, much in the same style as the nymphs at the Khajuraho temples. In one hand, she held a jewelled sword with a large stone at the centre of the hilt, in the other, she held a feathered quill. Marigolds were woven into the waves of her hair, falling over her neck, shoulders and breasts. At the nymph's feet sat a doe, looking up at her in absolute adoration.

And on her hip, as clear as day, was carved a star-shaped tattoo.

32

'It is an ancient tale,' the old man was saying. I had to fight to pay attention as my ears hummed – a sound I was sure only I could hear.

'Her name is Tara Devi. She is said to be an avatar of the divine nymph Maneka, who took the form of a concubine in the king's palace here in Kalinjara. She was an educated, fearless woman and the king was in love with her. Time and again, she saved his life and this is the spot where she sacrificed herself to save the king and the people of Kalinjara. It is said that the king had this carved in memory of her and as a shrine to her sacrifice. It is an auspicious place – they say that whenever a new ruler took the throne of Kalinjara, he came here to pay his respects to Tara Devi, so that she may protect him as well.'

I whispered to the old man, 'What is the name of the king who built the shrine?'

He shook his head. 'There is no inscription of any kind, so no one is sure when it was made. His name was never recorded.

The story has been passed down through generations. My father told it to me.'

I stared at him for a few moments and then turned back to the carving. My fingers traced the frame, the nymph's face, the doe and the star shape on her hip. Tara Devi, the divine avatar. I almost laughed out loud. I touched a marigold flower, remembering for an instant how Vidyadhara had brushed it against my skin that night. He had missed me enough to build a shrine for me. A shrine that included reminders of our time together. And he hadn't written his name on it. Such a public display of affection had remained, at its heart, completely private between us.

Finally, the tears came. It was over. I was back. And everything that had happened … it now only existed within me. The memory of Vidyadhara would probably never leave me, just as he made sure the memory of me never left him. Still, he had probably moved on and I needed to do the same.

I stroked the marigold with my fingers, leaned in closer and whispered almost soundlessly, 'Goodbye, Maharaj.'

The nymph smiled back lifelessly.

'Did the old woman tell you about this carving?'

Hari's deep voice startled me with its closeness. He was right behind me, peering at the carving.

I nodded, unable to find my voice for the moment.

Hari leaned closer to the carving and ran his hand over the star-shaped sign on her hip. I couldn't help let out a soft, involuntary gasp. Then I reminded myself that he had no idea I had the same tattoo on my hip. And definitely no idea that the nymph was a representation of me.

'I haven't seen this particular shape before. Looks quite modern actually,' he murmured.

I smiled. He continued without looking at me, his fingers moving down her leg to the doe. 'Unusual drape of the garment covering her legs as well. Looks more like pants.'

I looked closer and saw that he was right. Then I turned towards him and studied his profile as he ran his hand over the stone version of me without knowing it. Deep in my belly, I felt a familiar, and not entirely unwelcome, buzz of sensation. The same one I had felt whenever I stood close to him since I'd been a student in his class.

He turned his head and met my eyes. I realized in that moment that I had never looked this closely into Hari's eyes before. For a split second before he smiled the same non-committal smile he'd been giving me for years, I saw a spark of desire. A spark I would never have recognized before now.

I held his gaze. 'Should we leave?'

He nodded, leaned back and cleared his throat discreetly. 'Sure. Have you seen what you needed to see?' He stepped towards the entrance.

'Yes.' I turned towards the carving one last time and smiled. 'I'm ready to go now.'

We thanked the old man and walked back to the car in silence. As I sat down, I realized, for the first time, the magnitude of what I had done. I had saved lives. I had helped save the Khajuraho temples. I had helped shape history. Me. Tara Singh, loopy archaeologist.

'You Okay?'

I took a deep breath as I turned to Hari, who had now started driving on the narrow road down the hill from the fort. The past was over. It was time for me to look to the future. The one I didn't want to waste anymore.

'Hari?' I said softly.

'Hmm?'

'Did you know I have a tattoo?'

He glanced at me briefly with a slightly questioning look. 'Er, no. I didn't.'

'It's in a private place.'

The words hung in the air, suspended in frozen silence. He continued to look ahead at the road as he murmured softly, 'Okay…'

I held my breath. 'Want to see it?'

He stopped the car with a jerk. Right in the middle of the road. I heard him exhale softly as he turned to look at me. After a few moments of surprised silence, he said with a small chuckle, 'Yeah, I want to. Very much.'

I smiled but before I could say anything, we heard a loud honking from behind us. The vehicles lined up on the road were not happy about the abrupt halt.

Hari quickly set the car in motion again and continued winding down the hill. As we reached the wider main road, he murmured, 'For the record, I didn't mean that in a creepy way. You took me by surprise. Have dinner with me tonight?'

'You realize the team will see us, right?'

'Screw the team.'

I smiled again and peered outside the window at the north cliff of the fort, now fading into the distance. Then I looked at the road ahead. It stretched into the horizon.

Epilogue

A tickling on my lips woke me up from my jet-lagged slumber. I opened my eyes to see Hari's face just above mine, smiling at me.

'Sorry I woke you up,' he murmured, 'but you're going to need to stay awake now if you want to sleep at night. We're ten and a half hours behind India time.'

I smiled back and nodded, realizing I was curled up on the couch in his Manhattan apartment, my bare legs wrapped around a king-size pillow. I hadn't even unpacked yet.

Hari had picked me up from JFK airport in the morning. Not having seen each other in over three months, we'd barely got through the front door of his apartment before he'd hoisted me up against the wall for a proper welcome. The kind that necessitated a nap afterwards.

I stretched languorously at the memory as he tugged at the pillow I was cuddling on the couch. 'That's my spot,' he said as he threw the offending pillow on the floor and lay down next to me, weaving his arms and legs through mine.

He kissed me slowly and thoroughly before whispering, 'I missed you so much.'

'I missed you too,' I replied, kissing him back. 'But I'm here for a few weeks at least. I've been going over the coordinates again and again, and I'm almost certain the buried temple is under that commercial building I told you about. I just need an infrared imaging team to confirm it, so I'll be doing the rounds over here for a grant to fund an imaging expedition.'

He looked contemplatively at me. 'Are you sure you can trust the coordinates this … lady gave you?'

'Kala Devi,' I replied quickly. 'Yes, I'm pretty sure she knew what she was talking about.' I couldn't exactly tell him, or anyone else, that I was able to trace the coordinates of the buried Khajuraho temple because I had actually stood next to it when it was above the ground. When a king was being weighed against gold inside it. The time I spent there was something I could never talk about.

'Well, you're going to need a bit more in your grant application than just a tip-off from a local, no matter how well-informed she is. I'll put you in touch with a few people or feel them out before you approach them. I'll also ask my friends in the business to put the word out there.' He slid his hand up my thigh, over my butt and into my t-shirt as he began to nibble my neck. His voice was slightly muffled when he said, 'Once the images come out and *if* they show something buried under the building then you, Ms Rising Star Archaeologist, will have investors lining up to give you more money. We just need to keep our fingers crossed.'

'I have a better idea,' I murmured breathlessly as I arched my neck and began to undo the buttons on his shirt. 'Why don't I write the application, apply for the grant, get permission from the building owners and conduct the imaging expedition myself. If I need you, Professor World Renowned Archaeologist, then I'll just come back here and take your clothes off.' I smiled.

He grinned back at me. 'Sounds like a great idea. Why don't you start right now?'

I popped open the last button of his shirt. 'Way ahead of you.'

~x~

Author's Note

I love history and learning about the past is one of my favourite things to do. The Chandela Dynasty of Bundelkhand, builders of Khajuraho, were a fascinating study. I owe much to the books of Sisir Kumar Mitra ('The Early Rulers of Khajuraho'), R. K. Dikshit ('The Candellas of Jejakabhukti'), Upinder Singh ('Rethinking Early Medieval India' & 'A History of Ancient and Early Medieval India'), Kushagra Rajesh Sengar ('The Erotic Carvings of Khajuraho'), the numerous writings of Devangana Desai (https://devanganadesai.com/) and the websites http://www.bundelkhandinfo.org.in/index.html & http://www.asi.nic.in/ among other sources in my quest to absorb as much as I could about that period in history.

Many years ago, as a documentary filmmaker, I made a film about a group of lower caste women in the Banda district of Bundelkhand and was fascinated by the dynamics of that region. It's an interesting place to say the least, brutal and beautiful all at once. The people are incredibly resilient and their culture shines in vibrant contrast to the stark landscape. I feel honoured to have had the opportunity to write about them and many characters – Puppa, Kala Devi, Vijamba, the thakurain and kuwarani to name a few – are inspired by women I met when I was there.

As in any work of historical fiction, there are the facts and then there are the bits that totally flew out of the author's head. The information about the Kandariya Mahadeva Temple in Khajuraho is all true. King Vidyadhara, Queen Satyabhama, Prince Vijaypala, Thakur Jajuka, Mukhya Mantri Sivanaga and Vatsaraja were all real people who did exist, even though details about them are practically non-existent so I've had to cautiously imagine their characters. Sultan Mahmud of Ghazni is a well-known historical personality who is loved by some and despised by others – information, and misinformation, about him is abundant. Details of wars, battles and historical facts may be hotly debated in some circles but I've stayed true to what has been verified by experts in the field. Also true are details about forts, weaponry, clothing, folklore, feudal structures, religious practices and traditional customs as well as most facts about Kalinjar Fort and the Neelkanth temple.

So what bits flew out of my head? Sarvadasa is a fictional character – it's unclear who Vidyadhara's actual Rajpurohit was. Also fictional are Queen Vijaya and the 3rd queen from Bari – Vidhyadhara would have likely had more wives after Satyabhama, but we don't know their names or backgrounds. We do know that there are catacombs and reservoirs under Kalinjar Fort but we don't know the true extent of them or how difficult they may or may not be to navigate. However, like any Rajput fort worth its salt, Kalinjar would have had its fair share of secret tunnels and spaces. There is indeed a small door in the Neelkanth temple cave – only the priests know what's behind it. Maybe it is just a cupboard after all. There is no shrine to a tattooed Tara Devi in the fort. Obviously.

History, like life itself, is ambiguous. Everyone has a different perspective. The characters in this book express their points of view based on their own backgrounds and experiences and I've tried not to judge their beliefs. Clearly, Tara had no such compunction!

Some parts of this story may have made you uncomfortable. It is extremely unfortunate that issues like Sati, child-molestation, child-marriage, slavery, caste-discrimination, communalism, feudal hierarchies etc. are still alive and kicking today, a thousand years later. These are problems we need to talk about. So, if you've been disturbed by what you read, that's not necessarily a bad thing.

I do hope you've enjoyed Kama's Last Sutra. And I hope, in a teeny-tiny itsy-bitsy way, it's made you think about how time really is a wheel – what has happened before is already happening again and will probably happen repeatedly in the future. Until we change it.

Acknowledgements

I'm so grateful for all the help and support I've received for this book. My heartfelt thanks to:

All the wonderful people at HarperCollins India. You guys make dreams come true. Ananth Padmanabhan and Diya Kar, and my smart and sassy editor Swati Daftuar, who believed in this book before I wrote it. Her editing team, Rimli Barooah & Rea Mukherjee. Bonita Shimray, Shabnam Srivastava and their design and marketing teams. Along with everyone in sales & accounts who keep it going long after all the excitement has died down.

Jayapriya Vasudevan from Jacaranda Literary Agency, whose patience and foresight are remarkable. Helen Mangham and Pari Berlin.

The brilliant bunch at Weirdass Comedy.

Rajput friends (who shall remain nameless) for helping me learn about the Rajput community.

Rajiv Mehrotra, for his unwavering faith in me.

My tribe – relatives & friends – for surrounding me with support and sanity.

My family – Ma, who sets the bar in everything she does. Pops, who dreams bigger than anyone else. Vir, who works harder than everyone else. Shivani, who is always up for anything.

My husband, Deeps, who is the most honourable man I know.

My babies, R & J, who are everything to me.

And b, as always.